THE
VERY
ORDERED
EXISTENCE OF
Merilee
Marvelous

SUZANNE CROWLEY

Greenwillow Books
An Imprint of HarperCollins*Publishers*

The Very Ordered Existence of Merilee Marvelous
Text copyright © 2007 by Suzanne Crowley
All rights reserved. No part of this book may be used or reproduced in any manner whatsoever without written permission except in the case of brief quotations embodied in critical articles and reviews. Printed in the United States of America. For information address HarperCollins Children's Books, a division of HarperCollins Publishers, 1350 Avenue of the Americas, New York, NY 10019.
www.harpercollinschildrens.com

j

The text of this book is set in 11-point Berkeley Book.
Book design by Paul Zakris.

Library of Congress Cataloging-in-Publication Data
Crowley, Suzanne Carlisle.
The Very Ordered Existence of Merilee Marvelous / by Suzanne Crowley.
  p. cm.
"Greenwillow Books."
Summary: In the small town of Jumbo, Texas, thirteen-year-old Merilee, who has Asperger's Syndrome, tries to live a "Very Ordered Existence," but disruptions begin when a boy and his father arrive in town and the youngster makes himself a part of the family.
ISBN-13: 978-0-06-123197-1 (trade bdg.) ISBN-10: 0-06-123197-5 (trade bdg.)
ISBN-13: 978-0-06-123198-8 (lib. bdg.) ISBN-10: 0-06-123198-3 (lib. bdg.)
[1. Asperger's syndrome—Fiction. 2. Emotional problems—Fiction. 3. Family life—Texas—Fiction. 4. Dragons—Fiction. 5. Schools—Fiction. 6. Texas—Fiction.] I. Title.
PZ7.C88766 2007 [Fic] dc—22 2006050983

First Edition 10 9 8 7 6 5 4 3 2 1

Greenwillow Books

For Caitlin,
who believes in dragons
and all things magical

Me

Mama says change is God's way of showing us a tender miracle, kinda like the chocolate inside a Tootsie Pop. Grandma Birdy says hogwash; change is no good and it always comes in threes like plane crashes and natural disasters. It was after Weenie ate the giant Cheeto that my life began to fall apart. No, wait. This story starts before the dreaded Cheeto incident. Yes, way before that. Like when I was born. Precision.

But I'm not one for words, not conversations anyway. I have little to say to the outside world. My sister, Bug—she can talk the pants off ants in the rain. At least that's what Grandma (who doesn't mince her words) would say. If Grandma told the truth, that is. Though she wouldn't cause she adores her little Bug. Bug can't keep her mouth shut for ten seconds. She doesn't stop for nothing—she will talk in circles till your eyes roll back and you fall over dead and then she'll stand above you and keep on jabbering.

I do have words, though. Astonishing words, and ideas, too. They are trapped inside me where they spin around like the whirling hot dust devils off Highway 90, up and up, forever carving out my insides. But they stay mostly in. To try and get some of my words out, Mama gave me a beautiful black journal with a silver clasp in the shape of a dragon. It goes with me wherever I go.

People around here have always thought I'm not quite all there, that I'm missing a marble or two. They think I'm just good for picking up litter, reciting the train schedules, adding up their lunch tickets, or handing out those purple Tootsie Pops (my personal favorite). Just so you know, I have phobias, too, like bread crumbs in the butter tub, the word *Velveeta*, or having to stay perfectly still. Me, I move constantly.

One thing's for sure in Jumbo, Texas, population

1,258: if you are dumb as an old shoe or super, super smart, you get driven up to El Paso to see a specialist who can confirm what everyone already knows. I've been taken there twice, once because I'm smart and once because I'm dumb. After only a few years of life in Jumbo, I've come to a conclusion. There's a thin line between genius and bottom-barrel stupidness. I hover delicately on a tightrope between the two, wondering where I'll land if I ever fall.

Plasma hiccup. Sarcastic universe. A long time ago, they all thought I was a genius. Now I'm just known for being the weirdo who loves dragons. They even call me Dragon Girl. Although obsessions are common enough in podunk West Texas towns, dragons are not generally considered appropriate for young ladies. Horses, yes; dragons, no. But I can't stop drawing or thinking about my long, scaly beasts. Images of dragons litter every scrap of paper that comes anywhere near me—my black journal, my homework, my mother's store receipts, even posters nailed to telephone poles downtown. I scatter my dragons everywhere like pollen.

Chapter
1

It didn't take long to find out. News travels fast in Jumbo. Even on a hot Saturday morning when the world is moving slow. I was making my usual rounds with my litter stick and my binoculars, and I was at the old Dixie Dog Drive In picking up trash left by the teenagers who hang out there on Friday night. Bug and Tootie McKelvey came and told me.

"There's a new retarded boy," Tootie blurted out, and Bug pushed at her for stealing her thunder. Tootie has more freckles than face and that's all there is to say about her. "He's funny looking," she added, icing on the big-news cake.

This was not a surprise to me. I knew Biswick

was coming practically before he did. I felt it deep down in my dry bones that morning. A change was on its way and I didn't like it one bit. Not one bit.

"Humph," I snorted. "Marvelous." Lately my brain's been grabbing words and just throwing them out there to the world. My thoughts are clear. But when I try to speak, sometimes it sounds as if I picked up my words secondhand, like bits of tattered lace at an estate sale. And my voice sounds odd, too. Mama says I sound like an old soul while Bug is always screaming at me to stop "talking like a granny."

Anyway I have a tight schedule on Saturdays and I don't like to be interrupted, which Bug well knows. I lead a Very Ordered Existence, VOE for short. Everything is all lined up in my life and if anything is out of order, I get all "nervy," which is what Grandma calls it. It mostly feels like being on fire. I stared vacantly at Bug and Tootie, hoping that would be enough to make them go away.

"He's eight, supposedly, but Mary Alice Augustine saw him and says he looks more like a kindergartner. And he doesn't have a mother, and his daddy writes commercial poetry," Bug stated with the authority of a professional gossiper. "Which means Mama will invite the daddy over for dinner to get him to do a reading at the bookstore, which means we'll get to meet the kid first. And I bet they are gonna have to bring that funny little bus for retards over from Whiskey."

Whiskey is our sister town about ten miles away. It's got more stuff than we do, though, like the rinky-dink hospital where I was born and even a drive-thru McDonald's.

Bug's eyes got all big as she glanced down at my red high-top sneakers.

My "uniform" is a source of extreme embarrassment to Bug and she is always trying to mess with it. I wear the same things every day—a yellowy-orangey shirt with the words *Dilley's Chicken & Feed* emblazoned on the front (Daddy brought it back from some agricultural conference and I took to it), a pair of army green cargo pants, and my (rain or shine) red high-tops, which Bug calls retardo shoes because they have Velcro flaps instead of laces.

I had been missing my high-tops for several days because Bug had snuck in my room in the middle of the night and stole them. But this morning I found them sticking out of the Dumpster behind the Rexall Drug. Bug was pissed.

"You are an idiot!" she spewed, all flustered. "I bet the new kid dresses just like you."

"Spectacular," I muttered, spearing a Big Crush can with my litter stick.

"Spectacular? Oh Merilee! You are such a spaz!"

To which I replied, "It's *controversial*, not *commercial* poetry."

Bug stuck her tongue out at me, pulled Tootie along with her, and off they went to spread the exciting news to more enthused and grateful recipients.

I pulled the can off my stick and began looking for my next prize. I devote thirty minutes daily to picking up litter, two hours on Saturdays—9:12 to 11:12. I'm saving the world one Crush can at a time.

It's Merilee Monroe, my name. I know. Isn't it terrible? I would probably even snicker, too, and I'm as polite as you can get. You can't imagine how many times I've heard *"Mer-i-lee we roll along, roll along, ROLL ALONG!"* sung at my back. I'm not the least bit merry and everyone knows it. In fact, Grandma Birdy scolds me to get my butt off my shoulders and smile once in a while. Mama says I'm the moral compass of the whole wide world, and that I try to hold every sad thing there ever was in the palm of my hand. It's true. I think life is one big dream-squasher.

I also, by the way, don't look anything like Marilyn Monroe. My nose is so big and fat that if I lay down you could land a 747 on it. When Mama's not around, Grandma says someone hit me with the ugly stick up in heaven and the only time I should venture out is on Halloween.

Merilee. According to Grandma Birdy, my mother, high on the birthing drugs, spouted out this monstrosity of a name (or something similar), and the ding-dong candy striper wrote that down without consulting any of our kin. This all happened thirteen-and-a-half years ago. It could have been worse. Grandma Birdy thought for sure my mother said, "Mercy," which would have most surely stamped me with a holy name. I'm glad that didn't happen 'cause God knows I don't believe in him.

There's no middle name. I guess that candy striper thought Merilee was a mouthful and didn't ask for anything more, or maybe Mama finally passed out. The story has a murky-water tinge about it, like so many other old family stories.

When my little sister came along, Mama, being the visionary and stir-the-pot lady that she is, continued the dumb tradition she had started in her delirium, three-and-a-half years earlier. Mama has a unique sense of humor. Really, everything about her is unique, for Jumbo that is. She intended that we call my sister Bitsy, after "itsy-bitsy spider," but my father took one loving (and what must have been a very short) look at his new daughter and nicknamed her Bug. 'Cause she was "cute as a bug's ear," you see. Like a big fat domino falling and hitting another one down, this led to Daddy giving me the nickname Hug. I think he just wanted to be fair because that's how he is.

Hug is an even more preposterous nickname than my sister's 'cause I don't like touching or being touched by anyone. Touching makes me feel as though someone is plunging a thousand poisonous needles into my skin. All my senses are messed up, in fact. The whole world is like one big scratch-and-sniff, only I don't have to scratch to smell it. And I can hear a frog burp from a mile away.

By the way, it's not that I don't care for nicknames. Nickname-giving is a well-established pastime in Jumbo. Everyone has at least two, even the stray dogs. Unless you are an outsider, like Mama. I just think the nickname shoe oughta fit, that's all.

My sister got her a middle name, though. My mother wanted to birth all natural this time, and with no drugs she had the clarity to name my sister Bitsy Ruth Monroe, after my beloved grandma, Ruth, who lived in New York. Before she died. I guess Bug got the last laugh, 'cause she knows Grandma Ruth is the only one in the whole wide world who ever understood me.

* * *

Let me tell you I was not very thrilled that Bug got me off schedule when she came to tell me about that new boy. Not thrilled at all. I was off by ten minutes. Ten whole minutes. I should have already taken my paper and plastics to the recycling center over on Oak Avenue by now. VOE. Very Ordered Existence.

But there I was sitting on my bicycle at the corner of Fifth and Elm, in front of Myrtle Dean's house, staring blankly at my watch as though I didn't have a thing in the world to do. Suddenly Myrtle came screeching around the corner in her old yellow Cadillac, who she calls Mabel, and pulled halfway onto her driveway, halfway on the grass. She's blind as an old mole but refuses to get glasses.

"What's that?" said a high, squeaky voice. I knew it was the new boy even before I turned my head. And it was. He was indeed small for his age—looked like he was about five or six—and something about his face was not put together quite right, like his genes had been stirred a little too much in the mixing bowl. He had brown skin and unruly black hair, with a flat-as-a-board forehead and little brown eyes. His ears looked like someone had yanked them down an inch or two. Two lines of snot ran down from his nose, like a green eleven.

When I was little I had a habit of asking impolite questions. I wasn't able to read people's faces when they were mad at me, or irritated or perplexed. Back then I probably would have asked Biswick point-blank what was wrong with him. A couple of years ago, Mama decided I needed to work on my impolite question problem so she bought me a set of flash cards of people's faces for me to study and decipher from an educational store in El Paso. It helped some. But I still have to concentrate to decipher those deep meanings people have hiding behind a smile or a frown. I didn't respond to Biswick. I just kept staring at his face.

"That bike. It's funny looking. Can you ride with two people?" he said, pointing at my most prized possession.

I never learned to ride a normal bike, just like I never really learned to tie my shoes. I've always been all legs and arms, and since I turned thirteen they've stretched even more like I was a piece of taffy yanked in four different directions.

Daddy bought me this special bicycle last year so I could get around Jumbo. It's not exactly the sharpest-looking thing, I'll admit. It looks more like an old-lady grocery getter. It has two wheels in the back for extra support with two matching baskets for my litterbag, my black journal, my pair of binoculars (also a precious gift from Daddy), a supply of Tootsie Pops to give out, and whatever book I'm reading from Mama's bookstore.

"A special bicycle," I answered as I put my foot on the pedal and started to push.

"Did you know that frogs can throw up in space?" he offered to my back as I passed him.

I braked. I have to admit it almost made me smile. Almost. I retrieved my black journal and wrote it down and prepared to ride away.

"Did you know Betsy Ross was born with a full set of teeth?" he added.

I blew out an exasperated sigh. My VOE was already wrecked for the day.

"Marvelous." I cleared my throat and took a deep breath. I motioned for him to follow and started to pedal real slowly.

"Babe Ruth, Abraham Lincoln, and somebody else who I forgot, are the only real people heads on PEZ dispensers," he said as fast as he could.

Coincidence, I thought to myself. Life is full of them. "No," I told him as I tried to pedal on. "Horrendous. Not true." It was actually Betsy Ross, Daniel Boone, and Paul Revere. He was way off. I kept trying to pedal slowly so he could keep up with me, and I'm sure I looked like a grasshopper in a bug circus with my long legs.

"You know about PEZes?" he asked, clearly impressed.

"Yep. Stupendous." I have the best PEZ collection in the state of Texas. I'm not one to brag. But it's true. They take up four long shelves in my room, perfectly lined up and standing sentry.

"Me, too! I got my best one here!" he said, shoving his hand in his pocket. I stopped my bicycle. He held out a ghost head PEZ—worthless, but obviously priceless to him.

"Go away," I said. We were at the corner of Maple and Fifth, near Main Street, and I had forgotten where I was headed. Me, who has my whole year mapped out and planned, minute by minute. My heart started to beat faster and my palms were sweaty. I hate being off my schedule. Hate it.

"Me and Daddy, we're Irish," said the boy. "You know, like Lucky Charms."

I had never seen any Irish people before, but I can tell you he didn't look anything like the little guy on the Lucky Charms box.

"You want this?" he asked. He was still holding his ghost head PEZ out, all proud and grinnin' from ear to ear. "We can be friends."

"No, no friends," I told him.

I wasn't saying it to be mean. It was the truth. And I didn't need a ghost head PEZ, either. His face fell, so I rephrased my answer.

"No time," I said, pointing to my watch. I pulled out a purple Tootsie Pop and handed it to him. "Precision. Schedules."

He looked perplexed but I didn't have time to

explain. I felt dizzy and the sidewalk was beginning to tilt. I pedaled on with my eyes closed for a few seconds, trying to retrieve my balance. When I opened them and looked in my rearview mirror, he was standing there on the sidewalk, holding the Tootsie Pop down at his side, unopened.

Saturdays are special to me because these are the days when I visit Uncle Dal, Daddy's brother. He lives on the north edge of town in a rusted-out trailer on a patch of land where he's been sculpting a marble statue for seven years. But all that has ever emerged from that block of stone is a foot. I call it the Perpetual Foot.

Uncle Dal is one of the few people I like to be around. Him and Mama, and sometimes Daddy. That's about it. Uncle Dal is a little like me, I guess is why. In fact, he was the only one who had any luck with me when I was a crying baby and ruining everyone's lives. He reappeared after having disappeared for a long while, just in time to calm me down. I like to think he came home for me. He'd put me on his lap a few minutes each day, unwrap the mummy blankets Grandma Birdy had done me up in, and whistle a sweet song, old as the Chitalpi Mountains. I would stare into his eyes, still and calm as the summer blue sky. Mama would lay exhausted in her iron claw-foot tub, soaking like a pinto bean for fifteen quiet minutes all to herself before I would start bawlin' again.

I glanced in my mirror and saw the boy was no longer there on the sidewalk. Good. I had ditched him. I didn't want him barging in on *my* time with Uncle Dal. My heart, slowing and rhythmic, soothed me as I pedaled my three-wheeler toward Uncle Dal's trailer.

Chapter
2

Grandma Birdy says I was marked from the day I was born. Whether by the devil or God, she never specifies. She says I was tarred with the same brush as her Great-uncle Biedermeyer who had to be taken off in the middle of the night by men in white coats 'cause he stared at the same dollar bill nonstop for four days. When my family talks about my baby days, they do so with the reverence of old soldiers describing D-day. Apparently I screamed so loud in the baby nursery, the nurse on duty, Miss Veraleen Holliday, brought me in squallin' to my mother and told her I was making all the other sweet babies cry and I couldn't come back. And I didn't stop crying. Not for almost a year. Grandma said I had the gas cramps. She thinks everything in the whole wide world is related to gas.

The town doctor, Dr. Coyote Wilson, recommended all kinds of cures for crying, and of course everyone had their own brilliant ideas. Suggestions were even printed in the newspaper. Hot water bottles under the mattress, pacifiers dipped in sugar, lemon balms, tinctures, tonics, catnip tea, every nasty concoction you can imagine they tried on me. Both Mama and Daddy spent hours walking around our house in the dark hours trying to soothe me. They even put me on top of the dryer in my car seat until I vibrated off the side. Bug says that's why I'm funny in the head.

Next my parents ordered Dr. Homer Pitt's *How to Soothe a Squallin' Baby* off the TV. It was a waste of money like everything else. I made such a racket, Mama's pack of dogs (Beasie, Winkie, Weenie, and Stinky) hid under the beds, and when they would sneak out they'd slink around with their rears and ears hanging low like someone had swatted them and the whole wide world was ending. Daddy gave up trying to quiet me after several weeks and went back to his silent tomatoes at his hydroponics plant.

My crying was so loud, I think perhaps it was heard over in Whiskey, because one day that old baby nurse Miss Veraleen Holliday showed up at the door with a big smile and a mayonnaise jar full of moonshine water and fresh clover honey which she said would fix even a dead horse. Later Grandma Birdy dumped the jar in the trash, saying she wasn't gonna let some crazy ranch woman with voodoo cures get near her house again.

Mama told me that Grandma promptly got to work in the kitchen stirring up her own best cure-all, beet's breath with peppermint, otherwise known as Lady's Crank Water. She assured Mama I would sleep like a lamb that night, but after drinking a bottle I threw up all over the living room. I think Grandma never forgave me for it.

Dr. Coyote Wilson finally proclaimed that I was "wired" differently. He got that right. Sometimes I picture the wires in my brain, all crisscrossed and storm-tormented and wish I had my own cure-all for untangling the mess. When I look at the few photos of my early life, everyone looks bone tired and trying so hard to smile their lips don't show. Grandma says they look all like jackasses chewing cockleburs. I'm crying in every single photo, my little face all scrunched up, purple mad and ugly.

Mama never had the gumption to put together a baby album for me and I don't blame her. Who wants to be reminded of all that? Bug got her an album, though. It's full of photos of everyone smiling for real. All except me. Bug says I look like I'm staring into the great beyond. Now that I think about it, that's how I always appear in photos, sort of blank and vacant—not of this world, not of any world—like the hollow stare of someone fated a short life.

To make Mama feel better, Dr. Coyote Wilson told her a little story about how he got his unusual name. Seems he had been a strange baby, too, howlin' up a storm so loud three coyotes would come and sit in an arc outside his bedroom window and howl-sing along with him. His mother, part Apache, knew then it was a sign that he was destined for something good. Maybe I would grow up to be a doctor just like him, Dr. Wilson told Mama.

I guess she believed his story 'cause she tells it a lot. She says she knows, like Dr. Coyote's mama knew, that I'll turn out all right.

I rode on toward the outskirts of town, where the houses are a little more unkempt and unshaved, too-long grasses, ignored weeds, and rusty, broken-down objects cast forlornly in the front yards. My stomach was growling at me now. I was hungry. It was past my scheduled noontime lunch, which consists of a PB&J sandwich and a pickle, usually eaten en route to the recycling center. But I had forgotten all about it. I would have to scarf it down at Uncle Dal's.

Uncle Dal is full of mysteries. People ask me slyly sometimes, "So where was he all those years?" or "Does Dal have a sweetheart over in Whiskey?" or "What's that statue gonna be, anyway?" But my mouth is sewn up tighter than a sailor's knot. I wouldn't have an answer for them anyway. I've never asked Uncle Dal about anything like that, and he's never asked me anything, either.

That's why we are such a good pair. We have spent countless hours together with not one word spoken, only the sweet sound of his whistling breaking the perfect silence.

I do know lots of secrets about other people in Jumbo, though. I'm a good listener and a steady quiet presence, kinda like the town dog that everyone feeds but thinks they are the only ones doing it. It's amazing what people will tell you while sucking on a purple Tootsie Pop. I hand them out so that everyone will shut up and leave me alone, but all it seems to do is open up a whole can of worms.

I rode up to Uncle Dal's parcel of land, put the kickstand down, and looked around. Uncle Dal's pickup wasn't parked next to the barn, which was unusual. He knows very well how I feel about schedules and that I only have two hours with him—now only an hour and a half—before I have to go over to Mama's bookstore to help sort books.

I still felt a little dizzy. And I was annoyed. And hungry. I lay down despite the dusty dirt and let the ground red-sizzle my backside. I took deep, long breaths like I learned from watching Dame Fiona Friday, a turbaned lady who has a meditation show on at six A.M. every Saturday morning. "Breathe in! Breathe out! Expand your chest. Embrace the feeling of calm and relaxation." It works sometimes. I call them FF breaths in honor of the dame. After her show I tune in to the early morning classic movie on channel 39. That's the only TV I watch.

I lay there, my arms and legs sprawled out, staring up into the wide blue Jumbo sky. I looked at the clouds, wondering if I could find a dragon. The clouds were shapeless and long, like someone had stretched an ivory ribbon from the mountains to the highway.

A bird called forlornly and I blinked. I got my binoculars out of my bike's basket. I lay back down and lifted the binoculars to the sky. I was looking for White Feather. About a year ago, when I was out on my litter rounds at the railroad tracks, I spotted the hugest red-tailed hawk I've ever seen. He swooped down very near me, and I saw that amid his crimson tail feathers was one as white as snow. As I studied him through my binoculars, I thought that this would be as close as I would come to seeing a real dragon fly in this world. I haven't seen White Feather since that day. But I always look. Precision.

The slow rumble of Uncle Dal's pickup startled me. I turned my head just as the wheels of his 1956 baby blue pickup rolled to a stop.

I lay there, warm and lethargic, and watched his boots, crusted with dried-up mud, step down from the truck and walk over to me. I watched Flynn's paws arrive. I smiled at them sideways without lifting my head. I don't give away a lot of smiles, just like I don't give away a lot of words. Flynn licked my face with abandon, as though he had just found me lost in the desert. When he stopped his licking and I blinked a few times, I saw there was an extra set of legs standing next to Uncle Dal.

Little legs.

"What are you doing lying there in the heat, Hug?" Uncle Dal asked.

"Her name's Hug?" came an annoying voice

followed by a slurpy snort of a laugh. He was now sucking vigorously and happily on the Tootsie Pop I had given him earlier.

I scrambled awkwardly to my feet and wiped the dirt off my rear. I looked back and forth between the two of them.

"You're late," I told Uncle Dal, keeping my gaze just on him.

"Look what I found," Uncle Dal said with a big cheesy smile.

You would think he had found the North Pole or something. Uncle Dal doesn't smile often, either, so when he does, I tend to take notice. Once when I was very little, I asked Grandma why he was that way. "He could have been something . . ." she said, just like that, in her usual dismissive "nothing anyone can do about it now" way.

Uncle Dal had been a good baseball player. Everyone thought he was bound for the big leagues. But at the end of his senior year in high school, he fell out of the back of a pickup truck and broke his pitching arm. He and Daddy had been out joyriding in the brush when it happened.

Grandma never forgave them, but then again she never forgives anyone for anything. There's still a photo of Uncle Dal in his baseball uniform at the Sweet Home Diner, hanging next to a framed arrowhead collection and a photo of the 1952 State Champion 1A Jumbo football team.

"Work," I said, still doing my best to ignore the boy.

"This little guy has been looking for you, so I brought him along," Uncle Dal said. "He said you two were friends."

I shot Uncle Dal a look. He knows very well I didn't have, or want, any friends. He doesn't have any friends, either. Just me. I'm not usually someone that feels many emotions in either direction, but I could have rightly said I was madder than a wet hen. A hot wet hen.

"Did you know everybody has their own tongue print?" The boy stuck his long purple-tinged tongue out and flapped it up and down.

Uncle Dal laughed and rubbed the top of the boy's head affectionately. I couldn't believe what I was seeing. "Come on, you two can help me in the barn. By the way, little guy, what's your name?"

"Biswick O'Connor, sir," he said, following behind Uncle Dal. "I'm Irish and we are from Boston and Daddy is home sleeping right now. And I have a new striped bathing suit. Are there any swimming pools around here? Daddy said I should go find one and stay all day."

I followed behind. Biswick. Hmm. With a little bit of guilty glee I thought of what his nickname was going to be here in Jumbo. Bisquick. Or Biscuit. Pancake. Waffle. Ha.

We walked toward Uncle Dal's old red-washed barn where he works on his statue. The barn was built by a wheat farmer, Obedias Cuernavaca, a hundred and fifty years ago. Legend has it that he didn't have much luck farming in the hard ground outside Jumbo, so he became a stone mason, crafting all the headstones out in the old cemetery.

Since Uncle Dal doesn't have his own wife and kids, his work in that old barn has been his family. I can relate to that. I'm never going to marry, either; that mushy stuff is for morons. But I do want to go away from here someday, across the country, maybe to New York, or even England, where no one can bug me.

Our usual routine was that I would sit next to Uncle Dal in the barn as he did his pondering about his statue. Sometimes that's all he does. Ponder. Sometimes he stands and ponders and sometimes he sits and ponders in an old damask-covered wingback chair that Mama bought for him at an estate sale. Sometimes Uncle Dal whistles. Sometimes he doesn't. If it's a good day, he'll hold out his hand and I'll give him one of Obedias's old tools, which I keep in meticulous order, lined up on an ancient farm table. Today Biswick had run ahead and somehow knew exactly where I like to sit my own rear end. He was on my old milking stool, his face wide and happy. I wanted to reach out and straighten Biswick's face and pull up those droopy ears.

"What is that?" Biswick asked, pointing to Uncle Dal's statue. Uncle Dal didn't respond. He was already pondering, his forefinger on his lip, standing in front of the marble block.

When Uncle Dal reappeared after disappearing

all those years, he showed up with a six-foot-tall piece of white marble in the back of his pickup. It was the talk of the town for weeks. It's been here ever since on the dusty hay-scattered floor, right smack in the middle of the barn. And after all these years, only that rough-looking perpetual foot has emerged. People come out here periodically to stare at it. They take bets on what it's gonna be. Some say it's Bigfoot, others say it's the Venus de Milo or the Statue of Liberty. Or even Davy Crockett or Sam Houston. And of course they all try to pry it out of me, what I think it's gonna be. But I don't know, either.

"So, Hug, what are we going to do next?" Biswick asked.

"Shhhh," I said. "And it's not Hug," I said as I optimistically handed a chisel to Uncle Dal, who was watching me funny with his forehead all scrunched up.

"Well, what is it?" asked Biswick. He had one finger in his ear, picking at it.

"Merilee. Horrendous." I hate my name. Hate it.

"Uncle Dal, are there any swimming pools

around here? Daddy says there's nothing to do here in this jerkwater town."

Oh great. Now he was calling *my* uncle "Uncle Dal."

"Oh, we have lots of interesting sites here. We have the Balma hot springs nearby, and the Jumbo Ghost Lights." He walked around back of the marble and stood there.

Oh Lord. Why did he have to bring up that? We have some strange things around here that have been part of the landscape for so long people pay no mind to them anymore. There are mirages off in the desert that look like cities floating in the sky, and whirligig dust devils that seem to chase cars on the side of the highway. But what we're most famous for is the Jumbo Ghost Lights. There's even a viewing point off the side of the highway halfway to Whiskey. Supposedly the Apache Indians saw them, too, and believed they were spirits coming to take their ancestors home. The old-timers, they'll tell you a good story or two about the lights, if you'll listen. We even have a corny festival every year near Christmastime called the Jumbo Lights Festival.

"Ghost Lights? Whatya mean, whatya mean?" Biswick asked.

I broke in with some satisfaction. "Nothing worth seeing. They're not real. Phosphorous. Luminescence."

"Whaaat?" His voice quavered. "Why does Merilee Horrendous talk funny?"

Uncle Dal frowned at me, something he had never, ever done before. "The lights are beautiful, magical lights," he said. "And some say they are the ghosts of the Indians looking for their loved ones."

"Indians?" Biswick uttered, and I thought I saw a quick shimmer of something slide across his face.

"Maybe your daddy can take you sometime. They come out in the middle of the night," Uncle Dal said as he walked back around to the front of the statue and knelt down. My heart leapt. Maybe today was gonna be one of those good days where I got to hand him a tooth chisel for some smoothing. A couple of weeks ago, we'd had a breakthrough. We'd refined the baby toe and you could even see its little toenail now. The other toes still looked like fat sausages, those kind always in a Crock-Pot at parties. Uncle Dal ran his hand reverently over the pits and curves of the foot. Sometimes he could spend a whole hour doing this. So I sat down in some scattered hay and leaned back on my arms.

I stared up into the rafters. Old, rusty wheat-farming tools, remnants of Obedias's farming venture, hung down. Cobwebs were strung across from tool to tool like party streamers. Ferdie Frankmueller told Uncle Dal once when she came to stare at the foot that he could make a small fortune selling all those old tools up there. But Uncle Dal said no, he liked everything just as it was in Obedias's barn. And I did, too. I glanced further up to the old hayloft, which I'd never explored and which I was never gonna explore. Sometimes while Uncle Dal was pondering, I liked to imagine a dragon lived up there, guarding a nest of eggs.

Biswick ran over and peered down at the foot. "It's ugly," he stated. I narrowed my eyes at him.

Uncle Dal smiled a little. But I didn't. I was

insulted. It's true the foot is ill-formed and a little bumpy, but so what. Maydell Rathburger says she's sure it's her late great-grandmother Mamie's bunion foot resurrected. But I think it's beautiful and I don't find many things beautiful. And I know that Uncle Dal knows what he's doing. He has a vision. I'm just living for the day when he's gonna be ready for me to hand him the rasps and the rifflers for the truly fine carving, and then the sandpaper for the final finishing.

"Did you know that elephants are the only mammals that can't jump?" Biswick did a few stiff hops around the statue to illustrate. I wasn't going to write that one down in my journal. I was furious.

"Hey, go hand me that first chisel over there," Uncle Dal said as my face burned. Biswick ran over to the worktable and starting pawing all of Obedias's tools. I had to take an FF breath as I watched him scatter them around. Uncle Dal continued, "You know if you don't like getting up in the middle of the night, there's always the Conquistador tree you can go look for."

"I've seen trees before, Uncle Dal," Biswick said as he picked up one of those prized rasps off Uncle Dal's worktable and made a face that seemed to say "duh." He dropped the rasp, just missing his feet.

"This is a special tree, Bis," Uncle Dal started, and I winced at the nickname. "A conquistador planted one from Spain and then buried a treasure underneath it."

"Has anyone ever found it?" Biswick asked, his eyes wide.

Uncle Dal kept staring at the statue while he talked. "The Goat Herder tried. Died trying."

"Died?" Biswick repeated.

I rolled my eyes. We all had grown up hearing the legend of the Goat Herder. It was a bunch of bunk.

"His name was Jonah. He herded his goats up and down Cathedral Mountain, always on the lookout for the Conquistador tree as he did so. One day one of his goats got lost way up and the Goat Herder had to venture up farther than he'd ever gone. When he finally made it down the next day, shaken and pale white, he told his wife he'd seen the Ghost Lights and they seemed to beckon him farther up the mountain. But it was too steep for a simple goat herder to climb. 'Go back,' his wife demanded. 'They will show you the Conquistador tree and we'll be rich.' 'I do not want to go back," he told her. 'I don't want to tempt fate. I'm lucky to be alive.' But she made him go and his goat herd followed him up the mountain."

"And did he find it?" Biswick asked, his eyes big, as he rolled the rasp under his foot back and forth like a log. The sound grated on my ears.

"He never came home," Uncle Dal said as he plopped down in his chair. "The goats came down the mountain the next day. But he didn't."

For some reason this story really makes Grandma bristle more than any of the other stupid legends around here. "Saved once," she says mysteriously. "Not twice."

Biswick plopped down on my milking stool, mimicking Uncle Dal. Neither of them said a word.

I had had enough. I went over, picked up the rasp, which is used for final shaping, and slammed it back down where it belonged. Then I lined the other tools up quickly in a nice straight line. I walked out of the barn without looking back. Why fill a kid's head with a bunch of superstitious hogwash? There's no treasure, no goat herder, nothing magical around here, and there never will be.

Uncle Dal appeared in the doorway of the barn. "Hey, where are you going?"

"Off my schedule," I mumbled, and tried to stifle "horrendous" under my breath, but it came out anyway, loud, echoing behind me. I got on my bike and rode off down the road.

Grandma Birdy always knew when I came home. Today she was standing on her front porch with her hands on her hips and her lips pursed. About two years ago, Mama finally got fed up with Grandma living with us and made Daddy and Uncle Dal build a house for her out back of our house. Daddy was fed up, too, though he wouldn't admit it. It was Mama's idea to turn Grandma's new house on the side and have it face Third

Street so Mama wouldn't have to look at her all the time out the kitchen window and feel guilty, but all that ended up doing is giving Grandma a first-hand look, like a fat spider squattin' in her web, at all our doings every time we left the house.

At first Grandma said she couldn't wait to get away from Mama's mangy dogs. But more than once, I saw her wagglin' a T-bone out her new back door, trying to lure the dogs over to her. She managed on getting Weenie, the surefire dumbest one, to live with her permanently.

After my whole life of Grandma lording over our world, the loss of her came as a shock. It was an extra book out of line in my shelf, crumbs in my butter tub. Plus we lost all Grandma's good cooking.

Cooking is not one of Mama's strong points. We haven't had a decent meal in two years and I think that gives Grandma great satisfaction.

Grandma made Daddy buy her two white low-slung garden chairs so she could sit outside with her friends, but her companion chair is usually empty 'cause the only person who ever wants to sit next to her is Miss Fleta Bell, Grandma's longtime friend from the Holy Hands Baptist Church. Grandma won't go to church anymore 'cause she says the pastor, the Reverend Ham, has trailer-trash eyes and sticky fingers in the collection plate.

Miss Fleta Bell is battier than Grandma 'cause she insists on being called "Miss" and her mind has gone back to the old days before she was married. She can't hear worth a darn, which of course makes her the perfect companion to Grandma, who doesn't seem to care if anyone's listening as long as she's the only one doing the talking. Miss Fleta's caretaker brings her around once a week so she can sit with Grandma and Weenie in the shade of Grandma's sycamore tree, drink mint tea, and talk about the good old days.

Let me tell you something about "Grandma's tree." When she was first married, my grandfather asked her what she wanted for a wedding present. All she wanted was a tree out back of the house but she wouldn't tell him why. He planted it for her all those years ago, and it gave her the shade she needed when she sat outside watching everything, knitting her useless, rainbow-colored, snowball hats.

Daddy said Grandma'd gone around the bend since we moved her. But I wasn't so sure. Grandma was as sharp as a tack. Just meaner. Cat-scratch mean. I'd seen her watch me with those hard little eyes and I knew there was still lots going on in there.

Mama told me to write down all those slinging barbs from Grandma and it would make me feel better. Mama had written the first line in my journal in a cheerful, loopy scrawl: "When life gives you lemons, make lemonade." I have filled pages and pages with Grandma's stingers and all the interesting quotations I can remember. But when I wrote Grandma's words down, I can tell you, they still tasted blue bitter and nothing like sugar lemonade.

I rode by Grandma's house and before I could get past her she whispered, "Is he still working on that damn foot?" I ignored her but she went on. "I've heard about that boy. I bet the two of you will be thick as thieves." She had a strange grin on her face. Weenie, the traitor, barked at me. He's quite fat now, bloated like an overcooked hot dog 'cause Grandma had been feeding him all her good cooking. As Weenie has grown thicker, Grandma seemed to have shriveled like an old green grape. Then she added, "Brush that nasty hair." My long brown hair has a mind of its own. Grandma says it's full of tumbleweeds and brickleberries. Bug's soft and curly blond hair, of course, is always perfect and it smells good, too. She sneaks Mama's Love's Baby Soft Perfume and sprays it all over her hair.

I brought my bicycle to a stop and wrote "thick as thieves" in my black journal, feeling my tummy grumble as I did so. Without saying a word to Grandma, who was still standing there with her hands on her hips, I pulled out my sack lunch from the back of my bicycle and went inside our house.

I went to my room and sat at my desk. I ate my PB&J sandwich and opened my journal and started to draw dragons.

Chapter 3

About a week after Biswick's arrival, Miss Veraleen Holliday came to town in the midst of an unforeseen morning rain. Grandma says unforeseen rains are no good: like a cicada's dance, they're soon over. Miss Veraleen had always had a bit of mystery about her, since she's only been around these parts twenty years or so. She'd never married, at least not that anyone knew about, so she was still a "Miss," but Grandma said she looked more like a "Mister."

Miss Veraleen drove down Main Street in her metallic gold Pontiac GTO, with a trailer the size of a suitcase. It was kinda sad seeing the trailer get rained on, all her belongings in the whole wide world exposed and wet. I don't know what Miss Veraleen could have stuffed in there. Herbs, maybe. Concoctions. She didn't have many clothes. No one had ever seen her wear anything but her nurse uniform.

The rumor going around was that Veraleen got fired from the Whiskey hospital, where she'd been taking care of babies all those years, including me, because she tried one of her famous home cures on one of the babies and something bad had happened. People said that the hospital found out the only qualifications Veraleen had for being a nurse was her old-timey nurse uniform. People said the hospital had never been happy about what Miss Veraleen called the "ranch doctoring" she did on the side—working on cowboys *and* cows out on the nearby ranches, midwifing poor women's babies, and home curing every fool from here to Whiskey. The hospital just looked the other way until something happened. So people said.

Veraleen came from somewhere up in the Panhandle originally and she was as tight-lipped about her past as a tick on a pup's ear. When she showed up in Jumbo, all the old speculations got stirred up again. Someone even visited Dr. Coyote Wilson to "express her concerns," but he said don't bother with Miss Veraleen. Her way of doctoring has been going on for hundreds of years.

Lots of people come to Jumbo to escape, you see. I don't know why. It doesn't seem like a good hiding hole to me, even if it's out in the middle of nowhere. Jumbo is not discreet. It might take a while, but eventually everyone knows a little something about you, whether you want them to or not.

Jumbo lies on a high grass-plains desert, its little white Art Deco buildings dwarfed by the enormous Texas sky. No dark shadows here to melt into and disappear. The desert air is crystal clear like it's been bleached of all its sins. People who come here come to be cleansed. That's what the old-timers say.

Used to be we had only two types of people in Jumbo: the old-timers and the Mexicans. That's how it had been since way back when Jumbo was just a water stop on the old Union Pacific railroad line.

That all changed about fifteen years ago when Harvard University set up a poet-in-residence, taking over Old Man Porter's house. He died in his bathtub and no one knew it for two weeks. The poets who come seem to like it here because, well, everything in Jumbo, despite its name, is pretty minimal. And I guess poets like that.

Other artist types followed, a trickle of silent tortured souls in black turtlenecks. My mother arrived in the midst of this cultural awakening. She wanted to be an artist and Jumbo was the place to be at that time. But I have never once seen one of my mother's paintings. I'm pretty sure she never picked up a paintbrush after I was born.

I watched mesmerized with my face pressed against Mama's bookstore window as Miss Veraleen paraded down Main Street a few days after she arrived, her sturdy leather satchel wagging at her side. I'm not one to stare, but she was kinda a spectacle here in Jumbo; really though, she'd probably be a spectacle anywhere. Everyone else was staring, too—nonchalantly as they went about their business. And it was raining again, like the day Veraleen first arrived, misting shy and slow over everything.

Veraleen Holliday is all Bs. She's BIG—not fat big, not at all. Just big all over. And taller than any lady I've ever seen. Big boned. Big head. Gentle giant hands. I imagined just one of them could cradle a baby. Big feet. Only person I've ever seen with feet bigger than mine. And she really isn't that old, not like Grandma. She'd just been wizened like an old plum tree after all those years of ripening in the Panhandle sun.

Veraleen's blond hair, streaked with peppery gray, was scraped back in a long ponytail, and at her age, Grandma says, she oughta know better than to be wearing a girly ponytail. What's strange is, she has no other hair—no eyelashes, no eyebrows, nothing. Myrtle Bupp said Veraleen told a friend of hers over in Whiskey, in the strictest confidence, of course, that she has "hormone problems." And that's why she's so big all over and hairless.

Today Veraleen was wearing men's ole dusty Levi's and a plaid cowgirl shirt tucked in. The only sign of her old nurse uniform was her big white nurse's shoes that looked like sailboats careening down the pavement. Grandma Birdy says, "Hormone problems, my butt; she's a cow who ought to be put to bed with the night herd." I thought, as I watched her parade down the street, head high, her ponytail braided down her back, that she had a noble radiance about her.

First she went into the Cut 'N' Curl, then the Rexall Drug, then the Dairy Queen, and then Putt's Chicken Hutt, which has a big giant chicken whose eyes and beak open and close mechanically.

Veraleen seemed to get madder and madder each time she came out of a store. When she turned abruptly and strode into Ferdie's Doll-O-Rama (formally Ferdie's Five & Dime), she picked up a companion. Biswick hopped into the store behind her.

So far I had managed to avoid Biswick, so to speak. Every day after school he had been waiting for me in the same spot, as bothersome as a booger you can't flick off. He would follow along a little while, with a confused look like no one had ever rejected him before, until I lost him. I was not going to change my VOE for him. No sir.

I lifted my face from the store window. There was a smudgy nose smear left on the glass, just below the word *Hole*. Mama's store is called the Hole in the Wall. She started it with hardly any money at all. Now she even has a frozen ice cream cooler, and poetry readings and a coffee bar with wine tastings ("for hooligan sinners," Grandma says) on Thursday evenings.

The door opened and Lorelei, Mama's assistant manager, raced in. "Guess who I just met!" Lorelei stammered. Lorelei isn't her real name. It's Lettie Lee Carmichael, but she reinvented herself into the sophisticated type even though she's never left Jumbo. You can't count a visit to the mall in San Antonio as a cosmopolitan reincarnation. She changed her Texas accent, too. Tries to sound like Audrey Hepburn, her favorite movie actress. I hear her practicing sometimes in the back when she thinks no one is listening: "That's lovely. That's brilliant, my dear. Lovely."

Lorelei says she's going to open a chichi pooh-

pooh hair salon. To prove to herself she can do it, she styles her hair differently every day of the year. We were on Day 160 now and believe me, she was running out of ideas. She used to be what Grandma would call the town floozy, even though, for all I knew, she'd never had a boyfriend; she just looked like she's had lots of them. Grandma says there's no way Lorelei's hair color was real; it's as red as a fox's butt during pokeberry season.

Mama looked up over her cat-eyed glasses but continued to unpack an order of new books we had received today. I guess you could say Mama has a uniform, too, like me. She wears embroidered peasant blouses from Mexico, flowing skirts with long fringes from India, and last but not least—clogs. Most days she wears her hair in two pigtails—high—like a little girl's. Let me explain something about Mama. You tell her one thing, and she does the other. You say high, she says low. She's "artsy-fartsy *and* from New York" as Grandma says, and that's it for Grandma. Mama doesn't have a nickname, like everyone else here. The old-timers call her "Hell-in" instead of Hel*ene*, which is her real name. One of those half-friendly, half-insult kind of things.

"Miss Holliday?" Mama asked Lorelei.

"Is that Miss Veraleen's last name? Holliday?" Lorelei asked. "How lovely. Makes one think of canals and starting over like in *Roman Holiday*." Lorelei got that far-off look, like she's prone to. I wasn't about to tell her that she was thinking partly of Katharine Hepburn, partly of Audrey, and there's no canals in Rome. "I did see her today. Who could miss her . . ." She paused awkwardly, as people do when they've barely caught themselves from saying something insulting.

"She's looking for work and has hit almost every store on Main Street," Lorelei continued. "She was even in the Sweet Home Diner asking if they needed a cook."

I started doodling dragons in a copy of *Country Life* magazine next to some Holstein cows grazing in a green field.

Lorelei came behind the counter, picked up a book that was lying there, and started pivoting it back and forth in her hand. "No, the person I saw is the new poet who was having coffee, writing his delicious poetry, and oh my God you wouldn't believe who he looks like!"

Mama paused, but only for a second, and we locked eyes. Sometimes all we have to do is look at each other and know what the other is thinking. Mama smiled.

"James Dean!" Lorelei rolled her eyes, like we should have guessed from all her clues. "Just like in the movie *Giant* with his white T-shirt, jeans, slicked back hair, and that brilliant brooding intensity."

"*Rebel Without a Cause*," I mumbled under my breath. "Stupid. Stupendous." James Dean was a cowboy in *Giant* and Lorelei would rather be dead than be interested in a kicker, even though that's all there is around here. Kickers, cows, and a smoldering poet or two.

"Oh really." Mama smiled. "Well, I hope that's a clue that he can 'brood' good poetry. We haven't had a decent reading in here since Lovie and Lulie read from their *Great-grandmother Bupp's Cookbook of Southern Delights*."

Lorelei continued, throwing a frown at me, "And I left out the best part—he was wearing dark sunglasses in the middle of the diner." She laughed. "How brilliant is that!"

"Perhaps he's a bonafide poet, and not a graffiti artist," Mama said. The last poet got run out of town by the sheriff for painting "Life is Nothing" in drippy vermilion letters on the side of the Sweet Home Diner.

Mama opened a new carton, set it aside, and nodded at me. I knew what it was. My monthly dose of the classics. I walked over and pulled out a leather-bound book. It was a copy of *The Faerie Queene* by Edmund Spenser. I held it up and breathed in the leather.

It was Mama who brought me back from the silent world. After all that infamous crying, at about age one I just simply stopped. No crying, no whimpers, no "ma-ma," no "da-da." Nothing. So quiet, I was silent as the grave, Grandma says. Months went by and at first everyone just enjoyed the peace. Eventually Mama became very worried.

"Be glad that squallin' stopped. You should be praising the Lord on your knees like you do over at that Mezcan church," Grandma told her. Grandma doesn't like that Mama is Catholic and goes to the Church of the Divine Mercy on the wrong side of the railroad tracks. Grandma doesn't really like anything about Mama. Never has. Never will.

Mama says that in my second year, I watched and absorbed everything. My guess is that I was taking the whole world in for a while, withholding judgment. Mama says I'd crawl up on Daddy's plaid easy chair and stare out like an old blind dog she used to have.

But when I was two, even Daddy became worried. He closed the Jumbo Tomato Plant for the day so he and Mama could take me in their old red Buick, the Red Rocket, on my first trip to El Paso. Daddy's always with his tomatoes, so this was quite something for him to be closing up shop for the day. He bought Jumbo Tomatoes from Fleet Perkins a few years before I was born and he started growing organic tomatoes. Problem is, everyone expects huge tomatoes because of the name, so he has to ship them all off to the East Coast where they appreciate organic things and don't care that their tomatoes are runty. He doesn't ever make much a profit. Grandma says Daddy doesn't have the sense God gave a goose.

Anyway, everyone was sayin' as how I must be a mute 'cause I was silent as the desert wind that blows in like a ghost several times a year and spooks everyone. I don't think that first doctor had any answers for Mama. She doesn't talk much about those days.

Since she couldn't get any answers, Mama went into high gear to save me on her own. Ordered every book she could about child rearing and odd children. She brought me to the store every day and let me follow her around as she told me everything from the teachings of Aristotle to the sublime rhymes of Dr. Seuss. She talked to me as though I was listening. And she bought me endless fairy tale books and I would stare at the pages for hours.

Mama's project must have done some good. Finally I started to talk and once I did the words just poured out of me. By age three and a half, I was reciting full soliloquies from Shakespeare and entire chapters from classics like *Treasure Island* and *Moby Dick*. I could even recite the phone book at will. I was child genius. Girl extraordinaire from Jumbo, Texas. Everyone agreed I'd leave and be famous one day.

But Mama still worried. She says I spent hours outside in the backyard, pacing around and around in a figure eight, talking to myself. From her view out the kitchen window, it looked like I was talking to my only friend in the world. Grandma would stand over Mama's shoulder and shake her head. "Hell-in, I told you that girl is touched." Nowadays all that pacing is mostly camouflaged when I'm picking up my litter. But sometimes I just can't help myself. I charge up and down our driveway (where Grandma can't see me) like a soldier on night patrol.

When I was in third grade, my teacher, Miss Blevins, told Mama that even though I was spoutin' out all kinds of smart and wondrous things, that was all I was doing—spoutin' out.

And it wasn't that wonderful after all. I was just memorizing things, not really knowing anything true, Miss Blevins said, and I need to go to the specialist again. So Mama drove me back up to El Paso. Daddy couldn't come. It was shipment day at the tomato plant.

Mama filled out a pile of questionnaires, and they did all kinds of tests on me. As I drew pictures of dragons in a parade of empty rectangles, I overheard teasing snippets in hushed tones. All I got out of it was "qualitative" and "umbrella" and "high-functioning." When the doctor gave my mother the final diagnosis, he put me in another room with the broken stubby crayons and torn coloring books, and shut the door.

I can still hear the steady clickety-clop of the Red Rocket's engine as we drove home. Mama tried to find the right words. I could see out of the corner of my eye that she tried to say something for a long time.

Finally, "You are very special and always will be. That's all there is to it."

So there it was. Very special.

I knew she was leaving something out. Mama went on with a skinny smile. "You know the doctor said *lots* of famous people have the same thing. Like *Einstein* and *Beethoven*."

I'd seen both their freaky hair pictures in books and I didn't want to be in the same club with them thank you very much. I didn't care how smart they were. "This little trip will be our secret. Your daddy doesn't need any more worries, Merilee."

I knew what she was saying. Daddy could barely handle his silent, slow-growing tomatoes, much less deal with a daughter who has some sort of "qualitative umbrella problem."

Mama let out a long sigh. "Someday," she started, "when you're older, you'll leave Jumbo and the world will know how special you are."

At the time, frankly, I was only worried about Grandma finding out, I wasn't thinking about how I was special. When we got back I couldn't believe my luck. When we walked in the door, she was running around in a fit and fury clutching Bug at her chest. "She's got a rash on her neck!" she screamed at my mother. Mama quietly took Bug in her arms to make an inspection and Grandma collapsed on the sofa. She never even asked about the trip to El Paso.

I'm not sure what Mama told Miss Blevins. I think it had something to do with the prestigious Einstein Hair Club, because that teacher stopped staring at me with one eye screwed up.

Maybe I will leave here someday. If I ever gather the courage. Deep down, though, I'm too afraid to leave my VOE. I think I'd die without it. But Mama always says, "Sometimes when you climb a mountain, you discover it's just a molehill."

If I went, it would be faraway. Perhaps somewhere in upstate New York, near where Grandma Ruth once lived. Grandma Ruth. My nice grandma. She died when I was little, and I only have a few memories. I can barely remember her voice or face—only that she looked like Mrs. Butterworth, like the syrup container. My Mrs. Butterworth grandma. I think she's the only person in the world I would have ever let wrap her arms around me.

Chapter
4

I stayed late at Mama's bookstore to shelve the new books, and when I got home for dinner, the first hint I had that something was amiss were the tantalizing wafts of a home-cooked meal. One that's been simmering all afternoon—*real* cooked-food smells with exotic odors—echelons above what Mama's fish sticks, boxed macaroni, and store-bought casseroles conjured up.

My grandfather, Avery P. Monroe, built our house from a Sears Roebuck catalog kit in 1915. It's a Craftsman-style bungalow with four rooms on the first floor, four rooms above, and wide hall-ways that run down the middle. After he finished putting together his house, he went searching for a wife, and I guess they were pretty scarce in those days, because he came home with Grandma. He found Birdy Biedermeyer, as she was called then, sitting at the bus stop in Whiskey with one sad, ratty suitcase in hand, and no one to meet her. She must have had something special to snare him, because when I look at his old worn photos, I see someone with kindness and intelligence in his eyes. He died way before I was born.

Anyway, since we have this large hallway that runs down the middle of the house, I can stand in the front doorway and detect all kinds of things—what's cooking in the kitchen (nothing much since Grandma left), or if Daddy's snoring in his bed upstairs, or if Bug is about to pounce on me from around the corner. It was here, at the front door, that I was stopped dead in my tracks with the sweet smell of southern fried chicken. Oh my goodness. Oh no. Was Grandma cooking in there?

I put my things down on the hall bench and slowly crept back to the kitchen. The whole room seemed to be busting with people all squashed around our little table. And there was big Veraleen, standing at the stove and handing out orders like she was the head honcho chef at a swanky restaurant. Winkie and Beasie were lined up behind her, ready for a dripping of something good. I guessed Stinky was placing his bets from under the table.

"Get some more grits with that, baby," she said to—oh no!—it was Biswick sitting in *my* seat at the table. My eyes narrowed, following Biswick as he headed over to Veraleen, almost dropping his too-full plate. Mama, Daddy, and Lorelei were there, as were Bug and Snooky Venezuela, her latest try-on best friend. Bug has been searching for a best friend since I can remember and you can set your calendar to when a new wannabe will appear. She had actually gone through the full cycle of girls in the third grade twice and was on her third round.

I turned to leave. Fried chicken or not, I didn't want to be there. I felt like a worm in a beehive.

"Hi, Hug," came Uncle Dal's voice. A calming wave went down my back. I stopped at the door.

"Merilee! There you are, honey," Mama said all cheerful between bites. "Come sit down. You wouldn't believe our luck! Miss Holliday is going to be our cook! Seems she used to cook for the cowboys back on the ranch." They all looked up at me with faces as full as dog ticks.

"Well, here she is herself," Veraleen said, turning from the stove while holding a black spatula in midair. Pale blue eyes twinkled at me. "Hmm, hmm, hmm. Darlin', we called you Crybaby Monroe in the nursery." She had a husky voice that sounded salted and simmered over a campfire. "Looks like you stopped." As long as I live, I don't think I'll ever get away from that story. When I die, my grave marker is going to read, "Merilee Monroe: Cried All The Time and Made Everyone Miserable."

Veraleen had one of Grandma Birdy's little white eyelet aprons on and it looked like a postage stamp stuck over her tummy. She wore a white chef's cap that had flopped over in exhaustion. And those big ole nurses shoes, she was wearing those, too. At that exact moment, I saw Grandma Birdy peeking in through the screen door, her face all pinched up and her nose twitching, taking in the good smells. Then, like a silent specter, she was gone.

Veraleen handed me a heaping plate of fried chicken, mashed potatoes, a mosaic swirl of tantalizing creamy side dishes, and a pile of pinto beans. Oh, it did smell good. I couldn't resist. I took the plate and sat down in the only open seat at the table, next to Biswick.

"Gotta try my beans, baby," Veraleen said, her voice booming and I made a mental note to add another *B* to Veraleen's *B*s. Booming voice. "No ranch woman is worth her salt if she can't cook up a mess of beans." She smiled then, one of those smiles people smile when they got bad teeth.

"Hi, Huggy," Biswick blurted, a piece of food from his mouth propelling across the table, and everyone giggled like he was the cutest thing on two feet. I grunted and stabbed my fork into what looked like orange mush.

"That's sweet potatoes with pineapple, honey," said Veraleen, giving me, I noticed, a calculating stare with those piercing blue eyes. After all, she hadn't got a good look at me in a long time, not since I was a baby and screaming to high heaven. I realized after a second, she hadn't said "pineapple honey"—she had called *me* "honey." Ha. I just stared back at her blank-faced. I wasn't going to fall that easily, not like the other gullible fools and dogs lined up around the kitchen table, shoveling down her good food.

I wondered what Uncle Dal was doing here. He doesn't show his face much at our house, no matter how Mama coaxes him, for the fact that Grandma picks at him almost as much as she does at me. I guess Dal had smelled Veraleen's cooking from his sad rusty trailer home across town and couldn't resist.

Biswick piped up next to me. "I invited Uncle Dal over 'cause I didn't want him to miss this." Everyone went on eating as though Biswick always sat in my chair and had always been in charge of inviting the guests over to dinner. I also wondered if Biswick had been to Obedias's barn and helped Uncle Dal without me. "And I wanted to see Merilee Horrendous, too!" Everyone looked at their food. I just about died. Bug and Snooky laughed.

"That's real nice of you, Biswick," Daddy said. "We don't get to see much of Dal."

"So where's Mother Monroe?" Veraleen asked as she went bustling around the table. "I remember when Merilee was born, Mrs. Monroe looked like she was chewing on her own heart." I saw Daddy peer toward the screen door and I wondered if Grandma was there again. "Where is the little spitfire? We got enough to feed an army." My family passed several loaded looks back and forth. Oh Lordy, I thought, we don't need Grandma Birdy back in here and I'm sure that's what they thought, too.

"Grandma Birdy likes to cook for herself. As much as we try to, we can't get her over here to eat. She only comes on Christmas Day and for her birthday," Mama explained.

"And *my* birthday," Bug piped in, "but she always bakes a chocolate cake just for me at her house, too. Whoops! That's supposed to be a secret." She grinned. Grandma has never once, in my entire life, given me anything true. There have been a few recycled birthday cards, and once a teddy bear she bought at a garage sale. Nothing else. Not even one of her butt-ugly snowball caps she's always knitting.

"Well, all you need to know is that we're starving most of the time," Mama explained, deftly shifting the conversation away from Grandma. "I'm at the bookstore most of the day and my cooking never much progressed beyond Tuna Helper."

"I know all about that," Veraleen said. "Working hard and raising children. Hard work keeps the fences up." She was like a one-man band, all synchronized and shifting just right—topping off one person's sweet tea, plopping a dollop of potatoes—knowing what they wanted before they did—and sprinkling compliments about like she was sugaring strawberries.

Veraleen was making sure she was here to stay, I thought. The conversation started up again but I noticed that no one asked her about her children—if she ever had any and where they are now.

Back at the stove, Veraleen was stirring and muttering to herself, kinda sing-songy to her pots like they were her nursery babies and she was soothing them. It sent an eerie chill down my back, 'cause that's something Grandma used to do when she was cooking at that same stove. They were under-the-breath mutterers, or Under Mutterers—UMs. I'd seen Daddy do it, too, the few times we've been alone in the car together. I'm so quiet, I guess he forgets I'm there and murmurs Mama's name every few minutes like he's hiccupping old memories.

Bug started into one of her monotonous monologues, telling Snooky "and then you see I had a pencil already so I didn't need a pencil but she gave me one anyway, one more pencil which I didn't need" when I saw another specter in the darkness outside the screened door.

It was our new poet.

Filtered through the screen door, his face was incandescently handsome in the dark night. Where Biswick's face was incomplete, his father's was perfect to a fault—still it was an echo of something true. A soul that was searching. Someone that might write poetry. I'm not one to judge people. I don't read them the same way other people do. I summed him up right away, though, like I sum up infinite numbers—fast and definite. I knew him.

He walked straight in without even tapping. Everyone at the table looked up and the vision of him was enough to stop Bug in her pencil story— no small feat. He stood with a booted leg straight out to the side. "I'm sorry to interrupt," he said with an Irish lilt. "I'm looking for Biswick." At least that is what I think he said, because he didn't sound sorry, he sounded mad.

"Well, you'll just have to pull up a chair and wait a little. That child is as hollow as a winter coyote and I'm gonna see he gets a good home-cooked meal," Veraleen said. She was talking at Biswick's daddy like he was someone she'd known her whole life, but I don't think she knew him because she was giving him quick sidewinder glances like the rest of us. "And I'm working on a pot of cure here for that festerin' bug bite on his arm. Three weeds, chewed tobacca' juice, and baking soda. Best remedy for bites." She boomed back over her shoulder as she stirred, "It should have been looked to . . . before."

The poet watched her with hooded eyes and for a moment I imagined him pulling Biswick up by the arms and dragging him out of there. He seemed like the type who would. But he didn't. He left a defiant trail of red copper mud across our checked black-and-white linoleum and took the chair offered by Uncle Dal, who nodded politely to him. Everyone scooted to make room and Veraleen dropped a full plate in front of him as he sat down. It clanked and wobbled a little and some mashed potatoes ran over the side like an angry lava flow.

Bug asked, "Do you chew the tobacco up, Veraleen?"

"I've been known to take a chew every now and then." She smiled without really smiling again, and I noticed her lips were lined with a makeup pencil. In fact, everything was pencil-lined on her face. Her nonexistent eyebrows, her eyes, her lips.

"Hi, Daddy," said Biswick. His daddy didn't even look up from his plate of food as he shoveled it in, barely grunting an acknowledgment. He winced at his first bite like someone had fed him skunk oil with onions (I think he was smelling Stinky from under the table) and I saw this didn't win many points with Veraleen, either.

I felt Biswick change. I couldn't pinpoint whether it was fear, happiness, or anger—but something powerful washed over me. I kept chomping my food, trying to ignore the shivers. An embarrassing stillness settled around the table.

Veraleen started clanking dishes around loudly. I can't stand loud noises. Breathe in. Breathe out, Merilee. Breathe in. Breathe out.

"So, Mr. O'Connor," my father began amidst the clatter.

"Jack," he interrupted.

"Jack," my father repeated. "So you've moved into the Porter house."

"That I have," he replied with his Irish lilt that even I had to admit had a nice sonorous ring to it.

There was a long, flat silence. I wondered lots of things about the poet, and I'm sure everyone else did, too. But in Jumbo you don't ask direct questions. You wait till later when you can specu-late with others and build up your own embellished truth. I wanted to know if Mr. O'Connor was indeed Irish, and if he was, why didn't Biswick sound or look like him? Where was Biswick's mother?

"So are you from Ireland?" Bug asked. Bug doesn't follow the normal conventions.

"I'm from here and there," the poet said. He still had not made eye contact with one single person in the room.

Lorelei, the idiot, couldn't keep her eyes off him. Veraleen shook her head slightly as she stirred, her lined lips all pursed down and wrinkled, like the spokes of a sad setting sun.

"Yeah, we're from Ireland," Biswick said in his little distinctly non-Irish voice. Mr. O'Connor gave Biswick a queer look, his eyes meeting mine for a brief second. If eyes are the windows of the soul, he had a chasm in his core, and he was all there was between Biswick and the whole wide world. I shuddered and glanced over at Biswick and was ashamed. Ashamed that I had rejected him.

"Merilee used to think leprechauns were real." Bug laughed. I shot a look at her.

"Well, they are!" Biswick interjected. "Aren't they, Daddy Jack?"

"Yeah, if you believe in the damn tooth fairy." Bug and Snooky's eyes grew wide. They started to giggle.

"Merilee even built a leprechaun trap out in the backyard." Bug laughed again.

"Did she catch anything?" Veraleen asked over her shoulder from the stove.

"Just a bunch of chocolate gold coins." Bug snorted. "From Daddy."

I looked over at Daddy. He'd put the coins in my trap and the next morning I believed for a whole half-day there were indeed leprechauns until I saw a jar full of chocolate coins on the cashier counter at Ferdie's Five & Dime.

"Merilee still believes in dragons, though," Bug teased with a big grin and Snooky giggled. "They call her Dragon Girl at school."

Daddy frowned at Bug and it got quiet again. Mama was studying the poet. Mama likes contrary people 'cause that's how she is, but I could tell she wasn't sure what to think of him. Daddy was watching Mama. I saw his face darken and wondered if he'd say something, because unlike Mama, he doesn't like anything contrary. I knew he probably wouldn't, though. Daddy doesn't react to much. He's a lot like his tomatoes—solid on the outside, full of all kinds of mushy things inside.

"So tell me, Jack," Mama asked. "What kind of poetry do you write?"

"The kind that gets me in trouble," the poet replied as he tried with his tongue indelicately to get some food out of the side of his mouth. Daddy scooted his chair away, then walked out of the kitchen. Stinky, who had been licking my ankle, ran out from underneath the table and followed him.

"I run the bookstore in town and we would love to have you do a reading," Mama said as she watched Daddy leave.

"I'll give it some thought. My experience is people don't like hearing the truth."

One of Veraleen's penciled eyebrows arched in disbelief.

"Did you know that it's impossible to lick your

elbow or stick it in your ear?" Biswick said. He caught two big dumb fish with that one. Bug and Snooky, after thinking about it a second, both started fiddling with their elbows.

"Well," Mr. O'Connor said. He scooted out his chair with one loud ungracious screech. "Biswick and I will be going."

Biswick immediately stood up.

"You ain't going nowhere till you have had my Old Cowboy Buttermilk Pie," Veraleen said with a half (you knew she meant business) laugh. But Mr. O'Connor meant business, too, because he and Biswick left, the screen door slamming behind them.

After dinner when I was helping Veraleen with the last of the dishes, she said out of nowhere, "You don't have to keep frownin' at me, Miss Merilee. I only gonna be staying a little while, then I'll be movin' on. I'm going to Nigeria to cook in an orphanage." Just like that. And she didn't even have a Tootsie Pop in her mouth when she told me.

Later, when she had gone on home, I stepped

outside in the cool air where I saw lights dancing, and for a brief thrill of a moment I thought that the Ghost lights had come down from the mountains to find me. Then I realized the lights were nothing but fireflies, their star-shaped radiations teasing and pirouetting among the branches of Grandma's tree. What were fireflies doing here in September? I stood there puzzled. I wished I could be like them—dancing in the dark—wild and free in the world, instead of trapped in my VOE.

"A bad penny always returns."

It was Grandma, of course. Sitting in her garden chair sly-dark in the night.

"Grandma? Do you see the dancing lights?"

"Crazy girl, seeing things."

"Grandma, go to bed. It's cold out here."

"I seen that Holliday woman before. She ain't up to no good. She just pickin' cat fur to make kitty bridges. Just stalling." Weenie's eyes gleamed, luminous and knowing from under the garden chair.

The hair on my arms stood up and I clasped my arms to my chest. "Go to bed, Grandma," I bellowed to her, my voice cracking. I turned around and ran inside. *Crazy girl, seeing things.*

One Sunday when I was about five, I wandered by myself down to the train tracks to watch the trains. This was way before I knew the train schedule by heart and I didn't know they don't come on Sunday. I waited and waited and no trains came so I lay down in the tall grass and took a long afternoon nap. A soft breeze stirred me awake and I sat up. Something caught my attention way off in the distance at the base of the mountains.

It was a dragon, partially hidden in the purpled shadows. I could see him well enough to know that he was beckoning for me to come. I stood up and started to walk But he winked at me before slowly disappearing. I collapsed back in the tall grass and lay there for a long time, not wanting to let go of what I'd seen.

When I got home late that evening, Mama and Daddy were in an uproar about my disappearance. Mama just held me and all I could get out was that I had seen a dragon by the mountains.

"Crazy girl, seeing things," Grandma pro-nounced. Daddy just looked at the floor, helpless.

Mama told me it was a mirage I saw. Just my luck to be born in some stupid place that happens to have mirages that can explain away everything.

"No," I told her. "I saw a dragon."

"No, darling," she assured me. "It was a mirage. A dream. There are no dragons. They only exist in stories. They are not real."

"It wanted me to come," I said. *And I would have gone. I was going.*

Mama says I cried for two days nonstop and it was like when I was a brand-new baby. My world started to dim, like old-timey movies that fade slowly into black, till all that is left is a little sad prick of light. I didn't want to believe Mama, although I knew she wouldn't lie to me. And I couldn't imagine wanting to live in this world if dragons weren't real.

Chapter 5

Like Bug predicted, Biswick took the little bus for retarded children over to Whiskey. It came for him early in the morning, its too-little engine purring through the sweet ebony stillness. I would often picture him getting on that half bus and riding off to school where everyone is different. Grandma Birdy says there's an ugly one in every bunch, meaning every little town has its bona-fide retard. She looks at me, knowing as she says it that I'm Jumbo's lone ingrate. As I lay there, looking up at my ghostlike PEZ dispensers, I wished more than anything I could run and get on that bus with Biswick and go where I would be on the same side of ordinary instead of the other.

That morning, a Monday, I sat in my seat before the first bell rang, drawing in my journal an elegant medieval dragon with an extra-long tail that curled and spiraled through several pages. There's not much for me to do here at Jumbo High (which encompasses all twelve grades of school), because I've already read all the textbooks through twelfth grade.

Gideon Beaurogard (previously known as Bowl-a-Lard when he was a little fat boy) was also working at his desk. The other kids ran around the room like wild animals. Mr. Bonaparte (known as Mr. Phone-a-Fart) was upstairs doing his usual: drinking his coffee, picking his nose, and finishing the morning's crossword puzzle. I'm not his favorite student. I daydream all the time and he has to yell, "Come back from Dragonland, Miss Monroe" really loud before I'll pay attention. But I know a big secret about him. When he was a teenager in El Paso, he was so dumb he tried to sneak home late by going down the chimney and got stuck upside down and a fire truck had to be called to yank him out.

"Hey, Dragon Girl!" Romey yelled. I kept on drawing as a shower of trash cascaded over my head. I didn't blink or even flicker. Romey's one of my Three Tormenters—Romey McKelvey, Cairo Romaine, and Mona Lisa Venezuela. Three Barbie girls, stuck together like glue, who have been tormenting me ever since I can remember.

"Pick that up!" Scooter Stunkel, sidekick to the Three Tormenters, yelled in my ear. "Where's your stick, trash girl?" he yelled again, even closer. Scooter's daddy, Otis, has a pet skunk named Pooter (against the law in Jumbo—the skunk, not the name) hidden under a trench coat he wears all-year-round.

"Stupid. Stupendous," I muttered low under my breath.

Cairo threw a wad of paper at me which missed my head and landed at my feet. I kicked it toward the trash can. Cairo Romaine's daddy, Bobo, won the Jumbo Chilimpiad three years in a row for his Possum Tail Chili recipe, but it was just chicken he was putting in there and he got found out and had to return his prize—a gift certificate for a free pancake breakfast at the Sweet Home Diner. And her brother, Rio, is serving time over in Huntsville, even though everyone's been told he's off in the military. Cairo's own mother, Mama Peaches, known for her famous peach cobblers, told me all of this and even confessed to me that she once stole a package of sponge curlers and a Snickers bar from the H.E.B. over in Whiskey when she was a teenager.

Romey threw another paper ball. It hit me in the head, but I ignored it. Romey has an aunt that collects dead frogs and puts them in velvet-lined collector cases in their living room. Grandma Birdy remembers when Romey's granddaddy, Mooney McKelvey, crazy as a loon (and buck naked, too), walked downtown with a divining rod shouting, "The water will save us all!"

"Dragon Girl!" Cairo yelled again. The Idiot Sheep Followers giggled. I call them the ISFs. There's Yello Brown, named because all he'd eat was yellow Jell-O till he was six. And Truman Dearlove, who refuses to take off his cowboy hat and is going to be pulled out of school next year because his daddy owns the biggest ranch outside of Jumbo and thinks there's nothing good to be learned here. And Ramona Grace Callahan, who developed early, way before any of us other girls, and smooches with the sophomore boys behind the bleachers in the gym.

The bell rang, and my classmates scurried to their seats. I happened to glance at Gideon, who was peering at me intently from behind his thick glasses. He looked down and started to write again on his paper. Grandma says his daddy was a no-good, slicker-than-snot-on-a-doorknob scoundrel. He came to town way back when in an old pickup filled up in the back with his Finkle's Purifying Tonic. He sold bottle after bottle to practically everyone in town. It was years before someone realized it was really just bottled tap water with vinegar. Myrtle Bupp still swears by it, saying it's the only thing that will get dog puke out of her carpet.

Buddy Finkle married Elma Beaurogard and they promptly had Gideon a few months later. Elma gave Gideon the Beaurogard name because her grandfather was "distinguished" and a hero from the Civil War, and Gideon was the first boy born since. Buddy seemed to mend his ways for a few years. He worked at the gas station pumping gas while Elma raised little Gideon. His mother, Grandma Finkle, came to live with them, and for a while she was a constant ramrod fixture in the front pew of the Holy Hands Baptist Church.

Mona Lisa, oddly, was quiet today, too. Grandma Birdy says the Venezuela family came from the Whispering Pines Trailer Park over in Skeeterville, although they claim to be royal Castilians from Spain. Mona Lisa, named for the famous portrait, so they say, has a secret birthmark that no one outside her family knows about except me. It's the shape of Frankenstein's head—complete with bolts—and Mona Lisa has been wearing long pants ever since I can remember to cover it. I saw it once on the playground when we were little and she begged me to never tell anyone. Like I would. There's something even more peculiar about Mona Lisa. When Romey and Cairo were at cheerleader practice, she'd sneak into Mama's store and pore over obscure medical and history books and the classics. The same books I like to read.

Mr. Bonaparte came in and sat at his desk. A giggle simmered in the room. Mr. Bonaparte looked around. "I see you have a trash problem again, Miss Monroe." He pointed to the trash can next to his desk. It went this way time after time. I was expected to clean it up. I really didn't mind.

Then the unbelievable happened. Gideon Beaurogard spoke. "The other kids did it, Mr. Bonaparte. They should clean it." He pushed his glasses up his nose and glanced at the open-mouthed cretins.

I was as astounded as everyone else. None of us had heard Gideon utter more than a word or two on his own since second grade when his no-good daddy, Buddy Finkle, skipped town and disappeared with a whole bunch of money swindled from several elderly women who thought he was a financial wizard and then his mama turned all weird and Gideon was taken away for a while.

"Miss Monroe! Come back from Dragonland,

please!" Mr. Bonaparte yelled. "Who did this to you?"

I swallowed hard. I didn't want to cause any trouble. But Gideon stood up for me. I owed him that.

"Romey McKelvey," I whispered and then, as quietly as I could, "horrendous."

Mr. Bonaparte snapped his fingers and pointed to the trash can. Romey stood up and walked down the aisle, whispering under her breath to Gideon as she passed him by, "Freakoid!"

At lunchtime, after I'd eaten my PB&J sandwich and pickle, I drew another dragon in my journal. A sinuous serpent with two tusklike teeth roared up out of the sea, ready to pounce on a helpless ship. I sit in the farthermost corner of the cafeteria every day, far enough that food bombs launched in my direction cannot reach me.

I glanced up to see Gideon had joined my far corner at the next table and was staring at me from behind those bug glasses as he ate a sorry-looking squashy hamburger. There was a time when he could only eat wheat-free stuff and slimy tofu mush. Back then his mother claimed he was allergic to everything in the whole wide world, especially sugar, and she would come to lunch every day and monitor what he ate, just in case. During recess, though, Gideon would scarf down Jujubes and Sugar Babies behind a tree on the playground and nothing ever seemed to happen except his tongue turned different colors and he got fat.

Eventually one of their neighbors—no one ever knew who (except for me, it was Mama)—alerted the authorities that something wasn't quite right at his home. The social worker from Whiskey discovered a house filled to the gills with filth and muck, newspapers, and old *Life* magazines stacked like the wall of China with little mazelike pathways in between. Gideon was taken away and it was discovered he wasn't allergic to anything and never needed glasses, but now he did since he had been wearing them since he was three and his eyes were ruined, and also he had never broken his arm in kindergarten when he wore a shoulder-to-finger cast for six months.

It was finally decided that Gideon's mother was better than no mother, and there was still Grandma Finkle, who had stayed on even after her no-good son ran off. Gideon was returned, changed forever, months later. He looked like a normal little boy, a slimmed-down version of his former self.

I glanced back down at my journal. I had drawn glasses on my sea dragon. I smiled a little at the juxtaposition. Before I could say anything, though, Gideon got up with his tray and stomped off just as Romey walked up behind me.

"Wow!" she proclaimed. "It looks just like him," she said smoothly. I was surprised. None of the Tormenters had ever shown any interest in my journal. Still, I shut it. I looked up in time to see Cairo appear two tables over, and another Tormenter two tables beyond: Scooter. I grasped the journal to my chest protectively, but it was too late. Romey grabbed it from me in one swift move. It was tossed to Cairo and then Scooter, like a stone skipped across a river.

Chapter 6

Grandma thinks it's a sin to cling to anything in life. It saves you heartache later when God takes it away from you, she believes. She never liked my journal anyway; full of chicken-scratch mishmash (not even a full proper story in there), she proclaimed one day after looking over my shoulder, and if I didn't watch it, God was gonna snatch it from me like Minnie Dean's pearls. When Minnie Dean was a teenager, she made a trip all the way to Port Aransas to show off her Lauren Bacall cultured pearls that she'd won in a real Hollywood contest. But they were taken straight off her neck in the shallow surf by a huge, sudden wave, never to be seen again. And now some blowfish at the bottom of the sea is wearing those fancy-smancy pearls. It's divine retribution, Grandma says.

It's true I'd never written a full story in my journal. That was for someday. Right now I am just keeping parts, snippets, fragments—mostly beginnings. But they are precious to me, those beginnings. Someday I'd sit down and finish those stories. But for now they are in my head, wound and wound so tightly I didn't think I could ever unwind them. But what would it matter anyway? I'd lost my journal.

All during class the Tormentors exchanged knowing glances and smirks, but there was no sign of my journal. And after school I'd looked for the Tormentors but they'd skedaddled and run off in different directions and I wasn't able to follow any of them. It was gone. Gone forever.

"What's the matter?" Biswick asked when I found him at the corner of Maple and Fifth, our usual spot.

"They took it," I said, my eyes darting around, thinking dumbly that perhaps I'd find it just simply laying on the sidewalk. "Marvelous. Just marvelous." I felt the sting of tears but held them back. I had an image of a cow with Scooter's face, pawing through my beautiful black journal, laughing and reciting bits. "When life gives you lemons, make lemonade." Ha, ha, ha.

Biswick looked at the back of my bicycle. I was never without it. "Your journal?" he asked.

"Yeah," I said. "Get on." It was time for my litter patrol.

He jumped on the back. "Aren't you gonna tell anyone?"

"It's gone," I told him.

Later Biswick followed me home for dinner, cheerfully telling me they were having fish sticks, which he didn't like, again at his house. Grandma opened her door as we walked past and yelled, "Keep your friends off my property!" Then she slammed the door shut. Weenie appeared in her window barking up a storm at something in the yard before Grandma hushed him and pulled him away.

"Come on, Biswick," I said as we went in our

back door. Veraleen was stirring at the stove, talking away. "And if you'd seen what I'd seen you'd know it was nothing but a foul-smelling boil . . ." The kitchen smelled of a long-cooked spiced stew, one of my favorites. Mama, the recipient of Veraleen's story, was home early, setting the table. I avoided her eyes. If our eyes met, she would know, and there was nothing she could do about it. It was just another one of my fabulous disasters.

"Wash up, darlins'," Veraleen said over her shoulder to us, and then went on: ". . . that any backyard fool would know you don't touch with a ten-foot pole much less with an unsanitized needle. So I told him, whatya thinks gonna happen . . ." I plopped down at the table.

"Merilee, what's wrong, honey?" Mama knew. Of course she knew. She was Mama. Biswick grabbed a cookie off the counter and sashayed just out of Veraleen's reach with a giggle.

He sat down next to me and announced, "They stole her journal." He took a giant bite out of his cookie.

"What the blazes?" Veraleen cursed.

"Who took your journal?" Mama asked as she put the last plate down with a whap. I knew without looking she was staring at me over her cat-eyed glasses. She seemed to see more clearly over them than through them.

I took an FF breath.

Veraleen moved over to the table. "Get it out, honey." She slapped me lightly on the back. "It's no good to keep things in, it just festers up like that boil."

"It's no use, Mama," I said. "It's gone for good. Spectacular." I didn't want Mama marching over to any of those kids' houses like she'd did one time way back and I begged her never to do it again.

Suddenly Weenie was barking wildly in the backyard. Veraleen peered out the window. "He's got something cornered up Ms. Monroe's tree." She laughed. "Come look."

Biswick and I got up and Mama followed behind me, her hand briefly touching my shoulder. Weenie was barking up a storm and dancing around at the base of the tree.

Veraleen opened the door and we all followed.

Bug rode up on her bicycle from the side yard and joined us.

Grandma Birdy opened her door and yelled, "Get in here now, you ingrate fool!" Weenie wagged his tail, whined, and paced a bit in front of the tree before following orders. Grandma's door slammed behind him.

I walked in front of everyone straight to Grandma's tree and looked up through the limbs. Near the top, nestled in the V of a thin branch was a black shadow. I thought perhaps it was a bird's nest, but when I tilted my head slightly, I knew. It was my journal. I let out a huge sigh of relief.

Everyone else had joined me, their heads tilted back, too, like my PEZ dispensers.

"What's your journal doing up Grandma's tree?" Bug asked. A raindrop fell directly in my eye. I blinked and looked up farther. There was a small rain cloud hovering just above our yard like in a cartoon. Marvelous. Rain.

"Well, my goodness gracious, why'd they do that?" Veraleen asked. She tried to shake Grandma's tree but it was like Grandma, thin

limbs but sturdy in the ground—never leaving.
"We could call the fire department," she suggested
with a laugh. We didn't have much of a fire department. Just a couple of volunteer old coots,
Grandma called them, who drove an ancient fire
truck. More rain drops, long, thin, warning ones,
the kind that's telling you "We are about to multi-
ply fast. You better go inside."

The initial feeling of euphoria of seeing my
journal again was now replaced by an intense
wanting. I needed it, even if it was a sin. I needed
that journal. And before it rained and ruined all
my beginnings.

Mama was taking off her clogs. She stepped
closer and swiveled her head back and forth,
studying all the branches. She couldn't. No way. It
wasn't a good climbing tree. Bug and I had tried it
a few years back. The limbs were never quite
placed right for holding the heels and hands of a
climber. It was almost as though Grandma had
willed it to grow this way.

I glanced across the street as a few more raindrops teasingly splashed on my head. Marva

Augustine's ragamuffins, three little barefooted boys, all a year apart and under the age of six, were standing there, holding hands and watching the spectacle. It wouldn't be long before everyone knew. Their big sister, Mary Alice, was the town crier.

"Mama's gonna climb the tree!" Bug squealed.

"Go get your grandma and tell her you have a huge Kool-Aid stain on your sheets," Mama said to Bug. Grandma's favorite thing in the world is to conquer stains. "Cleaning up the devil's work," she calls it. She sneaks in when we're not home and later we find bleach marks all over the place like a dusty ghost has left its mark. "Go now, hurry," Mama said. Bug ran to Grandma's house and twenty seconds later Grandma marched out with her cleaning kerchief tied around her head, holding a bucket and a jug of Wipe-Out Bleach, Bug toddling behind her with a conspiratorial grin.

Mama turned to Veraleen as soon as the two of them went in our house. "Give me a shimmy," she said.

"You sure you know what you're doing?"

Veraleen laughed low as she cupped her hands. "Broken bones from a fall are the hardest to set." Mama bit her lip in determination, stepped in Veraleen's hands, and up she went.

Biswick pealed in laughter at the sight. There was now a group of about ten kids, wagons and bicycles in tow, staring and pointing at Mama. Mama was like a monkey, clambering up the tree, her free-flowing skirt flapping widely around her. Mama's limber. She started the one-and-only yoga class at the Church of the Divine Mercy (actually probably the only one this side of San Antonio) with two whole members, Mexican ladies who don't speak English but understand good posture.

One of the kids from across the street, Dooley Augustine, had joined us at the base of the tree for a closer inspection.

"You can see her underwear!" he announced. "They're purple!" he yelled even louder, cupping his hands around his mouth for projection. He was right. And they were lacy, too. My face flushed. I looked up again. The rain had changed its mind. It was now a soft mist. Mama. Mama's the only one in all Jumbo that would climb up Grandma's tree.

"You wanna go, too, honey?" Veraleen asked. I looked back up at Mama. She was nearing the top, where the branches became really thin. I nodded my head. Veraleen cupped her hands and up I went.

"Dragon Girl is going, too!" Dooley announced to the watching crowd.

"I want to go," Biswick said below me, but Veraleen hushed him.

I made it about halfway. I stopped and caught my breath. I looked up. Mama was reaching for my journal. But it was too far. She sat back and took a breath, too.

"She almost fell!" the little boy announced.

"You go home!" Biswick said beneath us. "Busybodies!"

"What do you know, Pancake!" Dooley taunted. "Ooooow! Someone pinched me!" I glanced down. Veraleen had a look of satisfaction as the boy ran back across the street, holding his elbow. There was now a sizable crowd with even grown-ups, and Mama's dogs had gotten out and were at the base of the tree whining for her.

"Need some help, Hell-in?" shouted Bobo Romaine.

"Mama?" I called as I clung to my branch. I couldn't look up or down. I'd suddenly developed a fear of heights from out of nowhere.

"I can see clear all the way to Whiskey," Mama said serenely. "It really is beautiful—this land."

"Mama?" I whispered.

"We're just having us a little adventure," she said happily, as though we were sitting at the kitchen table. "I can feel you're scared, Merilee. Don't be, honey." If either Bug or I fell down and skinned our knees, she felt a shooting pain go up her leg. Or if we had fevers, she felt hot, too. But with me, it was even more. She could feel me like I lived inside her, she told me once.

"I'm just catching my breath a moment, then I'll be able to reach your journal." Suddenly I was lurched forward and I grabbed the branch in front of me for dear life and scrunched my eyes shut. I suddenly had a vision of a dragon swooping down from the sky and taking me far away.

"It's okay, Merilee," Mama said soothingly. "We're fine," she repeated. She took a deep, cleansing breath, like one of my FF breaths, and I did, too. "Why, I can see all the way over to Ferdie's. She's got flip-flops on sale for ninety-nine cents. How nice. And someone over on Maple has a parachute hanging on their clothesline." We were so different, Mama and I. She always looked at the bright side of things and me the worst.

I held on even tighter, my eyes squeezed shut. I thought for sure we were gonna fall.

"We're not falling, Merilee," Mama said. "Have some faith, honey. God won't let us fall."

Ha. I shook my head. I didn't believe in God. We were gonna fall. For sure.

The upstairs window flew open. "Hell-in Monroe, you get out of my tree now or I'll flay your butt!" Grandma screamed. The crowd across the street roared with laughter. "And you, too, Merilee!"

Suddenly there was a flash. It was a reporter, Lola Mae Spivey, taking a photo for the *Jumbo*

Times. It wouldn't be the first time Mama had made the paper. She'd once staged a sit-in for world peace in front of the courthouse. Bug even keeps a scrapbook of Mama's escapades. Mama's hand was on my shoulder. I opened my eyes. She held down the journal to me. I grabbed it and clung to it with all my being.

Chapter 7

It was a big, giant, oversized meat eater, phosphorously orange, nuclear grown . . . Cheeto. "Where did you get that?" I asked him. I saw the thing even before I spotted Biswick. He held it out in his palm. He was waiting for me in our usual spot after school at the corner of Maple and Fifth, with the look on his face that said now this time he held the cards—a solidified, petrified snack.

"I found it in my chips bag at lunch today," said a beaming Biswick. "Do you think I could make the *Genius World Book of Records*? I'd be famous."

"Maybe," I told him. "Serendipitous." Stranger things than giant Cheetos had made it, although I had heard about a guy who picked his nose for three days straight but still didn't make it in because they didn't want the world emulating unsanitary stuff. "Be careful. Put it in a box or something."

"Do you think someone will try to steal it?" Biswick asked, his fingers quickly closing over his prize. "To try to be famous like me?"

"Nah," I answered, even though I knew a lot of people in Jumbo who wanted to be famous. Carmen Esparanza, the secretary at Jumbo National Bank, has fantasies of being in a Broadway play, and Dorwood Milton has been secretly writing a novel, in the "John Steinbeckian style" he told me, and hermit Bum "Chicken Pox" Fox (aptly named for his pock-marked face), has been sending in epistles to the editor of the *Jumbo Times* under the pen name "A Gentle Reader." We do have one famous person in Jumbo already— Louis Smeather, who wrote a book about talking to mushrooms. It was hailed in *Agricultural Times*, which Daddy subscribes to, as "a landmark of environmental sociology." I didn't think any of them would try to steal Biswick's giant Cheeto.

Of course there's Mama Peaches, Snickers stealer, but I doubt she'd want a giant Cheeto.

"I once had a two-headed Frito," Biswick said. He was following alongside me as I rode my bike slowly. "Where are we going?" He still held the Cheeto, his hand extended straight out in front of him.

"Litter patrol. Mondays I go to the trains. What happened?" I found myself asking him.

"Huh?"

"To the Frito."

"Oh, I ate it."

"Marvelous." I nodded knowingly. "I once found a piece of popcorn in the shape of George Washington's head complete with powdered wig. I ate it, too."

"Wow!" Biswick said. "That's a lot of words for you, Merilee Horrendous."

"It's not Horrendous," I told him as my face flamed up. "It's Monroe. Merilee Monroe."

"Then why did you tell me it's Horrendous?" he asked, still holding the Cheeto out in front of him like a butler with a tray.

"I didn't mean to," I told him. "Malfunction. Sometimes I malfunction."

"Like the robots in the cartoons?" Biswick laughed.

"Yep," I responded. "Marvelous."

"Who is George Washington?" he asked.

"The first president," I answered.

"You ate the president?" he asked, his eyes not moving one iota from the Cheeto.

"No, the president was a piece of popcorn," I said.

"Who was?" Biswick said, tripping over a lift in the concrete. He stumbled slightly, bellowing a little as though it would help. It did. The Cheeto didn't move.

"George Washington," I repeated, now regretting that I had stopped for him today, Cheeto or not. "Stupendous."

"Is that a good word?" he asked.

"Ah," I answered him.

"Is *marvelous* a good word?"

"Yep."

"I'm going to call you Merilee Marvelous." He had a big grin on his face.

"Please don't."

"Who is George Washington?"

"I told you," I said. "The first president."

"Is he on a PEZ?" he asked with all earnestness.

Everyone knows who the first president is. I wondered if he had ever been to school before he came here. "Wait, stop," I said. I had spotted a big Piggly Wiggly plastic bag. I stabbed it with my litter stick and deposited it in my basket in one quick move.

"I get to go to school *now*," he said, seeming to read my thoughts. "And I get to ride the special bus."

"Yes," I said, pedaling on. "But in Ireland. Did you go there?"

"I've never been to Ireland," he answered. He leaned down levelly, his arm still parallel to the ground, and picked up a piece of paper.

Biswick told me for a fact that he was from Ireland the first time he met me. I let it pass, though.

"What's this?" he asked. He handed the paper to me.

I stopped my bicycle and took it from him. It was a twenty-five-cent coupon for Wonder Bread. "I'll put it in my basket."

"I want to know what it says," he pouted, and grabbed the coupon back.

"Nosybody. Read it then," I said. "Can't you read?"

I saw it in his eyes, but he answered smartly, "It's in cursive. I can't read cursive."

I swiped the coupon from him and the gesture made a slight breeze, causing the Cheeto to rock back and forth a little. Biswick's face lit up in horror as he tried to steady it.

"What does it say?" he asked.

"Haven't you ever seen a coupon before?" I put it in my basket with the rest of the trash.

"Where are we going?" Biswick asked again.

"I told you. Trash. Train tracks. If we hurry we can see a BNSF Seven-Forty train."

"Are those ghosts going to be there?" His voice sounded faint and faraway.

He had stopped about ten feet back. "What ghosts?" I asked. "Stupendous."

"You know, the Ghost Lights." His face was painted over with fear.

"No. Only at night. Near the mountains. And they're not ghosts. Luminescence."

"My people think spirits come to take you home."

"The Irish?" I asked. "They believe that?"

He wasn't good at hiding things; I could see the lie crouched on the edge of his eyes before he spoke. "Yeah."

I heard a bird in the distance. Maybe a hawk. I lifted my binoculars and couldn't find it. We were standing on Elm Street not far from downtown. From Elm we would go along the old highway till we reached the train tracks. I stared at Biswick and wondered about his fear of the Ghost Lights. What would he have thought about seeing the September fireflies the other night? Were they tiny ghosts who had come to take someone home?

"I want a Dilly Bar at the Dairy Queen," Biswick whined. I sighed.

"I told you, Biswick, trains on Mondays. It's *my* schedule. My VOE. It's all in here." I pointed to my journal in my basket. "And I stick to it no matter what."

"Can I have a Dilly Bar afterward?" he bargained. "What are you gonna be when you growed up?" he asked without a pause.

I shrugged my shoulders. "I don't know." But suddenly I blurted out, "I'm going to go away from here someday. Probably New York, where my Grandmother Ruth used to live." It somehow sounded truer by saying it.

"Did you know they speak a hundred and thirty-eight languages in New York City?" he asked. "Do they speak English there?"

"Probably," I answered with a smile.

"My daddy says I'm not ever gonna grow up," he said matter-of-factly. "I'm gonna always be small."

I nodded and tilted my head toward the back of the bike. "Why New York?" he asked as he climbed on.

"Because it's faraway."

We turned onto the old highway, Biswick and me—and Cheeto.

*   *   *

I had to compromise on the Dilly Bar. Biswick just wouldn't stop whining. He was the king of whining, I decided. King Whiner. Bug could be Queen Whiner and the two could rule Whinerland. We went to the Dairy Queen first to make King Whiner happy and then headed over to the train tracks. Biswick was eating his ice cream too slowly; black and vanilla goo swirled down his wrist. Ugh. By age two I could eat an ice cream cone without getting one drop on me. I had a double vanilla dip cone and I was licking it all around trying to make it as symmetrical as I could. It resembled one of Lorelei's teased hair-dos from her floozy-looking days. At least I had finally talked Biswick into putting Cheeto away—it was carefully wrapped in a Dairy Queen napkin and tucked in one of my bicycle baskets. He wasn't very happy about that and I wasn't very happy about almost missing the BNSF 740.

The trains were one of my early obsessions. It started with anything mechanical. First it was ceiling fans, then windmills, and then the oil drills that pop up and down on the plains like giant pecking birds. But like my dragons, the trains caught and have held my fancy as they roar through Jumbo on their way to Whiskey. When I was little, Daddy sometimes took me down to our special spot out where the soft grasslands converge with the old steel tracks of the Union Pacific Railroad to watch them. I was in awe of the power, the sound, and the routineness of them. Even then I knew instinctively from the whirring vibrations beneath my feet exactly what was coming—whether it was a BNSF 740 or a mighty Union Pacific 9215 engine. I loved the trains then and I still do. The trains run like clockwork, like I used to before Biswick came along and pushed me off-kilter.

Biswick and I stood near the tracks and looked out over the wide plains that seemed to roll from the mountains to the other end of the earth. Cacti dot the grasslands, and an occasional rolling tumbleweed brings movement to an otherwise silent and still world. Biswick bellowed "Helloooo" to see if there was an echo and suddenly a roadrunner darted from behind a cactus nearby. He tried to chase it but realized he would lose the rest of his ice cream so he came back, panting and excited.

Above us the pink and purple sky looked as if it had been stroked by some mighty paintbrush. God's paintbrush, Mama says. It almost did seem possible that magic could happen here. Almost. Mama says deep down inside I know there is a sliver of magic in the world. It's embedded inside me, a tender miracle, waiting. Ha. Marvelous.

"Why's that one taller than the rest?" Biswick asked, motioning his head toward the mountains. "It looks weird."

I followed his gaze. Cathedral Mountain, the showpiece of the Chitalpi. With its long, tall, spire formations and turreted peaks, it resembled an abstract, ancient Notre Dame. "That's just Cathedral Mountain," I told him. "Supposedly there's a trail there, the Goat Herder's trail." Hikers had found it and marked it, Maydell Rathburger told me once.

"Did you know I can barf on cue?" Biswick

offered between licks of his Dilly Bar. He had a little Charlie Chaplin chocolate moustache. "Sometimes it just comes by surprise, but other times I can make it come."

I didn't answer him. The train was coming. I could feel its vibrations under my feet. It was the 740. I felt calm. Serene. Like I'd taken a thousand FF breaths.

"I can show you right now."

"No, Biswick." There was more ice cream on his arm than in his stomach. Just to be sure, I threatened, "I'll take you home. No trains."

"Can I have your Mr. Smiley Pez? I saw it in your room the other day."

"My room?" I was very annoyed. No one is allowed in my room.

"Bug let me in there to look at your collection. I saw Mr. Smiley head and it made me think of my daddy. He calls me Mr. Smiley 'cause I'm smiling all the time." He smiled in a perfect half arc, just like the smiley face. "Can I have it?"

"No," I answered flatly. I could never let go of one of my PEZes.

He took another lick of his Dilly Bar. "I could trade you my ghost head one."

I rolled my eyes. "Oh, marvelous." I could go over to the Piggly Wiggly right now and buy one of those for less than a dollar. "Worthless."

I could see it now, up ahead on the horizon. It came toward us with all its wondrous ferocity. Usually I would just stand there, my eyes clamped shut, letting it push me back with the force of a hurricane. For some reason, maybe because I was standing there with King Whiner Biswick, with his dripping ice cream cone, and because everything was off-kilter, I opened my eyes and watched. Something was not right. There was a movement. *Crazy girl, seeing things.* I squinted. Someone was hanging out the door about to jump. I glanced at Biswick. He was licking up the dribbles on his arm. I stood frozen as everything unfolded.

The train swooshed past and my eyes shot to the other side of the tracks to see if anyone was there. By a small copse of mesquite trees I caught sight of a figure running off toward town. I recognized the distinctive blue-and-gray flannel shirt and my stomach sank.

Uncle Dal.

He wears the same two shirts even in the heat because he believes, as many cowboys do out here, that the heavy clothes deflect the sun. My hands went down to my binoculars but I did not lift them up. Biswick was still lapping up his arm. He had missed the whole thing. Thank goodness for the Dilly Bar.

"Come on, Biswick," I said. "Finish up your ice cream. We need to get to work." I watched Uncle Dal disappear in the mesquite brush, getting smaller and smaller, then averted my gaze. Grandma says if you watch a person out of sight, you'll never see them alive again.

I walked over to my bicycle to get my litter stick. I stabbed a paper cup and thought about Uncle Dal. I shook my head. It was none of my business anyway.

"Are we going to make money doing this?" Biswick asked as he brought a pull tab from a can over to me.

"No. We do it to save the planet."

"What's wrong with the planet?" he asked. "Are we all dying? Daddy says life sucks and then you die."

"Poetic. Very poetic," I said. "I'm trying to do a good deed and pick up all the trash I can." I was quite irritated with him by now.

"What good does that do?" he said, holding out the pull tab, which I admit looked microscopic and useless against the wide land. "Why don't you try to make some of the sad people happy?" he asked.

"Oh spectacular," I said as I picked up several more pieces of trash, stabbing them extra hard. "I'm not a people person, Biswick." And I laughed to myself as I thought about how the statement "lacks social interactions" had appeared religiously on my report card my whole life. "Why don't *you* make the sad people happy?" I stopped and looked at him.

I could tell he was chewing on that. "Why doesn't Uncle Dal have a family?" he asked.

I let out a deep, exaggerated sigh, leaning on

my litter stick. "He has a family. He has me, Bug, Mama, Daddy, and . . . Grandma."

"No, why doesn't he have a wife and children?" he asked again.

"I don't know, Biswick," I said. "Some people just don't want children. And it's best kept that way." Grandma Birdy was barren until her fifteenth wedding anniversary and then suddenly two boys in a year and a half. She says it was a bona-fide miracle, that God was just testing her patience. I think Daddy and Dal were just biding their time, too scared to make an appearance in the world.

Biswick blew the hair off his forehead and bit the side of his lip. For the first time I noticed his eyelashes, long, black and beautiful, a singular perfection on his imperfect face. A tear ran down his cheek and he swatted at it like it was a bug. Now he was crying. Stupendous.

I raised my binoculars to the sky to catch the flight of a large bird. But it wasn't White Feather.

Biswick pulled the napkin out of my basket and unfolded it. Cheeto. He stared at it a moment, touched it gently to his lips, wrapped it back up, and stuffed it in his pocket. "Can we go see Veraleen now?" he asked. I looked at him through my binoculars, his little lips oranged with Cheeto dust. We got on my bike, with Biswick perched on my back baskets, and rode off.

Chapter
8

To everyone's surprise Veraleen had moved into a tiny three-room adobe on Pecos Street over on the Mexican side of town south of the train tracks. No one was surprised that *she* moved there, it was just that this little ramshackle hovel had no takers when it was offered for a thousand dollars on the steps of the courthouse five years ago. One time a poor family of six lived there but the children had all grown up and the parents had sought a better life elsewhere. The house was good enough for Veraleen, though.

Biswick and I found her out back on her knees, planting things in the hard ground that looked like nothing alive had ever prospered there. She wore a big wide-brim garden hat that had a little shovel and garden pick crisscrossed on the sash. It didn't look right on her—like a rhino wearing a sombrero. In her rear pocket I could see the outline of a tobacco can.

Veraleen looked up and shielded her eyes. "I'm planting me a healing garden," she said. She leaned back and slapped the dirt off her hands. "All my own. It's been many a year since I've had my own herb garden." She was smiling, all big and happy and I saw, for the first time, as it twinkled in the sun like treasure, that she had a gold-sheathed front tooth. It had the cutout of a star in the middle, colored a robin's egg blue. "Over here we're gonna have some willow herb, some cow lily, thimblehead, and some chamomile. And over here we're gonna have bitterweed, black haw, button willow, and persimmon. And maybe some dewberry." She took a long, long FF-type breath and she muttered low, "Dewberry for pinkeye, always dear. Mud from a hog wallow. Linden flowers will cure the nerves. Don't rub it. Never rub it."

Biswick ran over and hugged her. She wrapped

her arms around him and held him tight, rocking back and forth like a ship on the high seas. "You are a sweet, sweet boy."

"Don't most people plant in the spring?" I asked. "Mix match. Flip-flop," I mumbled. She had her seasons all wrong. I plopped down on a tiny patch of parched grass. Biswick grabbed a little shovel and started poking at the ground.

"Yeah, I guess most people do," Veraleen said, looking at me strong and hard, those eyes like sapphires embedded in her wrinkled peach pit of a face. She sure liked to stare. "Oh, and I have to see my Panhandle wildflowers again. Star thistle, flea-bane daisy, goatsbeard—that's a pretty one—sweet everlasting, beard tongue." Biswick was starting to make funny faces at the names. "Pig nut." Here he burst out laughing. "Blazing star, curly-cup gumweed, hog potato, and sweet smelling lemon horsemint." Now Biswick was rolling on the ground, holding his stomach, saying he might pee in his pants. Veraleen ignored him. She murmured, "Lemon horsemint. It's what we used on Mama when we laid her out." She started digging again.

Biswick got over his laughing fit and crawled over to her. "Why does your face have so many lines?" he asked. He was covered in dirt. He was grinning impolitely.

Veraleen let out that low, gravelly simmered laugh of hers. "The sun, baby." She took a deep breath. "The sun been shining on my pretty face my whole life. I don't mind it. I'm not looking for a cowboy no more." I saw a glimmer of sadness flit across her face. "'Kissing don't last—cooking does.' That's from my mama. Remember that, Merilee." Biswick snorted.

I wondered if she ever had a cowboy husband, where he was, if he existed. Guess he wasn't a good kisser. I wondered where her children were. Probably grown. I'm tired of knowing everything about everyone. I'm tired of listening. I'm not God. If there is one. I really don't believe so. I think he's sitting somewhere on vacation with the dinosaurs, the leprechauns, the fairies, and all the other things parents make up to make you think life is special.

Biswick was stabbing at the hard ground over

and over again. "Biswick, baby," Veraleen said. "Go inside and fetch me some water. And wash that dirt off your face, honey. And after, you can have a warm sugar cookie. They're on the counter." Biswick didn't have to be persuaded. He ran inside.

Veraleen started digging again. "Miracles happen, darling," she said.

I just blinked. She sounded like Mama.

"I know people will think I won't be able to get anything out of the ground, but I sure am going to try," she said.

"It's not spring."

"I don't have time to wait till spring," she said flatly. Her eyes squinted at me briefly. "I want to see God's garden before I go."

"You going somewhere, Veraleen?" I don't know why I was asking. I knew she was going to Nigeria.

"I told you, honey. I'm going to Australia to work in the Outback." She said it matter-of-factly as though she was reeling off her Piggly Wiggly grocery list. She kept digging, singing as she did.

"Whistling at the table, singing in bed, the devil will get you before you are dead."

I don't know if it was the heat or what, but I started to feel real dizzy as images of the September fireflies, dancing cicadas, devils, and early graves appeared before my eyes. I took two FF breaths.

I tried to follow Biswick into the house, but Veraleen stopped me, her big, hot, bearlike hand catching mine. I immediately felt better just as though I had eaten one of her warm sugar cookies. Me, who hates to be touched. Still, I yanked my hand away.

"That baby is okay, Merilee," she said. "Your mama wouldn't let me come work for you if that baby wasn't okay now."

I looked away. I didn't know why she wanted me to know this.

"Has Biswick told you much?" she asked.

"About you?"

"No, not about me, honey. About himself."

"No, only that's he's Irish. Not true though. Hoggywash. Hooey."

"Honey, you don't have to be Einstein to know that dog don't hunt," she said.

I thought of my Einstein Hair Club and smiled. I plopped down on my knees next to her.

"I don't like that daddy of his," she said. "Nothing but bad news dressed in tight jeans, lower than a snake's navel. I have my suspicions 'bout things over at his house."

She dug more intensely now and for a few minutes we were quiet. I wanted it to stay that way. She spoke again.

"You and I are going to keep an eye on Biswick. He needs us more than he'll ever know."

"I don't have time," I said. "No time. Can't deal with him."

"Oh yes, you can, sugar," Veraleen said, pointing her little shovel at me. "You have more strength than you know. I've been watching you, summing you up, and I know about these things."

"You don't know me," I said. "No one does."

"Oh yes I do. I can see you got the touch. I see it in your eyes."

"Marked. Grandma says I was marked from the

day I was born," I told her with a half grin. "Marvelous. Miraculous."

"That mean ole lady is right about one thing, darling. You're special and don't you ever forget it."

I hated being called special. What is special anyway? I'm not special. I've got red blood just like everyone else. "Blood. Vermilion" was all I could get out.

"Honey, I got red blood just like you but that don't make me just like you," she said, tipping her hat and wiping her sweaty brow. She lifted my chin and looked at me with those piercing eyes. "Yes, God gives us the same blood and he gives us gifts that make us different. He gave yours to you for a reason. And you can't stop it, honey.

"My mama had the gift, too," Veraleen continued. "She couldn't stop it, either. While she was washing dishes she'd see someone walk across the backyard, right and sure as daylight, dressed in their Sunday best. And our land was out in the middle of nowhere, I tell you. Nowhere. Our cattle dog Peabo was always sitting under the pecan tree watching them go, too. The next day that person always passed on to the Lord. Mama stopped doing the dishes—made me do them—always tried to keep poor Peabo inside. Cattle dogs don't want to be inside. It didn't stop anyone from dying, Merilee. God makes sure of that."

"I don't believe in God. It's all fairy tales." I started to walk away. "All of it."

"They call you Dragon Girl here, don't they?" she called after me.

I stopped and stared at her.

"Why dragons, honey?" she asked. "If you don't believe in anything else."

I turned and saw Biswick twirling around in Veraleen's living room, a sugar cookie hanging out of his mouth and one in each hand. "I suppose it's because when I was little, one came for me," I said. My eyes started to sting. "Stupendous."

"So you do believe in something," she said. "You believe in dragons, Merilee."

I hesitated, thinking about a bucketful of dreams before I answered. "No. There are no real dragons. Not here." I didn't know if what I said was true, but the words hurt just the same. I walked off, bitter at her for making me say them.

That night at home, I marched straight up the stairs to my room, stomping like a marauding elephant to let Veraleen know I wasn't coming in the kitchen for *her* dinner. As good as her cooking was, I really didn't want to sit through it with Bug and Biswick competing for every inch of chatter space and Veraleen staring at me with those eyes.

I plopped down on my bed. Why was Uncle Dal jumping off a train? Was this the first time he'd jumped off the train or had he done it before on the days when I wasn't there? I didn't know.

It was Biswick's fault. It was. He had to stir things up and change my VOE. I propped up on one elbow and started drawing a fierce horned dragon in my journal.

There was a knock on the door. Oh Lord, I hoped it wasn't more preaching from Veraleen about taking care of poor little Biswick. I pushed my journal away, rolled over, and faced the wall.

"Come in," I answered.

The door opened and I peeked over my shoulder. It was Daddy. I sat up. He carried a plate of Veraleen's food in one hand and a glass of milk in the other.

"Veraleen figured you might not be coming downstairs." He handed me the plate and I took it. He put the glass of milk on my night stand and sat down on the edge of my bed.

He brushed his fingers through his inky black hair and looked about the room, keeping his eyes from me. Daddy. He's what you would call old movie star handsome, somewhere between Errol Flynn and Tyrone Power, those old movie stars I see on Channel 39. Grandma Birdy says when Daddy was young, all the girls at church (and several who traveled all the way from Whiskey) used to turn around, rest their elbows on the pew, and just gawk at him through the whole sermon. But Mama says it was Daddy's green eyes she fell in love with. She said she could see the ocean in them the first time he looked at her. And in those ocean eyes was the soul of a good man.

"I'm fine, Daddy," I mumbled.

A look of relief crossed his face. He mussed up my hair affectionately, a really nonaffectionate gesture that he shares with Uncle Dal, and got up to leave.

I took a bite of Veraleen's Chicken Corn Casserole and watched as Daddy quietly shut my door. Grandma says men have a way of disappearing when anything difficult is afoot, and it's true about Daddy. But sometimes he tries to talk to me and when he does, it's like soft raindrops making hopeful marks on a desert plateau. It was Daddy who first took me to see the Ghost Lights.

He woke me up in the middle of the night, a time when folks here say it's so dark and clear you can reach up and pick a star from the sky and hold it in your hand. He took me to the viewing area, off the highway where a state sign marks the spot. I was still half asleep and pawing around for my own star, when Daddy sat me down on a large, cold rock. He wrapped a warm blanket around me and never said a word. I felt his strange quiet deep down in me, his hope. And then, there they were. A light. Not a star, a light, faraway hovering above the horizon, off toward the Chitalpi. Another appeared. They danced, twinkling and winking at us, turning first pink, then white, then yellow, and then pink again. They multiplied and shot up into the sky, disappearing into the dark night, teasing us with one last blink. I don't even remember the drive home or being put in bed.

The next morning at the breakfast table I said, "Daddy took me to see the lights, Mama." I didn't fail to catch a soft look that passed between my parents.

Grandma dashed everything. She always can be counted on for that. "Those lights are nothing but a bunch of car headlights." My eyes shot up toward Daddy.

"It's whatever you want to believe, Merilee," he said sincerely. Even I could see the silver flint of doubt in his eyes, though. Deep down, he didn't believe in them, either.

Chapter 9

Several days later we patched things up, Veraleen and I, over a discussion of butt spiders and shoe gum at the Piggly Wiggly. Our only grocery store, the Piggly Wiggly is run by Wadine Pigg and her son Pinell. They're no relation to the real Piggly Piggs. Wadine insists it was fate's sweet hand that pushed her to marry the late Hero Pigg, who later bought the Jumbo grocery. Their son, Pinell, never without his pink bow tie and armpit-stained short-sleeve white shirt, roams the aisles perpetually looking for spills, skid marks, and misplaced items, and he has been known to throw offending shoppers out of the store.

It was Friday, my regular day to turn in

bottles at the grocery store after my litter patrol. Veraleen was pushing a cart through the door into the store just as I was going out. Biswick jumped out from behind her and shouted, "Boo." It actually did scare me; he had been perfectly hidden behind her body. I got shivers and my hair stood on end, and for some reason the image of Veraleen's dog, Peabo, sitting under the pecan tree flashed through my mind. Veraleen pushed past me with the cart, Biswick now attached to the side like a happy bug. She motioned with her head for me to follow along. "We're having enchiladas tonight," she announced. I made a big production of looking at my watch and then hiding my arms. VOE. "Schedules," I muttered.

"You got time, baby," she said, pushing the cart on. I actually did have time. I have thirty extra minutes built into my schedule on Friday afternoons. I usually read the magazines at the bookstore. I shrugged and followed Veraleen and Biswick to the baking aisle.

A few minutes later, when we were strolling down the cereal aisle, Biswick stepped right into a huge wad of gum—must have been a three-piecer. There is nothing worse than stepping in a wad of gum except for stepping in steaming dog poo in your bare feet on a hot summer afternoon. Biswick tried desperately to scrape the gum off on the edge of the bottom shelf, right by the Cap'n Crunch.

"Why me, Veraleen? It was just waiting for me to step in it," he whined as he continued to scrape. He seemed to be making a spider web of pink gooey strings between his shoe and the linoleum floor.

"Someone in the world right now, honey, has gum on their shoe just like you and they're trying to scrape it off, too," Veraleen said as she grabbed a box of Boo Berry and threw it in the cart. "Now shoo and go run to the bathroom and scrape it off in there," she continued. "And take care of your business, too, sugar, so we don't have no more accidents like—"

Biswick shot her a look of pure horror. "I can't go in there, Veraleen!" he cried.

"Well, why not?" She gave him a stern look.

Veraleen didn't take much from no one.

"Because they have butt spiders here. Everyone knows that!" he screamed.

Veraleen burst out laughing. She sounded like a croaking bullfrog. I even smiled as we locked eyes. There's nothing like butt spiders and shoe gum to make one find a connection and forget other things.

"Now tell me, Biswick," she managed to say. "What in damnation is a butt spider?"

"You know. You sit down on the potty and they come up from the pipe and attack your hiney. They've been attacking butts in every Piggly Wiggly from here to New York. Everyone knows that." He hadn't moved. He continued to scrape at the gum, now leaving a long, pink strand across a box of Lucky Charms.

"Stop doing that, honey," Veraleen scolded him. "You're making a mess." I started looking around nervously for Pinell. That guy has radar for this kind of problem. "Now a ranch spider," Veraleen continued. "That's what you gotta be scared of. They're big as Dallas."

"Do you think it's Bubblicious or Bazooka?" Biswick asked.

"I don't know," I answered. "It's probably not Bazooka. I don't think Bazooka is very pliable."

Veraleen sighed, reached in her leather satchel, and pulled out a whole box of tissues. She seems to have everything in the world packed in there. She's even got a river stone in there she says is her touchstone. She told me she found it in the middle of the road in downtown Whiskey, like a meteor from another time and place. Veraleen says the idea that it spent millions of years on a river bottom being smoothed down by water and ended up in the middle of the road in Whiskey for her to find makes her believe there truly is a God.

"Here, baby, use this," she said, handing Biswick a tissue. True as blue, Pinell rounded the corner with a mop, Pine-Sol, bleach, and an industrial-size bucket. He'd been watching us from his supervisor's station, using the mirrors they have up in the corner of the store. He was blowing the whistle he had on a string around his neck. "Cleanup in aisle ten!" he shouted.

"Oh good Lord," Veraleen muttered.

"Little children that can't behave themselves should stay out of the Piggly Wiggly," Pinell bellowed, eyeballing Biswick like he was from the circus. "You should have left him on the quarter horsey ride out front." Pinell's face was all red and puffy. No doubt this was the highlight of his day.

"I don't have no quarters for no horsey ride, Mr. Pinell," said Veraleen, anchoring those big hands on her hips. "He's a good child. Someone left gum all over your store and look what it's done to my poor baby. He might need new shoes, and look, it's even on his socks. He's gonna need new socks, too."

"Now now, Miss Veraleen, I'm sure if he just goes to the bathroom we can get him all cleaned up." Pinell's eyes started blinking funny like a frog in a rainstorm.

"No," Biswick wailed. "They got butt spiders in the Piggly Wiggly potties!"

I thought Pinell's eyes were going to pop out of his head. "What?"

"You got butt spiders in your potty," Veraleen stated flatly, her voice coming out loud and low like the voice of God over the Piggly Wiggly loud-speaker.

Pinell picked up his bucket and mop and ran down the aisle. "Mama!" he yelled as he rounded the corner to the bathroom.

Veraleen and I smiled. "Here, baby, just take off your shoe. We'll take it home and stick it in the freezer, that'll get the gum off." Biswick leaned down and took his shoe off and handed it to Veraleen. A single strand of pink gum stretched from the cereal shelf over to her. Veraleen broke it off.

We walked over to the produce aisle, Biswick limping the one-shoe limp. I looked up to see the Three Tormenters—Romey, Cairo, and Mona Lisa. Nearby, next to the cucumbers, Wadine Pigg was handing out samples of her famous Pork-rind Casserole. The three girls were standing around crowding her.

They looked us over in unison. Of course, they had to look up high to give Veraleen a sweep over. Veraleen was scrunching up her nose at the store's herbs and muttering about foul-smelling pesticides and "Itching noses and kissing fools go hand in hand." Romey snickered. Cairo even laughed out loud and whispered something about "man purse" to Romey.

"Who are your new friends, Dragon Girl?" Romey asked. Mona Lisa laughed as she gingerly put her toothpick in one of the little paper cups Wadine had set out.

"You ladies don't like my casserole?" Wadine Pigg has been wearing the same hairdo since the sixties, a beehive that sports a little pig pin right at the crown.

"Your casseroles are great, Miss Pigg. Pure gourmet," Romey said. She turned and pretended to stick her finger down her throat.

Wadine frowned. "Scat then, girls, and quit loiterin' in my store."

"Nice outfit," Cairo said to me before they walked off.

We shuttled on toward the checkout counter. That's when I noticed Gideon. He was standing outside the front window, his face pressed right up against the glass, his hands cupped to shield the glare. There was a full cart of groceries next to him.

Poor Gideon. He has to do everything, even the grocery shopping, for his mama and grandma. A couple of times their cat, Jim, fat as a potato on toothpicks, has escaped and been found wearing cowboy and ballerina doll clothes. It's been rumored for many years that Gideon's grandma has a fear of getting hit by a space meteor if she leaves the house, and his mama is so obese she can't get out of her easy chair. The true problem, Dr. Coyote Wilson's nurse told me, is that both Elma and Grandma Finkle are agoraphobic, which means they are afraid of everything in the whole wide world and won't leave the house. Grandma swears, though, she saw Grandma Finkle rummaging through our trash cans late one night and when she turned on the back light, Gideon's grandmother scurried away like a startled raccoon.

"Whatya looking at, boy? See something you want?" Veraleen boomed at him through the glass. I just about died. So did Gideon. He pushed his glasses up his nose, turned around, and slowly pushed the cart down the sidewalk.

Veraleen made her famous Tex-Mex Enchiladas that night, and I couldn't help but wonder, as I glanced around the table at Mama, Daddy, Bug, Veraleen, and Biswick (who ate with us almost every night now), would it stay this way forever?

Chapter 10

Grandma Birdy says life is unpredictable—it can turn on you wild like a peach orchard hog and you never see it coming. When Sheriff Bupp was a little boy, his mama got a telegram on Christmas Day saying her husband, Johnny Bupp, had been killed by a Nazi in the big war. His mama folded the telegram up, walked inside, and keeled over right next to the Christmas tree.

It was little Henry who found her. Grandma Birdy says Sheriff Bupp's mother was a good woman and if those crazy aunts hadn't got a hold of him, he would have been a halfway decent person instead of the fool idiot he is. But faster than flies on butter, Lovie and Lulie moved in right after his mother's funeral and never left. There was no service for Sheriff Bupp's daddy; he'd been buried in France or Austria somewhere. But there's a bronze statue of him in his uniform over at the courthouse. It's a likeness from the last photo before he went off to the war, trying to be brave and serious, but still looking just like a kid.

Lovie and Lulie had some strange ideas about raising a child. Sheriff Bupp never got any affection; they were always harping on him, calling him "Dummy Bupp" or "Dodo Henry." He never had a Christmas after that day his mama died. Aunt Lovie and Aunt Lulie claimed they belonged to some religion where you don't give presents for anything. Actually they were just plain cheap. Sheriff Bupp made it all worse by marrying Minnie Dean, another harpy, and she moved into that little house with him and his aunts. And now Minnie has to care for those old aunts. She calls the sheriff in his car when one gets stuck on the potty or some other disaster, and he sets the phone down and she just keeps on jabbering.

Minnie Bupp has been feuding with her twin

sister, Myrtle, for years, mainly 'cause she thinks Myrtle stole her ventriloquist's dummy. She'd been honing her cornpone act with Leroy, a twin of Howdy Doody, since she was six years old. In all that time of practicing, she never progressed past an incredibly awful rendition of "Polly Wolly Doodle" which we had to listen to for years. Minnie thinks Myrtle stole Leroy out of jealousy 'cause Minnie was born with all the talent, and Myrtle never got over the fact that Minnie had won those Lauren Bacall cultured pearls. I know where Leroy is, though, like I know most things. Louis Smeather, the mushroom guy who got the worst earful 'cause he lives next door to the Bupps, has the dummy dressed in a little tuxedo sitting at his breakfast table. I guess in addition to talking to mushrooms, Louis talks to Leroy.

We never have any crimes to speak of, and never, ever any suspicious deaths, so Sheriff Bupp doesn't have much to do. Not that he'd be able to handle something if it happened. He once shot off his baby toe by accident and had to rest up in Odessa at Minnie's cousin Rudy's house so no one would know he can't handle a firearm. Minnie told me all this while she chewed on one of my Tootsie Pops. She also told me that the sheriff used to pee in his bed till he was twelve and his aunts used to make him sleep in the sheets for days before they'd wash them.

It took several weeks for Sheriff Bupp to find me and ask about Uncle Dal. It was almost the middle of October now, still hot as blazes, but with the optimistic hint in the air that things would soon change. Biswick and I were picking up trash at the old Jumbo cemetery after school on a Wednesday. I should say, *I* was picking up trash, because Biswick was too scared to come in. He was sitting outside the rickety cemetery gates sucking on two Tootsie Pops, one in each cheek.

I only come out to the cemetery every now and then, because nobody comes here much anymore and litters. Still, though, it was a pitiful sight. Obedias's finely carved gravestones were forgotten and abandoned, and like bad teeth they tilted and leaned this way and that to show their misery. Nearby was an old cotton field. For some reason last year it had sprung to life and intermittent clusters of cotton dotted the rows like white chocolate chips.

"You are not helping me very much from over there!" I called out to Biswick "We're doing a good thing for people, just like you said we should do."

He gargled a reply.

"I don't understand you," I called to him. "Incomprehensible."

Once again he gargled and I could see a purple line of spit running down the side of his mouth. "You are slurring your words," I yelled as I stabbed a Styrofoam cup.

Biswick spit one of the suckers out, and it hit the iron gates with a clang. "My daddy is a slurper, too, Merilee Marvelous," he said, and this cracked him up so much he had to spit the other Tootsie Pop into the dirt.

"Does he suck on suckers?" I asked.

"Do you think Veraleen does magic?" Biswick asked.

"No," I answered while picking up a beer bottle cap. One time I tried to collect bottle caps but Grandma had such a conniption fit because some of them were beer caps, I had to abandon the collection. "Why would you ask such a thing?"

"That's what Daddy said after my bug bite cleared up the next day. Says I should stay away from her. I like her." Half a second later, "I want to go home." His emotions change faster than bad news passes at a church social (or so Grandma would say).

"You are whining, Biswick. Did anyone ever tell you that you whine a lot?" I yelled. King Whiner.

"Those people are dead, Merilee. You are never getting me in there," he whined. "No way. There's ghosts. They're gonna be mad at you for tramping all over them."

"Preposterous. As you so rightly pointed out, Biswick," I said, "they are dead so they won't notice we are here." If anything, I felt more calm and serene in the cemetery, picking up my litter with the sure knowledge that no one would bother me.

"They know," he said quietly.

As I was turning to put the bottle cap in my

trash bag, a slight movement caught my eye. For someone who has just proclaimed she doesn't believe in ghosts, I jumped like the biggest scaredy-cat you've ever seen. When I came back to earth, I saw there was a blue-jeaned, booted leg behind one of the gravestones. Oh Lord. Was that someone dead lying there? Breathe in. Breathe out, Merilee. No, it couldn't be. Something had moved. It could be someone hurt or something. I tiptoed to get a better look.

There was a whole person lying there, sprawled out like he was taking an afternoon siesta, a gentle rise and fall of the chest letting me know he was alive.

I frowned. It was Biswick's daddy, the poet, Jack O'Connor.

A crucifix around his neck glinted in the sun. Except for the fact that there were five empty beer bottles lying around his body like spent bowling pins, he looked to be in complete harmony with his surroundings, as though he took a nap every day in a graveyard with his sunglasses on. I could picture dumb Lorelei saying, "Oh, but doesn't he look lovely?"

Biswick was standing at the gates, holding the bars, his little face peering in intently. He knew I had found something.

"What?" he whispered. "Is it a ghost?"

"No, no, Biswick," I said in a stage whisper. "Nothing here. Let's go home!" My voice cracked in a nervous staccato. I couldn't help myself. "Horrendous."

He was already opening the gate. "Shhhh!" He had his finger up to his nose. He had the look of someone taking their last walk.

I couldn't stop him. He did the dumb grave-yard tiptoe just as I had and looked down at my discovery. He burst out laughing. "That's just Daddy!"

"I know it's your daddy," I said, exasperated. "He shouldn't be here. Lying in the sun. Like this. We should get him home."

Biswick's face turned cloudy. "Oh no. Don't touch him. You can't touch him. You see, Daddy likes to take naps in all kinds of places. He says it clears his mind so he can write his poetry. He'll come home on his own when he's good and ready."

"Marvelous," I said. I looked down at the beer bottles and thought of the song, "Ninety-nine bottles of beer on the wall, ninety-nine bottles of beer, take one down, pass it around, ninety-eight bottles of beer on the wall." I wondered if that was the kind of poetry that Jack O'Connor wrote—"Ode to a Beer in a Graveyard" or "Graveyard Snooze with a Bottle of Booze."

"Does your daddy slur his words before he takes his special naps?" I asked. Breathe in. Breathe out. That was a long prying sentence for me.

Biswick was pretending to be interested in the different gravestones. "Yeah," he answered. "He gives me money and tells me to take a hike. He wants to make sure I get lots of exercise. Hey, how come this one doesn't have a lot of words on it?" he asked, pointing to a small marker that was set apart from the others.

I walked over, leaving our sleeping beauty alone for the moment. I read the marker out loud: "Mute Idiot. 1910-1918." That was all it said.

"It's an unnamed child," I told him. "It died a long time ago."

"You just said his name. Mute Idiot."

"Not his name," I said. "*Mute* means the child couldn't speak. Spectacular."

Biswick's lip turned down. He was more upset by the marker than his dad lying drunk in the grass. "Why didn't they put his real name?"

"Maybe no one knew it," I answered.

"Maybe it was a mysterious orphan that wandered into town and died right then and there on the spot," Biswick said.

"He?" I asked.

"It's a he. I feel it in my feet."

He was right. I could feel it, too. In my feet. It was a boy.

"It's really sad, Merilee," Biswick said. "Will you find out his real name?"

"Maybe," I mumbled. "I don't have time," I said. "Marvelous."

"Hey, you over there!" someone yelled from the gates.

Oh no. It was Sheriff Bupp. I glanced nervously at Mr. O'Connor on the ground and wondered if the sheriff could see him.

I motioned to Biswick to come with me. "Don't look at your daddy or we're all in trouble," I whispered out of the side of my mouth.

"I've been looking all over for you, girl. You been hiding from me?"

I took a FF breath. "No sir. I live right down the street from you."

"Don't talk back to me, girl, that's a slanderation." He took off his sheriff's hat and ran his hand across his smooth forehead. Sheriff Bupp's got no wrinkles. His face is as childlike and smooth as Veraleen's river stone. It's like he hasn't aged since he was a boy, since his daddy died. The only way you know he's older is he's bald and has one of those three-strand comb-overs that don't fool anyone. It starts from one ear and goes all the way over his bald head to the other side. The sheriff looked at Biswick and frowned like when someone smells sour milk in a bottle.

"Is that the retarded boy?" he said it just like Biswick couldn't hear him, just like people do with me.

I felt as though someone punched me in the

stomach. I opened my mouth to talk but could get nothing out.

"I'm not retarded, sir, I got a sin-drum," Biswick said. "Did you know that you got no hair on your head? Veraleen says if you would wear a cow patty on your head every night for a week, you might finally start growing hair."

"She said what? I oughta bring that voodoo witch in for practicing fool's medicine." The sheriff shook his hat at Biswick. "She can't cure what you got, though."

"Horrendous!" I blurted out. I wished at that moment I could have reached through the gates and grabbed him. I had never in my life felt what must have been fury. It burned deep down low and singed up into my throat.

"What's that?" Biswick asked innocently.

The sheriff shook his head like he was indeed talking to someone who was an idiot. "Where's your daddy, son?" he asked, his eyes slanting a warning at Biswick.

I could feel Biswick trying with all his might not to turn his head toward his prostrate, dead-drunk daddy. "He's at home sleeping." Biswick was blinking funny.

"Is that right, son," Sheriff Bupp said. "I want to ask him a few questions. Seems the BNSF had a stowaway a few weeks ago right outside of Jumbo and they are of course very upset about it. They asked me if I have any townspeople who might do some dumb thing like jump off a train and I tell 'em yeah, I have a likely candidate."

"Who?" Biswick asked, excited. He really wanted to know.

"Your dumb-ass daddy!" Sheriff Bupp said quickly with a chuckle.

Biswick chewed on his lower lip, his eyes flitting back and forth. I just stared at the Sheriff. I knew who jumped off the train but I wasn't about to say anything. I took another FF breath and felt the air, hot and sad, blow out through my nose. I closed my eyes.

"The engineer says he sees you every week, like watch work, out there picking up trash left by those migrants," Sheriff Bupp began. I opened my eyes a little. "He thinks maybe you saw something."

I shook my head no and mumbled to myself, "Watch work. Clockwork." The tips of my fingers tingled.

"I was there with her," Biswick offered.

"I didn't ask you, boy," the sheriff said.

"We didn't see anything," Biswick muttered.

"Is that so? I think someone as dumb as you would at least know how to lie right."

"He's—not—lying," I stammered out. "We—he didn't see anything. Horrendous." The tingle in my hands was now buzzing up my arms.

"Well I guess if either of you did, you wouldn't tell me anyway."

"That's right," Biswick spouted out.

"Boy, I have a right mind to take you in for public disorderliness on sacred ground and threatening a law official with a cow patty." Little did he know who was lying twenty feet away on "sacred ground," drunk as a skunk.

"You better scat and get home to your sleepy daddy." Sheriff Bupp put his hat square on his head and sauntered back to his car. He slammed the door and drove off.

"He used to pee in his bed when he was a boy," I muttered. "I'm sorry," I said, turning to Biswick. "He had no right to say that. No right at all. He's meaner and dumber than a rat's ass. That's all."

Biswick laughed long and hard at that. "You are so funny, Merilee Marvelous! It's all right. I've been called badder things before."

"Like what?" I asked him.

"Injun Joe or Biscuit, or Pancake or—"

"Are you Indian, Biswick?"

"No!" he declared a little too vehemently. "They just call me that 'cause I look it with my dark skin. I told you that I'm Irish, Black Irish Daddy says to tell nosy people, and you are supposed to believe me because you are my only friend in the entire world." His eyes teared up.

"I'm sorry, Bis," I said calling him that for the first time. "I really am."

He pouted.

"Doesn't your daddy have a poetry reading tonight at Mama's bookstore?" I asked. His gaze followed mine over to his daddy.

"He does?" he asked.

"Yeah," I said. "It's been in the newspaper and everything. Big crowd expected." What were we going to do with him? Could we drag him out of here? How would we get him to his house without everyone seeing?

"Don't worry, Daddy'll come around. He'll be there. I promise." I could see on Biswick's face, though, that he wasn't quite sure, either.

"Don't think so," I said. Biswick's daddy looked like he might just sleep through till next year.

"No, no." Biswick shook his head. "He always wakes up in time. He will. He always does." A wind blew through the cemetery then, making the beer bottles clink together like wind chimes and the hair on Mr. O'Connor's head wave gently. The poet didn't stir one bit.

"Should we wake him up? To be sure?" I asked.

Biswick contemplated this, pursing his lips. "Do you have any water?" he asked.

"Yeah, a water bottle. What do you want with it?"

"Just go get it." I went to my bicycle, retrieved the water bottle, and brought it to him.

"Get ready to take off as fast as you can," Biswick said.

I looked at him. "Preposterous."

"Don't worry, I know what I'm doing." He shooed at me with one hand and held the water bottle in the other like a weapon, ready to fire.

I started to feel a little silly, being the getaway driver on my three-wheeler. Then I heard a roar like a mad lion and Biswick came crashing through the gates. He jumped on and we took off faster than greased lightning.

Chapter 11

A long time ago, when the moon was full a dragon would come down from the mountain to show his mighty fire breath. It glowed like ancient fireworks in the sky. Crowds from the nearby village would gather 'round to watch, even though they knew the danger was strong. They couldn't help themselves. And one day, indeed, a child drew too close to the fire and was killed. The child's father prayed to the gods for no more full moons and his wish was granted. The moon dragon never came out of his cave again. But the next cycle when the full moon did not appear, the tides were altered, and the village was flooded by a great wave from the sea.

People will show up for anything if there's a spectacle on the horizon. Mama's store was cram packed that evening. Cram packed with small-town windblown hairdos, 'cause the wind still hadn't let up. Grandma says it was the desert wind that came through once a year and brought with it bad news—the "bad news wind" she calls it.

Mama had set up folding chairs between the big oak shelves carrying Natural History & West Texas and New Fiction. Already every seat was taken and it was standing room only for the late-comers. When Sheriff Bupp's old aunts Lovie and Lulie came tottering in, those smug chair sitters wouldn't budge an inch. Finally Carmen Esparanza and Miss Tunswell, our librarian, got up and gave them their seats.

Not only did we have the locals who fancied themselves literary, like Louis Smeather the dummy kidnapper and Dorwood Milton the John Steinbeck-wannabe, but we also had townspeople who had probably never cracked a book since their first-grade primer. Wadine and Pinell had even closed up the Piggly Wiggly for a couple of hours and were squeezed in with everyone else. And hermit Bum "Chicken Pox" Fox, was there, too, in the back row, shaking hands with people he hadn't seen a good long while.

Frida Pinkett, the owner of the Sweet Home Diner, fussed over a table of food and slapped Dr. Coyote's hand when he tried to take one of her famous pecan caramel pralines. A moment later when she had her head turned, Yello Brown helped himself to some orange slush punch.

Biswick and I sat on Mama's old chenille couch. The couch was supposed to make the store more sophisticated and artsy, but it just became a receptacle for the cheapos who never bought anything and just came in to read all the gossip tabloids for free. The couch did, though, give us a good view of the front door as we fearfully waited for Biswick's daddy, who was already half an hour late. I put the odds at a hundred to one that he would show—and if he did, I imagined him stumbling in, wet as a drowned rat and shouting obscenities.

"He'll be here," Biswick said, his eyes darting from the podium to the front door. I noticed Otis

Stunkel was there in his trench coat, the collar turned up like a gangster. Mona Lisa Venezuela sat at the coffee bar, her head bowed low over a book. Romey and Cairo were hiding in one of the aisles, probably pawing through a racy issue of *Cosmopolitan*.

"Yeah, he'll come," I said to reassure Biswick. "Is Veraleen coming?" I went back to drawing a dragon in my journal. It was a poet dragon with a long scraggly beard and John Lennon glasses. I glanced up in time to see Mama Peaches pocket a small paperback from the travel section.

"No, she's gonna go over to your house and cook for your daddy and Bug. She doesn't like poetry," he answered. "She says she can't understand why they can't come right out and say what they're trying to say. She says you can put boots in an oven but that don't make a biscuit." I nodded in agreement. For me, things are better if they are black and white with nothing in between to confuse you. I glanced over at Biswick. He looked like he was going to cry. He kept rubbing at something in his pocket like it was good luck or something.

"What's in there?" I asked as I glanced at the front door.

"Cheeto," he said as he continued to rub.

"Marvelous. I told you to put it away somewhere safe, Biswick. Stop rubbing it or it will disintegrate."

"It's *my* Cheeto. Not yours," he said. "It makes me feel better to have it with me. I used to have my purple poodle. Daddy Jack threw it away. Now I have my Cheeto. Besides, if I leave it at home, it's gonna get stolen."

I rolled my eyes. There was no use trying to persuade him. Let it disintegrate. I looked through the crowd and spotted Uncle Dal. Wow. He was leaning against the wall, his hands in his pockets, his eyes not seeming to fix on anything.

Lorelei appeared and sat on an arm of our couch. Her head kept craning toward the front door, too. She had her hair done up like Audrey Hepburn's in *Breakfast at Tiffany's*, complete with two Cruella DeVil frosted stripes in the front. And she had on her Audrey pink lipstick and a fake long fancy-smancy cigarette holder, which she artfully held and every now and then pretended to smoke.

Mama came over to us and asked Biswick very gently, "Is he going to be here soon?" She had on her special occasion silvery half-moon earrings that Daddy bought her for Christmas last year. They dangled halfway down to her shoulders.

"He'll be here," Biswick and I said at the same time. I started drawing a half-moon above my poet dragon.

"That's good, Biswick." Mama patted his head and went over to chat with Ferdie Frankmueller.

I glanced up and saw Gideon off in a corner by the children's books. He was staring straight at me, and I could tell that it wasn't just a mere glance. He had a question for me in his eyes. What did he want?

Dr. Coyote came over. "How are you doing?" he asked Biswick, as he chomped on a praline he'd finally managed to pilfer. Biswick nodded okay, but kept his eyes on the front door. I noticed Dr. Coyote studying Biswick's face with concern like a scientist studying a specimen. I wondered what he

SUZANNE CROWLEY

was deciphering. Then he winked at me and walked on.

Suddenly there was a commotion. Biswick perked up. Had *he* come? This was it. The big, slopping wet cussing scene I had been dreading. I closed my eyes but peeked through my lids.

"What are *you* doing here!" someone screamed. My eyes flew open. It was Minnie Bupp. The crowd quickly parted like the Red Sea, unveiling the object of her wrath.

"I have every right as you do to be here, Minnie," Myrtle, her sister, yelled back.

"Oh no you don't, you know perfectly well Mondays, Wednesdays, and Fridays are my days to be downtown. And you're probably double-parked as usual!" Minnie added.

"Mabel is too big to park in these dinky parking spaces," Myrtle fired back. There was a murmur of laughter. For years Myrtle has been double-parking her big, honking old yellow Cadillac 'cause she can't see the lines. She just ignores the piles of tickets her brother-in-law puts on her windshield.

"The only reason you drive that land barge is because you need the space to drive around my Leroy! And the only reason you double-park it is to catch the attention of my husband!" Minnie yelled. "And you are never gonna get him."

"Who's Leroy?" Biswick whispered.

"Her dummy," I answered. "She thinks her sister stole him."

"She stole Sheriff Bupp?"

I laughed. Yeah, Sheriff Bupp was a dummy, but she wasn't talking about that one.

"If you were lying here dead as a doorknob, I'd step over you and walk right past that crazy idiot, skinflint, cheap as used bubble gum of a husband!" Myrtle yelled. "And you never, ever once let me wear those pearls. Your own sister." About this time my mother started making her way over to the ladies, her arm raised to indicate they should calm down.

"Ladies, ladies," Mama said. "I think it is wonderful that you two are talking for the first time in years, but it would be best if you quiet down a little." She shooed at them to take it outside fast.

Myrtle pushed past her sister and went on out the door, letting in a big gush of wind that knocked a couple of books off one of the tables. Minnie started to follow her sister but froze, as did everyone else, because there, standing in the doorway, was Jack O'Connor.

He had cleaned himself up and now radiated the cool persona of a mysterious poet, just what everyone had come to see. He was wearing freshly pressed blue jeans and a crisp white button-down. I could hear Biswick's indrawn breath and I thought perhaps it was fear or disappointment. Instead I saw admiration. Admiration was mirrored on all the other faces in the crowd, especially Lorelei's. Fools. All of them fools. Except Uncle Dal. He slipped right past Jack O'Connor without even acknowledging him, and walked out the door.

"Well, here you are, Mr. O'Connor," my mama finally said. "We have been waiting for you—*for a long time*. I am so glad you could come." She hooked her arm in his. "Here's the podium," she said, smiling through clenched teeth.

"I'm not standing at no ———ing podium like a trained seal," Jack O'Connor said, pulling his arm out of hers. There was a murmur of shock from the crowd. I half expected to see people start marching out of the store but everyone stayed rooted where they were. They knew they were in for a good fire-breathing show and they weren't moving, not one iota.

"Just what kind of poetry does your daddy write?" I whispered to Biswick as his father made his way over to the coffee bar, tripping a little on the edge of the carpet. Someone got up and gave him his stool.

Biswick had his finger in his ear digging around.

"I don't know," he answered. "It's always about pain."

Mama Peaches handed Jack O'Connor a glass of wine, which he drank down in one violent gulp, and when he started to speak, his words danced across the room like sad and angry ghosts. He didn't have a paper or anything. He just recited from memory. I couldn't recall all he said to you verbatim but it had something to do with Hades, Berlin, rotting fish heads, ricotta cheese, with a whole bucketload of bad words perched in there. Romey and Cairo heads appeared, peeking around one of the bookshelves, their eyes as big as whoppers. I looked back at the poet, my eyes drawn to the base of his sunburned neck, where burned into his skin was the image of a crucifix.

He finished speaking and held his hand out. Mama Peaches gave him another glass of wine which he downed, and I saw Dr. Coyote shake his head in disapproval. But everyone else was mesmerized. Biswick was chewing his lower lip. Lorelei pretended to smoke her cigarette, her eyes narrowed like she was looking at a big piece of chocolate cake.

The poet recited another poem. This one was about Bolivia, the rumba, and JFK. And bad words. He finished with the line *"out of the wilderness we come, and to the light we rise."*

Pure, pin-dropping silence.

"Well," Mama said from across the room as she drew her hands together. She looked like she had clown rouge on her flaming cheeks. "Time for refreshments! And afterward Mr. O'Connor will sign his book of poetry, *Rising from the Ashes*." Mama's all for the First Amendment, but I think even she was surprised. People started standing up and moving around and talking excitedly like they'd just got off a roller coaster ride.

"Hold on there!" came a voice from the front door. Everyone turned. It was Sheriff Bupp. "I'm taking you in for foulation of the public sensibilities and public inebriatedness." The sheriff took out his handcuffs.

Jack O'Connor sat on his stool and smiled. He downed another glass of wine like it was Kool-Aid and waited.

It was deathly quiet and no one made a move. But then the poet got up calmly and walked toward Sheriff Bupp. The sheriff held out his handcuffs but the poet walked past him and out the door. The sheriff was so surprised he just stood there a moment, his mouth wide open, before running out the door after him.

The whole bookstore stampeded after them,

jostling like it was a fire sale at Ferdie's.

"Ten dollars says he calls for reinforcements from Whiskey!" Mama Peaches yelled.

"Twenty says the sheriff runs him out of town like that last one," someone behind me yelled. I desperately looked around for Biswick but couldn't find him anywhere.

"I was here first!" Minnie yelled as she and Carmen Esparanza became wedged back to back in the doorway. Bum "Chicken Pox" Fox, accidentally pushed forward by the crowd like a battering ram, hit them with such force they shot through the door like cannonballs. Everyone else squeezed through after them. By the time I got out, I'd missed the scuffle. Sheriff Bupp was picking the poet off the ground and putting the handcuffs on. I bent over and looked through the legs. I saw Biswick's feet in the doorway, one in and one out—tentative.

Then it all happened so fast. Mama was out front by the curb, holding her flowing skirt down in the wind and asking the sheriff something as he put the poet in the back of the police car. And then

Myrtle Dean came screeching out of nowhere in her big Cadillac. Mabel hopped up on the curb and the next thing you know Mama's flying through the air.

Although I don't remember moving, suddenly I was standing over her. Everyone else clustered behind me as the wind swirled around us. Her clogs were gone. When Dr. Coyote came over and checked her pulse, I could only stare at her earrings, which under the glare of Mabel's headlights cast shadows of tiny half circles across the sidewalk. There was no moon tonight. The wind had blown it away.

Chapter
12

I peered out of Veraleen's old GTO only briefly as we sped along Highway 90 up toward El Paso. Grandma was right. The wind had indeed been a powerful harbinger of bad news, and when it finally left a few days later unrepentful and arrogant, it sucked with it my mother.

"Your mama's gonna be fine," shouted Biswick from the backseat. He had his head stuck out the window. He was happy as a bee freed from under a Dixie cup. Since his Daddy was in jail, Biswick had moved in with us and was sleeping in my spare bed. And Veraleen was now showing up in the morning and staying all day. Sometimes she fell asleep on our sofa and stayed all night.

Bug sat next to Biswick bawling her eyes out, like she'd been doing for three days. "Stop crying, Bug," I pleaded. I focused on drawing an armored, spike-covered dragon in my journal. It was a Saturday and I had had to put aside my whole VOE to make the drive.

"She's gonna *die!*" Bug wailed.

"Ain't nobody gonna die, sugar." Even Veraleen had to bellow over the noise of the car. She had on her full nurse's getup, one big arm on the steering wheel, the other lying on the windowsill like a fallen tree trunk. Veraleen had an interesting way of driving. No brakes. Foot all the way down on the gas. If there was a dip in the road she kept the same speed and we'd all pop up off our seats like jumpin' beans.

Bug continued to wail. "Please stop!" I told her. I couldn't stand it anymore. "Please Veraleen, can we roll the windows up?" There were too many noises—wind, car, voices, crying—mixed together. I thought I was going to burst into a thousand pieces. FF breath. FF breath. In and out. In and out, Merilee.

Veraleen finally told Biswick to roll up his window and he did after whining about it.

"You haven't cried since you were a baby!" Bug yelled at me. "You got all your crying out and there's none left! No feeling. Nothing! You could care less if Mama dies! Because you don't care about anything except your dragons!"

I lifted my binoculars and looked out the window, the faraway mountains blurred but still looming. Perhaps I'd see White Feather.

"Hush, hush, darling," Veraleen said. "That ain't true and you know it. We all have our ways of dealing with things, that's all. Leave your sister alone." Her words were soft and yellow-buttery. "Sisters. Sisters are everything."

"Ha!" Bug bellowed, her wails piercing through me like ice daggers. "She's not a sister. She's not anything. She's a trash girl robot who always has those stupid binoculars on her face." I turned, focusing on a tear rolling down Bug's cheek. I lowered the binoculars.

Biswick leaned forward, resting his elbows on the front seat. "How come Myrtle and Minnie hate each other? They're sisters, aren't they?"

I rolled my eyes. Biswick's father was still in jail 'cause he had no money to get out and my mother was over in the hospital, but both facts didn't seem to penetrate Biswick's brain. And why'd he have to bring Myrtle up?

"I told you, Biswick, Minnie thinks her sister stole something from her," I answered, hoping that would shut him up. This was going to be a long, bumpy car ride. I wish I could've ridden with Daddy the first day. He wouldn't let me. He said I needed to stay home and take care of things, like I was really capable of that. He said he could trust me always.

"Well," said Biswick, mulling it over. "All she has to do is give it back and they will like each other again."

"She can't," I said. "Give it back."

Veraleen had one penciled eyebrow up a little. "Nope," she said. "Some things you can't give back." She sighed and I heard her mutter, "Broken hearts, cupid darts." And I thought about how Daddy sometimes mutters Mama's name. *Helene. Helene.* Oh Mama.

"Is Myrtle gonna be able to drive again?" Bug asked.

"Don't you worry about that," Veraleen said. "Sheriff Bupp took her driver's license and keys away. We won't be seeing Mabel on the road for a long, long time." Myrtle had spent a night in jail, too, before Minnie bailed her out the next day. Mama didn't want to press charges. She lives by the credo "forgive and forget." And Myrtle truly is sorry. She keeps leaving delicious food on the front porch for us on the hour, almost every hour.

I looked out the window and saw the beginning of a dust devil out on the desert plain. Biswick saw it, too.

"What's that? It looks like magic."

"It's just a dust devil," I told him. "Like a miniature tornado." I continued to work on my dragon, carefully shading in tendrils at the base of his pointy chin.

"The Indians believed they were born in wind-swirled dust, and that dust devils contain their ancestors' spirits. Some say it's lost souls dancing with the devil," added Veraleen. "Sounds fittin' to me."

Biswick looked straight ahead, not blinking.

I shook my head at Veraleen. How dare she fill his head with such crap. I looked back out the window, but the dust devil was dying down now, swirling like the remnants of the Wicked Witch of the West. I thought about Veraleen, how she had barreled into town like a dust devil, blowing up a storm in our lives. Biswick had come in quietly, like a sneaky thief in the night, Grandma would say.

We drove the next five minutes in blissful silence.

Then Biswick said, "I wish I had a sister. I wish that more than anything in the world."

"You do, baby?" Veraleen said. "That's sweet."

"No you don't," said Bug, who had calmed down to whimpering hiccups. "Not like Merilee. I wish I had sisters like Romey, Cairo, or Mona Lisa Venezuela. They're beautiful."

"Beauty comes in all packages," Veraleen said. I wondered what she looked like when she was young, before the sun wore its map into her face. Just then we came to a bend in the road and

Veraleen just kept going straight right off the road onto the dirt and back on the road again. Bug and Biswick spilled forward, almost coming over the front seat.

"Veraleen!" I shouted.

"Sorry. That's ranch driving, darlin'," she whooped.

Biswick plopped back into his seat and squealed, "That was fun!" One breath, then, "What's a dumb-ass?"

"What?" Veraleen asked. She turned to me for an explanation.

"Sheriff Bupp," I explained.

"Did he call you that, Biswick?" asked Veraleen.

"Yeah," Biswick answered, poking at Bug who let out a wail.

Veraleen shook her head. "I'm gonna fix his little red wagon. I'm gonna clean his clock. I'm gonna . . ."

I actually cracked a smile for the first time in three days, imagining Veraleen taking care of Sheriff Bupp her way. All she would have to do was sit on him and it would all be over.

"Sheriff Bupp has a red wagon?" Biswick asked.

"It's a colloquialism," I said. "An expression. He really doesn't have a wagon." I turned a page in my journal and wrote down Veraleen's sayings. She had a lot of good ones, just like Grandma Birdy. It was the only thing I could pull out of the whole universe that they had in common.

"Why don't we play the quiet game for a while. We all need some peace and quiet," Veraleen said. And then she muttered, "Quiet as a snowflake on a feather," which I wrote down, too.

Now all that was to be heard were Bug's sad hiccups, which only reminded me every five seconds of why we were driving to El Paso. A few miles later, Bug started crying again, and next Biswick, the whole backseat a chorus of wails. No one was gonna see me cry. No way. Bug was right. I used up all my tears when I was a squallin' baby. As I was about to stick my fingers in my ears we went over another dip in the road and got jostled again. Then I heard from the backseat, "Veraleen, I think I'm gonna throw up. Here it comes."

*　*　*

When we arrived at the hospital an hour later, the barf had dried in my hair. It was caked and crusty, still smelly. The aroma of barf hangs around for a long time—that's universal. Even an aborigine in Australia knows that. When Biswick threw up, instead of sticking his head out the window like he had just been doing a few minutes before, he leaned forward and sprayed me like Otis Stunkel's skunk. Since we were in the middle of nowhere, there was no place to stop and nothing to wash it off with anyway. There wasn't one spatter on my journal, which was all I cared about.

"We'll get you cleaned up, darlin,' right away," Veraleen told me as we all walked in through the front doors of the medical center. It was eerily quiet. There weren't many people, only two old lady volunteers sitting behind an information desk. "Later I'll mix you up some ginger shampoo with lavender oil," Veraleen continued. "It'll draw the smell out. Poor Biswick. There are worse things, Merilee." Veraleen asked the two old ladies where Mama was.

Yeah, right. What's worse than having dried

barf in your hair and all over your back? But as we walked down the long hallways, I saw that yes, things could be worse. There were old people walking along dragging their oxygen tanks, and crying relatives outside of rooms, sick children, and everywhere, everywhere, worried looks of bewilderment and confusion.

And suddenly all I wanted was to see Mama.

"Here we go," Veraleen said cheerily as she found a bathroom. She motioned for me to come in with her. I stood there. Bug's face was red and striped with tears.

"I can wait. Let's go," I said.

Veraleen looked at me for a moment. "I just thought you would want to get cleaned up before you see your mama," she said.

"I don't care," I said. "Let's go." She nodded and went on down the hall and Biswick, Bug, and I followed behind.

"It's all right," Bug said, brightening. "I've spent all night with throw-up in my hair. In fact two nights . . . I get so excited on Christmas Eve I've thrown up in my sleep two years in a row. Mama says it's from all the Christmas candy but I swear it's from that Christmas stew Grandma makes for me every year. . . ."

Veraleen pushed open the door to Room 211 and we all walked in. Mama's room was half darkened by pulled shades. A TV mounted to the wall was on, but the sound was turned down way low, buzzing. It was cold.

I did not want to look at Mama. I imagined her all shriveled up with tubes snaking all around her.

But she spoke first. "It's my darlings! Oh, come here and give me a hug." Bug and Biswick ran toward her bed and I shuffled slowly behind, my eyes cast down. From behind, Veraleen's big warm hand shoved me into the mix and Mama put her arms around me, too. I couldn't tell you if this was a good sensation, being hugged by Mama in the hospital—all I know is that it sent a stove-hot shock all the way through me, up to my head where it lingered. I stepped away.

There was a big gauzy bandage on Mama's forehead where she'd had stitches, and a few bruises here and there. She'd been unconscious for two days and even the doctors were worried. But when she came to yesterday, Daddy says she asked about Bug and me right and normal as though nothing had happened. I wondered about that. If she'd be any different now. And what she was dreaming about when she was gone. The doctors said it was amazing she wasn't injured more. But they said sometimes the body just knows right before impact and it turns into a giant Gumby doll. Mama had put on some lipstick, which she usually doesn't wear. She smiled over Bug and Biswick, whom she still held at her chest.

Daddy was sitting in a little chair in the corner. There was no sign of Uncle Dal. "Did Uncle Dal go to the cafeteria?" I asked Daddy. He shook his head no. He meant not at the hospital, either.

When I had ridden my bike over to see Uncle Dal yesterday after my litter patrol, he said he would be there. But I could tell by the way he had said it, his eyes not meeting mine, that there was a good chance he wouldn't. Daddy and Uncle Dal were a lot alike. At least Daddy was here. He was here.

Veraleen put her big strong hands on my shoulders and led me to the bathroom without announcing the reason, and that I was thankful for. As she soaped up my hair, I felt a stinging sensation in my eyes. I'm not sure what it was. Maybe the beginning of real tears, or maybe shampoo in my eyes. I put a stop to that nonsense. For some reason it was all of a sudden very important to me that Mama not know I had a mess in my hair and that I was about to cry. Veraleen dried my hair with a towel and then pulled a brush from her satchel and brushed out the tangles with long, gentle strokes.

When we came out of the bathroom Daddy was holding Bug to his chest. He was watching Mama, barely blinking. We stayed for a while and Mama chattered a lot, that kinda chatter people do when it's too quiet. Then Mama got tired, so Veraleen took us down to the cafeteria where we had some "chicken fried unidentified" with syrupy mashed potatoes and lime Jell-O.

Then Veraleen drove us home in the dark, dark night.

Bug and Biswick fell fast asleep in the backseat. I leaned into the car door, my face pressed into the cold window, searching the sky for the lights. All I could think about was Mama. How she could have died that day. How she *is* going to die someday.

Chapter
13

As I sat in class a few days after our visit to Mama, I wondered if there was any truth to the notion that what we do in life boomerangs out into the universe and then comes back to bite you in the butt—like a Piggly Wiggly butt spider. That's what Grandma thinks. Bad things happen to people who have sinned. But I haven't ever *done* anything really bad in my life except cry my head off as a baby. Maybe that was enough. That crying reached past Whiskey, past the Chitalpi Mountains, and up into the sky where it hit a star and headed back to me.

I had finished the geography test we were taking and was trying to draw a coiled, serpentine dragon, but it was just mishmash scribbles, with a horn and a scale emerging here and there. Gideon had finished his test, too. The cretins in the class were either sneaking looks at their neighbors' tests or scratching their heads and frowning. I hadn't had to pick up one scrap of trash (in class, that is) since Gideon stood up for me. My invisible antennae told me that it wasn't over. The class was simmering like one of Veraleen's cure pots, and the lid might blow off at any time. I noticed Gideon reach down and softly touch his little backpack on the floor.

About the time Gideon was brought home to his mother, he started showing up at school with a backpack strapped diagonally across his chest. Except for Cairo once proclaiming it looked like her meemaw's old stinky purse, no one really seemed to bother him about it or ask what was inside. It was no great secret to me. All I had to do was spend more than one minute at the photo counter at the Rexall Drug, and Maydell Rathburger told me that Gideon Beaurogard brings in film every week to be developed, thinks he is "Adam Ant," she says. "Always black-and-white film, what kind of artsy fool wants black and white? We have to send 'em off to El Paso to be developed."

The bell rang for the end of the day and Mr. Bonaparte went around picking up the tests. Everyone ran out the classroom door and shot off in different directions. I headed for the bicycle rack. I have to chain my bicycle to the side of the rack because it doesn't fit in the slots for normal bicycles. Gideon arrived at the same time.

"I'm sorry about your mother," he mumbled quietly, pushing his glasses up his nose. I knew he was sorry. I had seen him out front of our house a couple of times, watching like a shy sentinel.

I stuttered a moment before answering, "Thanks."

"Well, lookey here!"

It was the Three Tormenters. Of course. They stopped in front of the bike rack. Right legs out and right arms on hip. The ISFs stood back about ten feet watching.

"Is this the retard club meeting?" From Cairo. They giggled. All of them.

Gideon blinked and I looked away. In and out. In and out.

"Horrendous," I said before I could control it.

"What's horrendous, Merilee? Your face? Your existence?" asked Cairo.

"Where's the little retard?" Romey asked. Mona Lisa's arm dropped from her hip.

"Horrendous." I said it again.

"Why, are you hoping there's an extra space so you can join?" Gideon responded.

Romey's eyes grew big. Just then Scooter Stunkel walked over with a big shark grin on his face.

I felt like the ground was melting and I was falling. Horrendous. Horrendous. I knew all their secrets. Skunks. Dead Frogs. Snickers Bars. Prison. Frankenstein.

I tried to say the words. To throw their secrets at them. They wouldn't come. My mouth just hung open. I probably looked like a slack-jawed cow.

"What's the matter, Dragon Girl? Dragon got your tongue?" From Scooter Stunkel. More laughter. Gideon peered around at all of them, assessing the situation. "What you looking for, your daddy?" Scooter bellowed. "You ain't gonna see him again." No one's heard sight or sound of Gideon's daddy, Buddy Finkle, since he left all those years ago.

I blinked slowly a few times and felt someone trying to steady me. It was Mona Lisa. I brushed her hand off violently and kept my eyes fixed on one spot. Suddenly Scooter appeared in my line of vision, holding his hand to the side of his head. I looked up to see Gideon riding off on his bicycle, his backpack still swinging.

When I got home later, after making my litter rounds, I discovered that Grandma Birdy had seized her chance and slithered into the house. She had left a big suitcase in Bug's room and scoured the house down like a white tornado. She was now cooking up a huge pot of gumbo in the kitchen. She wore Veraleen's chef's hat as though it was a diamond tiara, but all she looked like was a fool with a pillowcase on her head. Even Weenie was in on the invasion. He lay confident and smug on Beasie's bed by the kitchen door. Beasie, Stinkie, and Winkie, already upset by Mama's departure, had retreated somewhere.

Biswick and Bug sat at the table scarfing down snickerdoodles. There were several trays of other baked goodies on the counter. I went over to get a drink from the fridge.

You should have seen the look on Veraleen's face when she walked in a few minutes later, her arms full of groceries. She looked like you feel when you discover a crunchy bug is in your shoe, after you have slipped your bare foot in.

"Ms. Monroe," Veraleen started, "that's real nice of you." She set the groceries down on the table hard enough so that one bag tipped over and an apple rolled to the floor. "You can go on home now. I'm here to take over." Veraleen put her hands on her hips. "Helene will be coming home very soon."

Grandma Birdy kept on stirring the gumbo pot real slow. Her upper lip twitched.

Veraleen blinked twice and licked her teeth.

Uh-oh.

A good full minute passed. Grandma was taking her time. I turned around to leave. My heart was starting to race.

"You can take *that* boy and go on home," she said it low and mean-sly like she was talking about something disgusting.

"Is she talking about me?" Biswick asked. "I'm the only boy in here." I stopped in my tracks. Oh Grandma, please don't.

I could see out of the corner of my eye Veraleen's big chest heaving to and fro.

"Grandma," Bug admonished. "That's not nice."

"Come here, my Bug," Grandma said, turning around and asking for a hug with her arms. Bug ran to her. She hugged her tight. I felt dizzy and wanted to sit down.

Biswick picked at his nose. "Come on, Veraleen, can we please go get my daddy out of jail?"

I wondered what Veraleen was going to do—fight Grandma Birdy for her place in our kitchen or take Biswick to the jail? I wanted her to stay and fight it out like the cowboys did in old westerns. Stay. Stay.

"Mrs. Monroe, we are finished here," Veraleen said, her voice gravelly and sure. Grandma ignored her. "I'll be back to cook breakfast in the morning." She gathered up Biswick and they walked to the back door. She grabbed her chef's hat off Grandma's head as she walked by. Grandma let out a little whoop.

The door slammed and Grandma turned on me. "What are you staring at, Merilee? Cat got your tongue, as usual? I'm only doing the right thing. This house has been falling apart and I gotta take care of my family. Something ain't right with that woman. She's as big as a killing hog, for goodness sake. Look at her. She ain't got no business coming in here wearing a proper nurse's uniform and pushing her voodoo cures on us."

Grandma wasn't finished. "She needs to go home. Veraleen Holliday is an ole bean-masher ranch cook and her food tastes like it's been cooked in a boot. Harley is gonna want a true home-cooked meal when he gets in and I mean to give it to him." It seemed strange to hear her say Daddy's name 'cause she usually just refers to Daddy and Uncle Dal as her boys.

"Aaaaaah!" I opened my mouth to scream articulate insults at her but that was all that came out. But it was enough to surprise Grandma. Her jaw dropped, and just as she was about to find *her* words I went running out the screen door. Veraleen's GTO was backing out of the driveway and I sprinted after it like a maniac.

Veraleen came to a screeching halt. I pulled open the back door and jumped in. Without saying a word, she stepped on the gas pedal and we rode off.

"Merilee!" Biswick exclaimed. "You coming, too?"

"Yep," I answered. "Stupendous." Biswick lay down on the seat, almost touching my leg. I debated scooting over, but decided not to. He was asleep within seconds.

"How come, Veraleen?" I asked after a few minutes of complete silence. "Why?"

Veraleen lit up a cigarette. My eyes popped

wide open. It was a real cigarette, not like Lorelei's fakey Audrey Hepburn one. "I don't smoke 'em very often." I frowned and she saw me in the rearview mirror. "Out on the ranch everyone smoked, Merilee. You figure something else is gonna get you before the smoke will." She took a long inhale, and when she exhaled it came out like magical mist into the darkness, stinging my throat. "I've been dealing with strong women like her all my life, Merilee. All my life," she repeated. I looked out the window as we drove down South Street.

"It's not for you to judge what I do or do not say to her," Veraleen continued. "A woman like that, and I'm sorry if this hurts you, a woman like that ain't ever gonna change. Those two, my mama and Birdy, are two of a feather, and I know for sure my mama never changed. She lived close to the bone on that land and it made her hard and mean till the day she passed. Something's hard in your grandma's blood, too, and no bitter-wood tea from my satchel is gonna suddenly make her sweet."

"I know that," I said as I watched out the window at the approaching ghostlike downtown. "Everyone is afraid of her."

"Oh, I'm not afraid of her, believe me," Veraleen said. "I just think there are better ways of dealing with her. You'll see. I'll be cookin' you up Good-night Biscuits tomorrow morning in *my* kitchen. Cookin' and curin' are all I ever known, Merilee. Cookin' and curin'. My mama pushed it in me, and her mama before that." She slowly blew a smoke ring out the window and muttered, "Hold your breath and bite your tongue . . . moonshine whiskey and heated syrup, in small doses." I almost felt like Veraleen's mother was in the car with us and I shivered. Biswick was waking up.

He sat straight up. "Huh?" he said.

"Go back to sleep, baby," Veraleen cooed as she held the cigarette out the window so he couldn't see it. He lay back down and fell asleep. Veraleen chuckled. "God, what I would give to fall asleep so easily. They say those without anything on their consciences can sleep like a baby."

Some babies, I thought. Maybe I was worried

about life as soon as I was born. "Are we really going to the jail?" I asked.

"Yep."

"Do we have to?"

"He's learned his lesson. I could have sprung him out a couple of days ago. I thought it would be better for him to sober up in there and think about things."

"You believe that?" I said. "Marvelous."

"What?"

"That he thinks about Biswick."

Veraleen laughed. "When you're in the pokey, things suddenly become clear." She pulled into the parking lot. The county jail looked like one big, lusterless cement block with little sliver windows teasingly placed too high to see in or out. We sat there a moment not moving, both of us staring at the jail.

"Did you know Biswick's daddy drinks?" I asked quietly. Very quietly.

"Is the Pope Catholic?" She snorted. "I could smell the liquor on him from ten miles away the first time he came to get Biswick. No good, he is. No good."

"Leave him here then. Take in Biswick yourself."

My suggestion hung in the air, unbalanced and unsure which way to fall. "I can't do that. I can't," she finally responded. "I'll be leaving soon. I'm going to be a fry cook on a cruise line. I'm going to travel the world."

She couldn't do it. Well, why not? 'Cause she was going away for no good reason to Africa or Australia? 'Cause she did something to a baby over at the hospital? I didn't think so. She'd told me herself that baby was okay. Well, why then?

"Sheriff Bupp is pea-brained," I warned Veraleen as she started to open the car door. It's how Grandma would describe him, and it fit.

"Don't worry about me, darling. I'll handle him. I've had a lifetime of experience dealing with cow-boys—real ones and ones that just think so. You stay here with Biswick. Stay quiet and I'll be right back."

I peered out the window into the velvety Jumbo sky and wondered if the lights would appear tonight. I looked down at Biswick. The starlight flickered across his hushed face, illuminating a tear S'ing its way down his cheek. I reached down to stop its path but held my finger a millimeter above his skin. I could feel a warm fire all the way through my fingers. I quickly withdrew my hand. I had always wanted it. Utter aloneness. Now I wasn't so sure.

"Just get in the car, mister, and be grateful I bailed your Irish butt out of jail," I heard Veraleen growl.

Jack O'Connor threw himself into the car and slammed the door as hard as he could. Then he slumped down.

Veraleen got in and started up the engine. Biswick's eyes fluttered open.

"Hey, Daddy," he said sleepily. "Where you been?" I rolled my eyes. "I missed you!"

"Why the blazes did you bring him?" Biswick's daddy roared at Veraleen.

"You ain't in no position to complain, Irish boy," Veraleen whispered, her voice cracking. "What kind of arrangements did you make for your son while you were on vacation?"

Jack O'Connor peered out the window.

"Unnn-huh," Veraleen muttered as she gunned the motor. The GTO, low to the ground and glistening like gold dragon's breath in the dark, barreled down the street.

Chapter
14

There's an ancient legend of a white dragon, the Songbird of Sadness, who lives in the middle of a great lake. Every fifty years the white dragon turns into a songbird with magnificent golden feathers. But no one wants to hear his song, a mournful howl really, because it always seems to foretell disease and famine. I awoke early the next Sunday to the sweet and soulful call of a mourning dove and wondered if, like the Songbird of Sadness, his song told my future.

I pulled up the covers and listened to the sounds of our house. Footsteps echoed across the wood floors downstairs, the back screen door slammed with a large whap, then two smaller tremors. And water creaked through the pipes when someone turned on the kitchen faucet. Outside, Myrtle Dean's rooster cockle-doodle-dooed intermittently and the McKelvey's dog, Quincy, joined in, barking so forlornly you knew he was chained. If I listened really good, I could hear the eighteen-wheelers roar past on Highway 90. When I was little I used to imagine those trucks were my dragons coming down from the mountains for me.

Then the best sound of all, a car coming up the driveway, the wheels making a wonderful sand-papery sound over the gravel. I got out of bed and walked sleepily to the window. But it wasn't someone coming, it was someone leaving. Daddy was backing out in the Red Rocket to go back to the hospital.

I could still hear water running and doors creaking and wondered who was downstairs. I stood in my doorway and tried to convince myself it was Mama. The smell of things being fried in iron skillets and floury baked goods in the oven wafted up to me. Breakfast with Mama never advanced past burnt toast and cold cereal. I quickly threw on my clothes.

I heard a dish breaking and the pieces scattering across the floor. But when I walked into the kitchen, everything seemed perfectly fine. Too fine. I blinked. I blinked again. Grandma Birdy and Veraleen were cooking—together. They displayed such a congruous, harmonious, melded synchronicity of domesticity no one would ever believe that they had never gotten along. Veraleen was wearing her nurse's hat and one of Grandma's little aprons and she was sashaying (as best as big Veraleen could) around the table, spinning place mats down like Frisbees. Grandma's friend Miss Fleta Bell was sitting at the table with her Sunday hat on, tightly fisting her purse, her eyes flickering nervously between Grandma and Veraleen. I knew how she felt.

Carefully Grandma took a tray of Veraleen's famous Good-night Buttermilk Biscuits from the oven. Fat Weenie was by Grandma's side and the other dogs were peeking out from under the table with smiling eyes.

Something dripped on my head. I glanced up and caught another drip on my cheek. I licked it off with my tongue. It tasted like pancake batter. There was a huge splash of pale buttery mush on the ceiling. I stepped aside as another drip came down and the dogs ran out from under the table to lick it up. Miss Fleta Bell had some spots in the netting of her hat that looked a lot like the batter on the ceiling. I spotted the broom in the corner. The dustpan held the shards of perhaps one or two of our Blue Willow plates. Apparently there had been a little scuffle. Although it would have made my insides coil, I would have paid a million dollars to have been a fly on the kitchen wall about five minutes earlier.

"Good morning, darlin'," Veraleen said, pulling out a chair for me at the table. I sat down. Already on the table there was butter, honey, an assortment of homemade jellies, and a plate of good-smelling sausage.

"Her name ain't 'darlin' *Miss* Veraleen," Grandma said as she wiped her hands on her apron. "It's Merilee." She said it as though she was chewing on something distasteful. "I fixed it," I heard her mutter. "It could have been worse." She brought over the biscuits and set them down on the table. What was she talking about? My name? Or had she "fixed" Veraleen's biscuits?

"I know what her name is, Mrs. Monroe," Veraleen said before I could get a word out. "I'm just trying to show some affection which seems to be lacking around here."

Oh no. Now I wished I was back in bed. Before Grandma could answer, which I'm sure she would have, Bug came in very quietly in her pajamas with her hair sticking up funny and sat down. Grandma leaned over and kissed her on top of the head. "Look what we got for you, Bug. A breakfast fit for a queen."

Bug has never been a happy camper in the morning. This morning was even worse; she pushed her plate out of the way with a rude shove. "When is Mama coming home?"

"Soon," Veraleen and Grandma chorused together. They frowned at each other.

"Your daddy is going to bring her home

tomorrow," Veraleen said. "He said she was up and walking mighty fine last night."

Bug brightened. "She was?"

"Uh-huh," Veraleen said, and she nodded. "See, I told you your mama was going to be all right. I've been curing up a concoction all night to make her head better. Can't hurt." Veraleen nodded to a big black pot on the stove.

"Those fool's potions of yours don't do anyone any good," Grandma Birdy said, coming over and sliding Bug's plate in front of her again. Grandma and I caught eyes for a moment and she smirked.

Veraleen put her hands on her hips and shook her head at Grandma. I wondered if there was going to be more batter on the ceiling. The dogs must have wondered, too, 'cause they started panting and wagging their tails.

Bug watched Grandma and Veraleen with big buggy eyes.

"Your mama's on the mend," Veraleen told Bug. "But this is gonna speed things up a bit." She started chopping some herbs on a cutting board, then she threw a handful in the pot.

"Where I come from," said Grandma, walking over to the sink, "they say you gotta take the bitter with the sweet and there's some hogs you just can't perfume." Then she muttered, "Hell-in ain't ever gonna be normal." She daintily dropped a biscuit for Weenie. "Some things you just can't cure. Especially with no spices or sugars." I remembered what Veraleen had said about there being no cure for Grandma.

Veraleen uh-huhed again. "Just where are you from, Mrs. Monroe, that has such a happy outlook on life?" Grandma had never discussed with us her days before Grandpa had found her at the bus station sitting on her suitcase.

"That's none of your business," Grandma said, turning on the water. "Just what you been hiding back up in the Panhandle? I thought a real cowgirl never left her ranch."

I saw Veraleen wince a little. She was making up a plate of biscuits and sausage. She put plastic wrap on top of it. "And that's none of your business," she said smiling, her penciled lips curling up slightly.

Grandma mimicked Veraleen's uh-huh noise and rolled her eyes like a four-year-old child. "Old, my butt. You got more wrinkles on you than an old steer and you look like one, too." Bug gnawed on a biscuit, her eyes on the action.

Suddenly Miss Fleta Bell came to life. "I was born right here in Jumbo. On a clear sunny day in April. My mama had no milk in her so they fed me milk from our old mare Annabelle." There was a moment of silence.

"Where were you born, Grandma?" Bug asked. "You've never told us."

Grandma waved the question off and muttered, "From here, from there, from everywhere." Bug smiled. Veraleen had a funny look on her face. She picked up the plate, which I guessed was for Biswick, and started for the back door. As she was leaving, Grandma said, "It's no good to look back on things, just stirs your heart around." Veraleen, stiff and upright, let the screen door slam behind her with a whap that reverberated through the kitchen like the sting of a slapped face.

I looked at my watch. It was time to go do my

Sunday morning litter patrol. After litter patrol I spend the afternoon lying around in bed reading novels. I grabbed two sausage patties and tiptoed out the back door before Grandma could say anything. She was staring out the kitchen window as I left.

We had breakfast food for dinner that night since there was enough food left over from Grandma and Veraleen's cook-off to feed the whole state of Texas. Veraleen had appeared again at dinnertime and she and Grandma worked side by side heating things up and unwrapping casserole dishes just as though they hadn't had words before. In their companionable silence, though, there was an undercurrent of something brewing.

Someone was following me. I thought I had left the house unseen. I guess not. I had to be alone. Alone but not alone. It's hard to explain it. I didn't want to have to say one word to anyone. And the only person that I could do that with was with Uncle Dal. So after dinner I snuck out and walked down the dark streets past Leroy and Dorwood

Smeathers', the Bupps' house, and past Lorelei's, where I could see she was in her bathroom scheming up another hairdo to impress us with tomorrow.

I could hear the patter of feet behind me. I stepped off the sidewalk and hid behind a tree. The footsteps stopped for a moment and started up again.

I jumped out from behind the tree. "Biswick?" I asked a small figure in the darkness.

"Unh-unh" came a negative reply.

"Bug?" I smelled her Love's Baby Soft before she answered.

"Yeah, it's me."

"What are you doing out here late at night?"

"What are *you* doing out here late at night?"

"Now scat and go home, or I'll tell on you."

"I'll tell on you to Grandma Birdy," Bug answered.

"Grandma's catching horseflies in Mama's chair," I told her.

"Well, I'll wake her," Bug responded.

We both knew that was the ultimate threat.

"You are spectacularly annoying. "

"Oh Merilee, why do you have to sound like that all the time?"

I kept walking and she walked quickly after me.

"Don't you say one word," I warned her.

"I don't feel like talking." We walked in silence listening to the chirps of the insects and the whir of a car in the distance. The sky was bright and full of low stars.

At last we reached Uncle Dal's. A faint slice of light escaped from underneath the barn door.

I pushed it open and Bug and I walked in. There was only one lit lightbulb hanging down from a rafter. It cast an eerie spotlight over the statue.

"Uncle Dal?" Bug called out. He was sitting very still and strangelike in his wingback chair. Flynn was asleep by the chair, but he opened one eye. Uncle Dal smiled and Bug jumped into his lap.

"What you girls doing out here at night?" he asked, so quiet, even for him.

"Daddy's not home yet from the hospital," Bug answered. She withdrew a little from his hug. "You working on your statue, Uncle Dal? When are you going to finish it?"

I don't think anyone had ever come right out and asked. No one dared to. Leave it up to Bug to go where no one had gone before.

In the low light of the barn, Uncle Dal's eyes reflected more sadness than they usually did.

"Someday," he answered Bug.

Something made me turn my head fast to the statue, as my stomach dropped. But it was the same. No changes. I knew that foot very well, every nick, bump, and curve, and it looked as though he hadn't done any work in weeks. Not since the last time I had been out there, that first day with Biswick.

"Someday should be tomorrow," Bug said. "I'll come tomorrow and help you finish, Uncle Dal." I sniggered. Like the statue could be done in one day. Ha.

The corners of Uncle Dal's lips turned up slightly in a pretend smile. "You do that, Bug. You do that." He rubbed the top of her head affectionately. I felt a deep sting of jealousy. I am the one who is helping Uncle Dal on his statue, not Bug. No way was she going to come over and take my place on the milking stool. First Biswick, and now her. No way. Breathe in, breathe out. Breathe in. Breathe out.

Bug squealed when she spotted a flashlight on the barn floor next to Flynn. "Can I go look for horned toads outside?" she asked. "Please?" Uncle Dal nodded and she was off waving the beam around in jerky arcs. Good, I said to myself. Go find one. Good luck. Ha.

I sat down on my milking stool and closed my eyes a moment. "Why didn't you come to the hospital?" I couldn't look at him as I felt my eyes start to sting, like I had been splashed with a salty wave from the sea. It was a very long time before he answered.

"I just couldn't, Merilee."

He had never called me Merilee. I felt I had grown to be a thousand years old in one microsecond. I swallowed hard and felt a tear roll down the side of my cheek. I touched it with my tongue.

Why couldn't you come? I wanted to ask. He answered for me.

"I just couldn't go to that hospital," he said.

My head shot up. What did he mean by that? His face was in the shadows. I have always had a hard time reading people's deep expressions anyway. I read people in different ways. I feel them, like Mama feels me, but in a different way. And Uncle Dal didn't feel very good right now. I suddenly wanted to go home.

"I don't have anyone," he continued.

"You have us, Uncle Dal. We are all family." As soon as I said it, I knew it was true. Even if I wasn't really one of them. Even if I was a distant cold moon to a warm earth.

He smiled a little then. "Your mama," he began. "I couldn't see her like that. My wife—" He stopped.

"*Wife?* You have a wife?" I almost wobbled off my stool.

"Yes," he answered, and I felt my heart start to fall.

"Where is she?" I asked.

"I go to visit her sometimes. That's where I had been when you saw me jump off the train," he said.

I looked up at him to ask silently, *You knew?* He nodded. The tears rolled down his face and I knew the proper thing would have been to hug him. That's what a normal person would have done.

"Your daddy and me used to ride the trains when we were boys. To get away. We'd jump on a train, have an adventure somewhere in the universe, and be back before Mama called us home for dinner. It was our way of escaping. . . ." He trailed off.

"Daddy?" I whispered. "Daddy went with you?" I couldn't imagine it. Daddy wanting to leave. My tangles tightened inside me, and I felt so dizzy and suffocated that I thought I saw lights, magical lights, dancing in the shadows of the barn. I heard a noise. My eyes shot up to the hayloft. But it was only Bug coming through the door of the barn.

"What's wrong?" she asked as she shone the flashlight back and forth between us.

"Nothing's wrong," Uncle Dal answered with a voice that sounded more like him now. I took a deep FF breath. Bug's eyes widened as she shone the light in my eyes. Unshed tears, almost ready to fall. She had never seen me cry. Tears from me were the stuff of legend.

"Marvelous," I mumbled. "Just marvelous."

"You are such a spaz, Merilee," Bug said.

"Come on, girls," Uncle Dal said. "I need to get you home." A few minutes later, as we backed out of his dirt driveway, the headlights of his pickup shone a beacon of shimmering truth on the barn. He was carving the statue for his wife—wherever she was. It was all for her.

Chapter
15

It hailed the night that Bug and I went to see Uncle Dal and I found out his big whopping secret. The hail, big as gum balls, sounded like a fairy tale giant pounding on our roof. And the next morning, everywhere you looked were little brown baby frogs, hopping over Jumbo like they'd been birthed by the sky. It was a sign, Veraleen said. Life is full of them, and like new friends, they are sent from God to show us something we need to know. The problem with signs, though, according to Grandma Birdy, is that they're all bad ones. And I didn't think it was a coincidence those frogs showed up. It was Oral Report Day, my most dreaded day of the year.

That whole morning Grandma had been guarding the stove, mumbling dire predictions about the hail and frogs, pestilence and famine, Mama's accident and the world coming to an end. Biswick ran around outside, delirious, trying to catch them. Veraleen had to coax him inside for breakfast, and when he walked into the kitchen with several passengers clutched on his pants, Grandma proclaimed, "Better swat them off, boy, everyone knows when a baby frog crawls on you, it's measuring for your shroud."

Biswick's face dropped. He should not have known what a shroud was, but he did somehow. Maybe by the way she said it. He just knew. He started to cry.

Grandma went to the sink and rinsed out a pot. Veraleen shot her a nasty look and soothed Biswick. "Come on, son, eat up, I think I hear your bus coming along." Then she coaxed him out the back door, discreetly picking the frogs off and tossing 'em in the grass so fast you'd think she believed Grandma. I followed behind after grabbing my backpack and Biswick's.

After Biswick left on his bus, Veraleen and I didn't bring up what had happened, even when a frog hopped right between us. Both of us kept our eyes off the ground.

"You don't have to go to school, Merilee. We all understand," she said.

I looked back at the house and saw a curtain move. I'd rather face the most dreaded day of the year than go back inside and hear about graves and shrouds. I pedaled off on my bicycle and braced myself.

Oral Report Day.

I've never been able to read aloud in class, no matter whether it's *Dick and Jane* or *War and Peace*. Even though the subject today was easy for even the dumb kids—our favorite hobby—I still was sure I was going to throw up all over the place.

When I got to class, after inadvertently running over an unlucky frog or two, most of the kids were gathered around the window. There were about ten little frogs clutching to the screen. Scooter kept yelling and banging on the screen trying to knock them off. The bell rang and everyone slowly walked to their desks.

Mr. Bonaparte announced we would be doing the reports after lunch. Great. Fabulous disaster. I'd probably toss my PB&J and pickle across the whole class. I decided not to eat lunch.

When we got back from lunch, the ISFs— Yello, Truman, and Ramona Grace—filed up one by one to do their reports. Yello and Truman talked about duck and deer hunting respectively and Ramona Grace gave a demonstration on makeup application. At some point Mr. Bonaparte fell asleep, mouth wide open, feet propped up on a desk. No one was gonna wake him; they all knew they'd get a good grade 'cause he wouldn't want to own up to sleeping through their reports.

But not Gideon. He made his way to the front of the room and dropped a book on the floor. Mr. Bonaparte sat up, wiped his forehead, and signaled for Gideon to begin.

He cleared his throat a couple of times. I glanced at the Three Tormenters out the corner of my eye. They had pulled out fingernail polish.

Scooter sat forward seeming to watch Gideon with genuine interest. Finally Gideon spoke. "Photography is a spiritual medium. It's the seen and the unseen, and the sheer beauty of nature fused in light and captured forever." Someone sneezed. Gideon blinked a few times and pushed his bug glasses up and I realized that underneath all that thick glass he was a teeny bit handsome. Perhaps. Someone coughed, "You suck." There was a smattering of giggles. Mr. Bonaparte told everyone to quiet down. Gideon went on. "The first actual photo was taken in 1826 by Joseph Nicéphore Niépce, a Frenchman who was experimenting with lithography. It's a view from the upper-story window of his country house." Someone made a snoring noise. Then someone farted. "All right. All right. Let him finish," Mr. Bonaparte said. Gideon went through a long time line of the history of photography and amazingly there were no more catcalls. He took his seat with a big grin.

I was next. At that moment I wished I had stayed home, even if it meant being home with

Grandma and hearing dire predictions. I steadied myself by lightly touching every other desk, like a duck on its way to its execution. Still, there were no catcalls, sneezes, or coughs. Nothing. It was deathly silent.

I stood behind the podium and cleared my throat. Mr. Bonaparte was asleep again. He was actually snoring now. Well, at least I'd make a good grade. I snorted. Maybe this would be okay after all, even if I screwed up some. I heard Romey say to Cairo, "Let me guess. Dragons," and they laughed.

The room started to wobble a little. I grabbed hold of the podium and took two FF breaths. I caught a glimpse of the frogs on the screen still hanging on for life. Their eyes bored into mine. *"They're measuring for your shroud."* I saw an image of a bandaged Mama in the hospital, smiling, her arms reaching out for me. "Horrendous."

"Merilee?" It was Gideon. I blinked and nodded that I was okay. There was a smattering of laughter. Mr. Bonaparte briefly opened his eyes, then closed them again.

I began. "There is no such thing as a dragon." It was eerily silent. No coughs. No catcalls. Nothing. I cleared my throat. "Yet he is everywhere in every culture in history . . . graceful and ethereal, ferocious and sometimes kind, saber-toothed monster or sleek-scaled serpent, he is myth, legend, and . . ." Wow. I couldn't believe I'd made it this far, even if I did have to take some FF breaths and long pauses. I continued.

"Why? Why can he be found in every form possible going back thousands of years in recorded history? From cave drawings to Egyptian hieroglyphics, to . . ." I paused and took another FF breath. I was waiting for something. Anything from the Tormenters. Gideon nodded for me to continue.

"Some scientists believe maybe we did know them—at least some form of them. Perhaps early mankind overlapped with the last of the great predator birds. Other scientists believe that dragons were formed by man's earliest fears . . . the feline, the reptile, and the fierce bird. He is there in all of us . . . a collective worldwide ancient memory." Big FF breath.

I caught Gideon's intense gaze. He smiled. "Horren . . . There are many types of dragons. The earliest recorded in history are the tail-biting Oroboros, serpentlike; they represented the cycle of life . . . life out of death. Eternal return . . . Creation out of destruction . . . Oh horrendous." I glanced up at the paralyzed frogs on the window screen. FF breath. It was then that I heard a light tinkling sound. It was something rolling across the floor, and I thought of faraway castle bells. I shook my head. I was imagining it. Then something touched my foot and I jumped. The cretins laughed. I saw a penny next to my shoe. There was a tiny note taped on top. It read: *Freak*. There were six more pennies rolling down the aisle, like charging warriors. One made a perfect arc around me. It said, "Dragon Girl." Scooter and Cairo high-fived each other.

Horrendous. Horrendous. "Then . . ." I began but couldn't remember where I had left off. More and more pennies joined my feet. *Weirdo. Ugly. Nerd. Geek.* They resembled the Necco candy hearts that come out at Valentine's Day. I looked back at the window and saw a shrouded figure peering in. Mama? She called my name, "Merilee!" Merilee!" I blinked. It was Biswick.

"Merilee, I need you!" he called, his voice muffled hollow and ghostlike through the screen.

"Hey, it's Pancake! Hey, Waffle!" Scooter yelled. The whole class laughed, Mr. Bonaparte woke up.

Biswick called for me again and I stood frozen. Another round of pennies slid across the floor. *Weirdo. Freak. Idiot.* I looked over at Gideon. "Go, Merilee," he mouthed.

"Miss Monroe, if you choose to leave the classroom right now, you will take a zero for your grade."

I glanced back outside at Biswick. I knew I had to go. Before I did, I cleared my thoughts and said, "The enigmatic dragon . . . he doesn't exist, or does he?" It was just one sentence. It felt so good. The cretins sat there slack jawed. Gideon started to clap, a slow, melodious staccato, a one-person ovation. I lunged for the door, skidding on the pennies.

"Miss Monroe, sit down, please."

I reached for the knob but it wouldn't move. I yanked as hard as I could. I yanked again and felt tears sting my eyes. Oh, why wouldn't it open? Suddenly there was a shadow behind me. Gideon.

"Gideon Beaurogard, please take your seat!" Mr. Bonaparte was making his way up the aisle.

In one deft motion, Gideon pulled the door open. I ran from the room.

As I raced down the hall I heard laughter and Mr. Bonaparte shouting, "Miss Monroe! Miss Monroe!" over and over.

I found Biswick slumped against the building, crying. I helped him up. "What are you doing here?" I asked him, out of breath. The bus from Whiskey usually didn't bring Biswick home until well after I got out of school.

He just shook his head. "I'm worried about your mama. I told 'em I was sick and they brought me home early. But Daddy won't open the door."

"Mama will be all right," I said.

"Do you think I will always have Cheeto?"

"Cheeto is going to be fine, Bis," I told him.

"I'm worried about Daddy, too. Can you help me get in our house?"

"I'm not so sure about that." I checked my watch. VOE. It was actually a half hour before school got out, a half hour before my litter patrol. "Uhhhhh," I stuttered. I checked my watch again. I bit my lower lip. "Uhhhh."

"Please?" Biswick pleaded. "He usually leaves the door unlocked for me, even when he's sleeping."

"Oh, all right." I sighed. "Marvelous."

As we walked toward the bicycle rack, I looked back and saw Gideon in the window, peering out at me. I thought of the tale of the baby dragon who left his cave for the first time and never looked back.

When Biswick and I reached the Porter house I suddenly had an image of Old Man Porter sitting on the front porch in his rocker splitting peas. That was something his wife Ola used to do, Mama told me. Ola would split peas or snap green beans and wave to the neighbors. Old Man Porter wasn't seen much after she passed away, that's why no one found him for a while after he died in his bathtub. But Mama had seen him one time on the porch, about a week before he died, and he had waved at her just like Ola used to do. And then a couple of weeks later he'd been found dead. Mama had always wondered what he'd been doing in that rocker. Maybe he knew.

But the rocker was gone, I noticed as we walked up the steps. Instead several baby frogs hopped around in its place. Biswick squealed and hid behind me. I inched toward the front door, with Biswick grabbing onto my shirt. I tried to open the door, but it was locked.

"I told you so," Biswick said, his face buried in my back.

I really wanted to go start my litter patrol. This was the last place I wanted to be. I sighed. "Let go, Biswick. We're gonna have to try a window or something. Where's your bedroom?"

"Uh, in the back" came his muffled reply. I tried to inch forward but he jumped on my back and I reluctantly grabbed his legs.

"Oh, all right," I said. I carried him piggyback as fast as I could, dodging frogs, to the backyard. I set him down and wiggled my shoulders back and forth. I had the double heebie-jeebies—goose bumps all up and down my body from carrying Biswick. I had to take four big FF breaths and lean over and put my hands on my knees.

The backyard looked like it hadn't been mown in a year. Even daisies grew among the tall weeds. I noticed a rocker, upside down in the weeds, its slats sticking up like wooden skis.

Biswick stepped on an upturned bucket and crawled in an open window. So I crawled in after him. When I stood up, he had already darted through a bedroom. I heard him yell, "Daddy! I'm home!" Right away I was struck with an odor—a rotten broccoli forgotten in the refrigerator crisper kinda odor. I had to breathe through my mouth. I thought I was gonna gag. I quickly glanced about Biswick's room. There was a bed with a dingy bedspread and Mickey Mouse sheets. A nightstand with a shadeless lamp. And clothes strewn everywhere. Taped on the wall was a hand-drawn picture—a stick figure with a bow on the head holding a litterbag.

I called Biswick's name but he didn't answer.

I walked down a hallway till I came to the den. I stood in the doorway. The odor was stronger in here. Much stronger. Like a whole bunch of rotten broccoli and dirty gym socks. Diet Coke cans, beer bottles, and wadded-up paper balls were scattered everywhere. There was a dartboard on the wall, with most of the darts stuck in the wall beside it, a brown and orange beanbag with some of the filling spilling out, and a poster of an old Walt Whitman, who looked like he could be in my prestigious three-member Einstein Hair Club.

The poet sat at a desk staring at the empty wall in front of him. His back was to me. Biswick stood next to him, motionless, his hands clasped like a praying mantis. "Daddy?" he whispered. I was frozen in my spot. "Daddy?" Biswick repeated. "There's frogs outside. Everywhere, Daddy." Still the poet didn't move.

I noticed an old upright piano against the wall. It looked like someone had taken a hammer to it.

Really bashed it in good. It used to be Ola Porter's pride and joy. Her daddy had it shipped from Louisiana for her when she married. Grandma remembers standing outside with everyone else in the town watching it be delivered and carried inside.

I walked into the room. I felt like I needed to be near Biswick. The poet slowly turned his head toward me. He had on his dark sunglasses.

"What's she doing here?" he said, his gaze aimed just above my head like he was blind or something.

I shivered and the heebie-jeebie goose bumps returned. I took an FF breath.

"The front door was locked, Daddy," Biswick said.

"No visitors," the poet said flatly. "I told you no visitors. Ever." Biswick curled his lower lip and clenched his teeth into an "uh-oh" expression. "I'm trying to write," the poet continued angrily. There was an old black Selectric typewriter with a fresh page on the cylinder. One word had been typed. I stepped forward to see what it said. The poet's arm shot out to block me but I still saw the word. It said: *June*. I quickly stepped back, way back.

Biswick ran into the kitchen and came back with a Diet Coke. "Here Daddy," he said, putting it on the table next to him.

"Get her out of here," the poet said.

"Daddy, Merilee likes to write, too. She writes in her journal."

"Good for her." He laughed. "Good for her."

"Mr. O'Connor?" I began as I peered around at the messy, stinky room. I had to breathe through my mouth. FF breath.

"Go get me a beer, Biswick," he said. Biswick ran back into the kitchen.

"What do you write?" the poet asked.

I realized he was talking to me. "Uhhhh . . . just stories. Snippets. Funny things. Stupendous."

"I wanted to be a poet," he said.

I didn't know what to say. "Your book sold out at the bookstore," I offered. "All thirty copies. Mama's gonna try to order more."

He didn't respond. I looked around at the

messy, trash-covered floor. "Do you want me to help you?" I shivered again.

Then I took another FF breath. And then another.

"Nobody can help me," he said.

"I meant clean up a little around here. Maybe that would clear your mind." I was itching to go get my litter stick and bag.

"It's already clear. Wiped clean. That's the problem." Biswick had come back with the beer. I noticed the top was off. He held it out to his daddy, who nodded for him to set it down on the desk.

"You need to leave now, Merilee," the poet said.

Merilee. Somehow he sounded more human in the using of it.

I didn't want to leave Biswick but I knew I'd see him later at our house for dinner. He followed me out the front. "What does 'June' mean?" I asked him.

He kept his eyes on a frog that was hopping around my feet. "That's my mommy." Then he turned without saying anything else and went inside.

As I walked away from that house, I couldn't shake the images of Ola Porter's upturned rocking chair and her bashed-in marriage piano. I got on my bike and thought about telling someone what I'd seen, but remembered Gideon, and how he'd been taken away for a long time. I rode on south, toward the train tracks.

All those frogs disappeared that night like they'd never been there, and the next afternoon Daddy drove up to El Paso to get Mama. I watched from my bedroom window as he helped her from the car. Bug ran outside and I could hear Mama's gentle laughter. Her bandage was smaller now, just a little white patch above her left eye. She looked good. She was home.

Chapter
16

They say dragons are good keepers of secrets. Who would dare pry a secret out of a dragon? St. George, maybe. No one else. I am the secret keeper of Jumbo. The holder of things no one else wants to hold. But I don't want the secrets, either. People give me their secrets because with me the secret stays dormant but not forgotten. I used to know funny cotton-puff secrets. But then everything changed and I knew sinking-anchor secrets that kept me awake at night. I knew that Uncle Dal had a wife somewhere that he had never told us about, and Veraleen was going to leave us someday, perhaps soon, and Biswick's daddy had a drinking problem much worse than anyone in this town guessed.

It was almost Christmastime. Life seemed to have almost returned to normal. Daddy had gone back to his tomatoes and Mama had gone back to work at her bookstore. Mama seemed to be all healed now. There was just a faint pink line on her forehead where her stitches had been. "God took care of me," she told me when she came home from the hospital. But something changed the day she was hit by a car. Sometimes I saw her watching me almost hungrily, like a poor child peering in a fancy department store window. She was yearning for something from me. Perhaps something she knew I couldn't give her, and it hurt me so much to know that I wasn't right even for Mama anymore.

And she started going to her church every morning for Mass. At Mass she discovers the tender miracles of life. She wanted me to go with her, I think, so I'd find my own salvation. I said no to her every morning before school when she asked me with her eyes. I didn't believe in miracles.

I hadn't been to Uncle Dal's barn in a long, long time. The last time was that eerie night when he told me his secret. I just couldn't go back. And what's worse is that I thought he didn't want me back. I caught a glimpse of him a couple of weeks ago. I was coming out of Mama's bookstore and he drove right past me in his pickup, his face frozen like Johnny Bupp's courthouse statue, even though Flynn was barking up a storm at me.

Grandma didn't completely return to her house when Mama came home from the hospital. She would go back at bedtime, but the rest of the time she was with us, her presence overwhelming us like a cloud. Veraleen still came at night to help with the cooking. She and Grandma seemed to have some understanding and they stayed out of each other's way. They cooked together and even were civil, although I caught all kinds of interesting things they said under their breaths that I wrote down in my journal and double-underlined with a special pink highlighter.

Grandma somehow knew, like she always did about such things, that Veraleen might not be around much longer. I could feel it when she watched her. That's why she was abiding Veraleen and being halfway polite to someone she would never even nod to on Main Street. Not that Grandma would nod to anyone. And for some reason she thought Mama was going away, too. "It'll all be over soon," I heard her say to Bug as she kissed her good night. "It will all be over soon, and I'll take care of you."

One morning Grandma appeared in her funeral clothes—black dress, black hose, and black hat with a big raven's feather sticking out the side. Grandma has always loved going to funerals— even funerals for people she didn't know. She usually checks the obituaries. But there was no funeral that day. Veraleen says our souls know a dust storm is coming and they just start to go a little haywire as a warning.

As Grandma predicted, Biswick and I became "thick as thieves." We were always together. Mama says when she saw us it looked like I finally found that imaginary friend I was talking to when I was a toddler. Was he part of me? Not truly. I wouldn't let him be. I was scared to let him inside me, to get too attached to him. He'd be leaving someday, and

I didn't ever forget that. The poets-in-residence only stay one year. One year. And they move on proclaiming their lives have been changed by West Texas and that real soon they'll be back. But they don't ever come back. "Be backs" don't come back. Mama has always said this about her customers who claim they'll buy the book another time, after sitting on her couch and pawing through the whole thing.

But sometimes when Biswick and I were together a wave of sadness so fierce would come over me I had to lean on my litter stick and take a bucketload of FF breaths.

Biswick claimed his daddy was behaving again and spending long hours at his typewriter writing poetic masterpieces. I was more than a little suspicious. Lorelei asked me a lot about Jack O'Connor, batting her fake eyelashes as though I was him and giving me messages to pass on, no matter how many times I told her that Jack O'Connor didn't allow any visitors. I never as much as stepped in that poet's house again. One day when I went past the Porter house, I picked up storm vibes that caused me to have wild dreams that followed me around the next day. Then Biswick appeared with a trail of small marks up his arm like a little animal had left dirty footprints. I wondered if Veraleen had a good cure for bruises.

One Tuesday afternoon about a week before Christmas, a couple of days before our Lights Festival, Biswick bugged me the entire time I was doing my litter patrol to take him to the Jumbo dump to shop for Christmas presents. It was really cold that day and I told him it was too cold over and over. Jumbo gets very cold in the winter just as it gets deathly hot in the summer. Jumbo even had a blizzard one time that came out of nowhere. The old-timers talk of it with reverence.

Biswick had it stuck in his craw that he wanted to go to the Jumbo dump because he overheard Maydell Rathburger, over at the Rexall Drug, say there were all kinds of good pickin's there. Biswick had a very long Christmas list that had practically everyone in the town on it. And I mean everyone. It started with me and went through most of the population, including Sheriff Bupp, and that tells you something about Biswick's sweet forgetful heart. He was perpetual in his cheerful belief that all was good in life, just as I was perpetual in my belief that life was one big dream-squasher.

"Well, have you ever been to the dump?" he asked me for the umpteenth time. I was picking up litter on the far west side of town on an old lot that the teenagers had found recently after being shooed off the Dixie Dog Drive In property by Sheriff Bupp.

"Yes. I just don't feel like going there right now."

"Give me a hundred good reasons," he said. He was sucking on one of my lollipops which he does all the time, helping himself to them without asking. I just knew he had a couple of purple cavities hiding in his mouth.

"I don't have to give you even one," I said.

"Well, let's go see Uncle Dal," he said, biting straight into the lollipop and chewing it up, making loud, crunchy, teeth-breaking noises.

"Give me *one* good reason," I muttered to myself.

"He misses you," he said as he unstuck the right side of his jaw. "Something ain't right."

I frowned at him. I started to pick up my trash again.

I wondered about that. For Biswick, who saw every glass as full even when it was half empty, to say that, maybe something was wrong.

"Well," I said leaning on my litter stick and thinking about it, "maybe we should go."

"Okay." His face lit up. "But he's not there. We can work on the statue ourselves. For him."

"Not there?" I asked. "Marvelous."

"I've gone over there several times in the last few weeks and he's gone."

"Was Flynn there?"

"No."

I got a sick little worry in my stomach. Uncle Dal was gone again. Perhaps he had gone to see his wife. Why wouldn't he bring her home? Was it because Grandma Birdy was so mean and would scare her off? Uncle Dal usually only disappeared for a couple of days or so. I remembered that time I saw him, his face dead, as he drove through downtown. Had he been gone since that day? I bit my lip debating if I should tell someone. Maybe Mama or Daddy. No, this was Uncle Dal's business. He chose to lead his life this way and I wasn't going to change it.

"Merilee?" Biswick asked, worried. "What's wrong?"

I shook my head. "We can't go over to Uncle Dal's while he's not there. That's not right."

"Why's he so sad?" Biswick looked at me, his eyes deep and clear.

"I don't know, Biswick. I truly don't. Let's go shopping," I said.

"Really, Merilee Marvelous?" His face lit up. "Okay. Afterward let's go see Veraleen 'cause she's sad, too. Just like Uncle Dal."

The Jumbo dump. It lies north of town a couple of miles off a dirt road that's strewn with trash from people who couldn't wait. I don't understand why people have to have so many things in life. Like snakes, they shed their junk and start all over on new junk, which will eventually end up here, piled on top of their old junk. I never come out here; it's one big litter kaleidoscopic and it sets my nerves on edge to see it. And it stinks to high heaven in the winter, the worst rotten odors stewed together and left to bake in the sun—gasoline; sulphur; moldy, mothball attic smells; and mushy, maggoty food smells. Besides, it's against the law to be out here. Sheriff Bupp would give us a dumpordination if he caught us.

Biswick's eyes lit up. "Wow," he said, surveying the littered landscape. "And it's all free!"

I sat down on a squashed box. I lifted my binoculars and started watching the sky for White Feather. Biswick darted, squealing and talking to himself. He went behind a stack of old dryers and mustard-colored appliances and I couldn't see him.

"Here's something for your mama," he yelled. I dropped my binoculars down to my chest. I saw the tip of a walking cane held up over dryers.

"Fabulous. It was her head, Bis, not her leg," I told him. Still, she could have died. She could have been paralyzed.

"I'm just thinking ahead," he said. "She might need it when she's old." I heard another squeal and this time he ran back to show me his next find. He had an unruly hot pink wig on his head. The ringlets went down to his ankles. I smiled.

"You think Veraleen is going to wear that?" I asked.

"Sure, and if she don't like it, she can wear it just for Halloween," he said. He ran off with the wig on, the tendrils waving behind him.

I wrapped my arms around myself and shivered. Veraleen was probably not going to be around for another Halloween. She would probably be gone before spring or she wouldn't be trying so hard to make a winter garden come up.

"Hey, look what I found!" He came running back again. He held up a rusty, old-timey toy fire truck.

"That looks like it's a goner, Biswick. Do you really want that?"

"No." He laughed. "It's for Sheriff Bupp, silly! It's what he's always wanted. Uncle Dal can help me fix it up."

I felt someone staring at me. You know the feeling you get when someone is beckoning you to turn around and look? Biswick had run off in the other direction so it wasn't him. I lifted my binoculars and looked around before quickly dropping them. They thudded on my chest. Oh, it was *him*.

Gideon. He was on his bicycle, his camera bag at his side. Our eyes caught. There was a tiny silken web between us. I fought the urge to lift my binoculars up again. I felt a trickling warmth slide down my backside. Biswick came back around the stacked appliances with a lampshade over his hot pink wig. We all passed looks like we were human points on a triangle. Finally Gideon pedaled away.

"Who was that?" Biswick asked, taking off the lampshade. He was very serious, for Biswick.

"Just Gideon Beaurogard," I answered, hugging myself tighter. I was cold again, suddenly so.

"Why was he staring at you like that?" he asked, throwing the lampshade on a pile.

"I don't know. Maybe because I'm so funny looking. Marvelous."

Biswick swished his lips to the left and to the

right. He lowered his eyelids like he was studying a pirate ship far away on the horizon.

"Nope."

"Nope what?" I asked.

"That's not why he was staring at you. Look, he's still there."

I followed his gaze and saw that Gideon was way up the road, stopped on his bicycle again. He was indeed staring. I looked away.

"Why don't you like him?" Biswick asked.

"I really don't like anyone."

We were quiet then, Biswick and I, as we stared off in the distance at Gideon.

"He likes you," Biswick said then matter-of-factly. "He wants to kiss you." He made a gross, slurpy kissing noise.

"Ha!" I coughed out. "Like in a million years."

"Veraleen says everyone yarns for someone."

"And do you know what the word 'yearn' means?" I said as I stood up and passed by him. I looked for Gideon again, but this time he was gone. Biswick shook his head. "It means to truly want something in your heart," I told him.

"Like a cherry Popsicle when it's really, really hot outside?" he asked.

"Yes," I replied. "Sometimes it's wanting something a lot bigger than that. Impossibility."

"Oh, I know. I yarn to find the Constipater tree. To be the first ever from around here to find it."

"Conquistador tree." I sighed. "Ridiculous. I told you, Biswick. That's all made up. There's no magical tree waiting to be found. They like to put that on the chamber of commerce brochures to lure people to Jumbo. Just like the Ghost Lights."

"I don't want the Ghost Lights. I want the Contwistador tree. I'm gonna find it someday. And they are going to rename it the Biswick tree."

"Fabulous. Finish up, will you? I'm freezing," I said. I started to kick my legs around 'cause they were beginning to fall asleep.

Biswick laughed. "You look like you are dancing," he giggled. "Did you know that grasshoppers do a little dance before they mate?" I was starting to get a little suspicious that he just made up his factoids.

"Marvelous."

"Are you gonna dance tonight with Gideon at the Lights Festival?" His face was round and pouty beneath his wild wig.

"No way," I said firmly. "I am not gonna dance with Gideon, tonight or ever. Ridiculous."

He seemed relieved at my answer. "Good."

I paced around and started to feel my feet again.

"Why do you always walk around and around?" Biswick asked me.

I thought about it for a moment. "It makes me feel better," I answered. "Lots better."

"Oh." And then, "What do you yarn for, Merilee?"

I looked up at the Chitalpi, beautiful Cathedral Mountain standing sentry over Jumbo, and I thought of Mama, her accident. Her wanting something of me that I couldn't give. "Nothing, Biswick," I answered. "Nothing at all."

Something colorful in the pile of junk caught my eye. I pulled at it. It was an Indian headdress, with lots of feathers and turquoise and white beads—part of a kid's costume. I held it up as if to ask Biswick if this could be a present for someone. He pulled his wig off, gave me a look like I had betrayed him, then threw the wig on the ground and ran off behind the appliances.

What was that about? I followed him and found him rolled in a ball at the base of an old dryer.

"Biswick?" I asked. I still held the headdress.

"Go away."

"I'm not leaving you here."

"You are just trying to make me admit it," he said so quietly.

"No, I'm not," I said.

He saw I still had the headdress in my hands. "Put it away," he said.

I lifted it up and threw it as far as I could, beyond a heap of old tires. "There," I said. "It's gone."

He sat up but he wouldn't look at me. "Biswick, I won't tell anyone," I said. "I keep really good secrets. Lots of them. Ask anyone." But a fear was coursing up through me. I wasn't so sure I could take on another secret. My box was full.

"My mama did this to me."

I waited for more but he was quiet. "Did what?"

"When I was in her tummy, she drank too much," he said. "She wrecked me."

"You're not wrecked," I told him. "And I'm sure she didn't mean to."

"Nobody means to do nothing," he said, and I thought for a minute about what that meant.

"Why were you so upset about the headdress?"

"Well, duh," he said. "I'm Indian."

I think somewhere I knew that. "That's cool," I said. He picked up a pebble and threw it.

"Where is your mother now, Biswick?" A sudden cold breeze whipped around us, stirring a pile of newspapers nearby. It destroyed whatever had made Biswick talk in the first place. I knew he would tell me no more, at least not for now. And I was glad. I plopped down next to him.

Suddenly there was a mewing sound behind Biswick. We locked eyes and waited for it again. There was another meow. Biswick started crawling over a pile of old clothes till he reached a cardboard box.

"Oh my," he said, lifting the lid of the box. "Look!" I peered over his shoulder. There was a scrawny tabby mama cat with four equally scrawny babies nursing on her. There were huge, fat fleas crawling all over the mama and her kittens.

"She looks real bad, Merilee. Do you think we could bring her home with us?"

"No," I said. "It's better if we leave her here and bring her some food."

"She looks so cold," he said. "They look like they are starving."

I said, "Hmmmm." I said, "Marvelous." I turned my eyes. I knew we couldn't bring them home to my house. Grandma says she's allergic to cats. "Maybe we could bring them over to Veraleen's. She'll know what to do."

"But Veraleen's sick," said Biswick. She hasn't gotten out of bed since yesterday."

Oh. I took a deep FF breath and thought about telling that nonexistent God that he needed to stop stirring up everything like Jumbo was a big pot of soup.

I frowned as I lowered the lid. "Since yesterday, huh?" I carried the box of mewling cats to my bike and realized we'd need a bit of rope to make it secure.

"I'll be right back," I told Biswick. I climbed over some old televisions and spotted some rope. As I was leaning down to pick it up I heard a noise. Gideon?

No. Someone was lying on an old yellowy mattress about ten feet away. And he held a whiskey bottle on his belly. He was out cold with a big goofy smile across his lips. You don't have to be in my Einstein Hair Club to figure out who it was.

I so wish I had known that this was one of those tipping moments, where one small breath, one small push, one small decision would change everything. But I didn't say anything to Biswick about his daddy. We got on my bike and rode away.

Chapter
17

A doorway can tell you all kinds of things about what's beyond. I could immediately feel that something wasn't quite right when we walked into Veraleen's adobe. The air was quiet. And although there was a pathetic two-foot-high Christmas tree sitting on a table, decorated with gold tinsels and cheap balls from Ferdie's, things didn't feel very cheery. There was a stale, mothballs-in-the-attic smell. Biswick called out for Veraleen and went running off to her bedroom to find her. I followed behind, and stood by the door when I got there.

She was lying on her side, with the covers drawn up over her like a pup tent. Her big bare feet were hanging off the bed and looking just like dragon's feet—wrinkled and spidery veined. Her toes were extra long and crooked, her toenails yellow tinged and in need of clipping. She'd told me once that all those years of wearing boots had done a number on her toes. Biswick knelt down beside her. "How you doing, baby?" I heard her coo in her crusty voice. She reached out and stroked his cheek. "How you doing, Merilee?" she said lifting her head a little. "Come over here where I can see you."

I sat down on a little threadbare stuffed chair across from the bed. I was afraid to look, knowing her eyes were on me, studying, deciphering as always. Finally I glanced over and was shocked to see that her hair was loose from her ponytail. Although streaked with pewter, her hair was beautiful. Her face, though, without the pencil lines, looked as bald as her river stone.

"Why are you still sleeping, Veraleen? Are you tired?" Biswick asked.

"Bone-tired, sugar," she answered him. "Just bone-tired, that's all." She wasn't tired, she was sad, just as Biswick had said earlier. She had the same hollow, gone, good-bye eyes Uncle Dal had that last night I had seen him. It crossed my mind that Veraleen might have a loved one somewhere who she was pining for, like Uncle Dal.

Biswick tugged on her arm. "Veraleen, what's wrong?"

She smiled at him and her tooth twinkled like dragon's gold. Biswick giggled. "Can I have your tooth someday, Veraleen?"

She laughed. "You sure are a sweet little boy. I wish you were mine. I sure wish you had been mine," she said.

"But I got a daddy," he said.

"I know, honey," she said. She looked at him with such love I knew then that there was family somewhere out there, beyond the mountains. And I was jealous.

A tear fell from her face and hit her pillow. It was like seeing a tear roll down from a peach pit. "Come on, Veraleen," Biswick said. "You can tell us."

We waited. Finally. "I saw her clear as day a couple of weeks ago. I was working on my little garden and there she was—walking across where the bitterweed is planted, wearing her Sunday dress, the one I gave her. Years ago. So long ago."

I waited. Biswick ran to the window and peered out.

"She's gone. And I never forgave her," Veraleen said.

"We can find her," Biswick said. "I'm real good at finding things. People, too. Maybe she's still in the garden."

Veraleen smiled, and I saw another tear run down her face. "No, honey. You can't find her there. She's gone to heaven."

"Oh Veraleen!" Biswick said. "You don't have any eyebrows!" He had come back to her side.

"No, Biswick. I don't have no eyebrows." She looked above him at me. "I got a letter yesterday. She's gone. Been gone for several weeks and I didn't know it. Can't believe I didn't know it. It took a while for the letter to catch up to me."

I sat there frozen, knowing I should say something, the right thing, like "I'm sorry." It never came out. It was all I could do to meet her sad eyes. She nodded that she knew. That it was enough.

"You aren't going to go away to her *funeral*, are you?" He mouthed it like it was an evil word.

"No. It's done and over."

I closed my eyes a moment and wondered why she wasn't going home, wherever that was, to be with her family. And who it was that died.

"I don't want you to miss Christmas, Veraleen," Biswick said. "I got you a perfect present and I'm going to wrap it up and put it under your Christmas tree."

"You do that, honey." She smiled. "And I bet it's the best Christmas present I'll ever get." I wondered if she'd really stay for Christmas, if she'd be leaving for Africa or Australia or wherever soon.

"Guess what we found at the dump, Veraleen?" Biswick said. "Guess!"

"I don't know, honey. I'm all out of guesses right now. Tell me."

"We found a boyfriend for Merilee!"

"No!" Veraleen laughed, her low simmering laugh. I didn't think it was very funny. "You have a boyfriend, honey? Remember what I told you 'bout kissin'." *Kissing don't last.*

"No, absolutely not," I stammered. "Horrendous."

"She's gonna get married to him someday!" Biswick made slushy, smooching noises.

"I will never, ever marry," I announced.

"What we really found, Veraleen, is a mama kitty with her babies!"

"Well, ain't that the berries." She laughed.

"In an old box," I added. "They don't look good. They've got bugs. We left them in your lean-to."

Veraleen thought for a minute, chewing our news in her mind. "Well, we'll just have to fix that," she said. She pointed with her head toward the closet. "There's some blankets in there, Biswick. Go get 'em." He ran toward the closet and started rummaging around.

Veraleen started to sit up, slowly, with determination. "We'll bring some warm milk, and . . . " She reeled off more items as she picked up a robe that was draped over the end of her bed and threw it on over her nightgown. She headed toward her bathroom. "There's an ole dog bowl out there, just at the back door, Merilee," she said, emerging from the bathroom door. "Will you go fetch it?"

She started muttering under her breath—things like "Warm milk under moon shadows" "Drink a couple swallows of the willow water and you'll be all better" and "Mud from a hog wallow, dried." I watched her carefully. Something wasn't quite right. And I thought about what she'd said when Grandma showed up in her funeral clothes. About the soul going haywire when it knows a storm is coming. And I wondered if perhaps, all this time Veraleen had been here in Jumbo, she'd been going a little haywire.

I stooped to pick up the dog bowl outside her back door, and as I stood up I was shocked to see her finished garden, little mounds all laid out in neat, promising rows waiting for the first green buds to poke through the hard earth. *When I see God's garden, I'll be ready to go,*" she had said that day. I walked over and knelt down, resting my hand on one of the little mounds. It was so soft. Somehow she had pulled this good earth from the stubborn hard ground. Of course she could. She was Veraleen.

I picked up the bowl and brought it inside. "You all right, Merilee?" Veraleen asked.

I plopped down on her old chair and stared out her garden window. "I'm sorry we brought the cats here," I told her, eyes on the garden. I couldn't even feel the words come out of my mouth. I prayed then, my first-ever prayer to the vacationing God. I hoped he could hear me from so far away.

Don't let that garden grow, ever.

Chapter
18

$\mathcal{A}$ couple days later at school, there was a little mystery. Someone had left piles of neatly stacked pennies, in the shape of five-pointed stars, on Scooter, Romey, Cairo, and Mona Lisa's desks. It was as though a leprechaun had come in the middle of the night and left piles of gold. Scooter pocketed his pennies while Romey and Cairo scraped theirs off into their purses. Mona Lisa just sat and stared at her pile until Scooter, seeing that she wasn't going to take it, pawed it off her desk and filled up his other pocket.

Mr. Bonaparte, who is usually about as creative as a fence post and who usually puts our assignments on an overhead projector and who quite often disappears up to the teacher's lounge during the day to sneak food out of the other teachers' lunches, came in and announced, "In honor of the Lights Festival tonight, let's have a rousing debate on the scientific and mythic explanations of the Jumbo Ghost Lights."

Everyone perked up in their seats.

"Anyone?"

No one wanted to speak first. I slunk down in my chair.

Finally Romey McKelvey raised her hand. "My mama thinks the chamber of commerce club goes up there with flashlights and mirrors." Everyone giggled. "To bring in the tourists."

"Could be," Mr. Bonaparte said. "But was the chamber of commerce around in the eighteen hundreds when ranchers first started spotting the lights?" No one answered.

"Some people think it's swamp gas," Cairo offered. Scooter Stunkel muttered "phone-a-fart" under his breath and Ramona Grace snorted.

"There hasn't been a swamp around here in three million years," Mr. Bonaparte said. Cairo hung her head down.

Truman spoke up. "It's car headlights in the distance reflecting phosphorescent mineral deposits in the soil. Or perhaps static electricity. My daddy says he sees static charges between the cows and their horns at night on his ranch." Everyone giggled at the image of cows with static electricity sparking across their horns. Yello mooed.

"How about the myths and folktales that surround the lights?" Mr. Bonaparte asked.

"I read somewhere it's ghosts up in the mountains," Mona Lisa offered. "My daddy says don't ever go near the mountains or beyond the mountains. He says an Apache tribe of old women and children were fleeing the cavalry and they got lost up there on Cathedral Mountain and were never seen again. The lights are their souls looking for each other in the dark."

It was quiet a moment and then Scooter added, "Spooo-key!" Everyone laughed.

"Yes, there are lots of folktales with Native American themes," Mr. Bonaparte added. "And what happened to the Goat Herder, if the tale is true?"

"My daddy says he just ran off from his nagging

wife," Truman Dearlove offered from under his cowboy hat. Everyone laughed.

"Maybe the lights got him, the Indian spirits," said Ramona.

"Maybe," Mr. Bonaparte responded. "Now, have any of you seen the lights?" Most of the class started to raise their hands. "I know we have all seen the lights at the viewing area. They're there almost every clear night. Have any of you seen them somewhere else?" Most everyone lowered their hands except for Scooter, who probably had a made-up story to tell. Gideon had his head down, not making eye contact with anyone.

"How about you two? Gideon and Miss Leaves School Early. Do you have an opinion of the Jumbo Lights?" Mr. Bonaparte now had a new nickname for me. Even though I'd only left school a half hour early on Oral Report Day, I'd gotten three days of detention, which was no big deal, since I'd just be picking up trash around the school.

Gideon shook his head no.

I shook my head, too.

I noticed then, that there was a lot of fidgeting

going on. Scooter was scratching the back of his hands and so were Romey and Cairo. "Oh my God! What's on my hands? OH MY GOD!" Romey yelled. She held one up and I could see a bright, angry red rash spreading across it like a marauding march of army ants.

I looked at Gideon. He still had his eyes glued to his desk, a serene smile tucking up the corners of his mouth.

Mr. Bonaparte sent the hand-rashers to the school nurse and then whipped out a spray bottle of 409 and started spraying all of our desks down. Although Romey, Cairo, and Scooter didn't say nothin' on their way out, they all looked at me with surprise and wonderment, and I knew that whatever had happened, in some small way, I had won.

"So she thinks she's in high cotton now? Doesn't have time to come over and cook?" Grandma said when Biswick and I walked into the house after school that day. I don't know why Grandma was complaining. The whole kitchen counter was loaded with food; real good-smelling foods like crispy-fried okra, fried chicken, and smothered fried pork chops. We really didn't need a big supper since there would be food at the Jumbo Lights Festival. Biswick and I joined Bug at the table.

"Well?" Grandma asked me.

"Veraleen is not feeling good, Mrs. Monroe," Biswick answered.

Grandma ignored him and sat down. "Feeling poorly, is she?" she said to no one in particular. "Well, well, well. That woman's got the constitution of a beef steer." She snickered.

"Veraleen's not coming tonight?" Bug asked.

"Hot damn," Grandma said, hitting the table with her fist. "I'm gonna fix her my Granny's Sick Chicken Soup." I followed Grandma with suspicious eyes as she pranced over to the refrigerator and started taking vegetables out. "Show her what a real cure is," she muttered under her breath.

"What was your granny like?" Bug asked. "Was she pretty?"

Grandma cackled. "No. Not pretty at all." She started throwing baby potatoes in a pot on the stove. "Ugly as sin. Had a big ole nose, like Merilee. And busy. Busy as a stump-tailed cow in fly time. She had to raise me herself. It wasn't good then. Never was." Then under her breath, ". . . sadder but wiser, you are, Birdy Biedermeyer."

"What was her name?" Bug asked.

"Whose name?" Grandma said coming out of her reverie.

"Your grandma's," Bug answered. "The ugly one."

"That ain't nice to call someone ugly," Biswick said. "Ain't nice at all. I know that for sure."

"Well, ain't that the pot calling the kettle black."

"Grandma!" I bellowed. Something in me had cracked, like a hairline fracture in an iceberg. We locked eyes. I grabbed Biswick by the elbow and pulled him toward the door. He was frowning, trying to figure out what Grandma had said that made me upset. Daddy was coming through just as we were pushing out.

"Hold on, Hug," Daddy said. "Where are you going in such a hurry?"

"I'm taking Biswick to the Lights Festival," I said, trying to hide my angry, scrunched-up face.

"I thought I was taking you and Bug and Biswick," he called after me.

"We'll meet you and Bug there," I yelled, letting the front door slam behind us.

The night air was as still as a grave, no meddlesome wind to stir people up. All the lights were turned off in preparation, and it was dark as midnight. People were already lined along the sidewalk several feet deep. I breathed in the sweet aromas of caramel corn, cotton candy, and slow-cooked meats as Biswick and I walked along the sidewalk trying to find an open spot. Frida Pinkett was handing out fluorescent light-up necklaces and I grabbed two for Biswick and me.

"We're gonna miss the parade," Biswick said grumpily.

"Keep going," I told him. Why was he in such a funny mood? Did he know Veraleen was planning to run off? Or that his daddy had passed out at the dump? Where was the poet anyway? Any minute he'd probably show up, swaggering down the sidewalk above us all, with no hint that he had taken a little siesta on an old yellow mattress.

I stood for a moment on my tippy toes, trying to see if there was an opening across the street in front of the Sweet Home Diner. But it was just as crowded over there. I peered through people's legs to see if there was some room somewhere on the curb. Someone was wearing big inflatable furry shoes with claws. Even though Halloween is long gone, people put on all kinds of kooky stuff. It's a tradition. Pinell Pigg wears a huge blue felt top hat and actually thinks he looks good. And Bobo Romaine used to dress up as "Bobo the clown," till he got told to stop it 'cause he was scaring the little kids.

Suddenly the mayor, Ferdie's husband, Frank Frankmueller, wearing a Santa suit with a lit-up cowboy hat, climbed a platform across the street. Everyone got quiet. He held his arms up like a conductor. I plugged my ears. "One!" he shouted. "Two!" everyone shouted with him. "Three!" the crowd roared. All the teeny-tiny sparkling lights, gazillions of them, came on up and down the street. Then the lights on the buildings came on.

There was popping noises as everyone snapped their light-up fluorescent necklaces and bracelets. I snapped Biswick's and mine. I put his around his neck just before he crawled between Dorwood Smeather and Otis Stunkel, who moved over for him.

"Marvelous. Excuse me," I said to Otis, who was wearing a plastic Viking helmet in addition to his usual trench coat. He moved over and I'm positive I heard his skunk, Pooter, squeal as I joined Biswick at the curb.

The first entry was already rolling by on a flatbed. It was the mechanical chicken from Putt's Chicken Hutt.

"Tonight is a night of magic," said Biswick, beside me. "I can see twinkles in the eyes of everyone, Merilee. Can't you?"

"It's the twinkle lights reflecting in their pupils, Biswick."

"Oh." He frowned as the Jumbo marching band went by, followed by the Knights of Columbus on John Deere tractors.

"I see things as they are, Biswick. Cut and clear."

"I wanna go find the Conquistador tree. Tonight. On this magical night. Will you come with me, Merilee Marvelous? Look!" he said excitedly, pointing to the volunteer firemen, the old coots, who rode by on the old fire truck.

To drop everything and run. Like Veraleen was gonna do. I had thought about running many times—beyond the mountains. It was a distant thought that moved farther and farther away like a dream attached to a falling star. I knew I couldn't do that to Mama. I was tied to this place, like it or not.

"I want some funnel cake," Biswick said, pouting.

"There's no Conquistador tree," I snapped, sounding mean, just like Grandma. Sheriff Bupp rode by waving his hat, as he sat on the back of a '62 black convertible 'Vette.

I glanced over at Biswick and saw he was staring at me, like I had a big glob of food on my face or something. "I wanna leave," he said. The baton twirlers marched by. Their batons had lit sparklers on the ends. I frowned. Was all this because I wouldn't go look for the Conquistador tree?

The last entry rode by, an old Model T Ford covered in lights.

"What's wrong with you?" I asked. The crowd started to disperse and Biswick ran off ahead of me.

I caught up with him in front of the pork rib booth on the lawn of the courthouse. People had set up folding chairs and were eating watermelon slices and buttered corn on the cob. "I thought you wanted funnel cake," I said, out of breath. In the distance, old Rondo and the Ronettes' live band started up playing "Unchained Melody." They had blocked off Main Street so people could dance to the music.

"I thought you said one time you wanted to go far away," he said. "I want pork ribs," he told Ferdie, who was manning the booth. I reached in my pocket and pulled out a dollar and handed it to her. She had on felt antlers and a light-up Rudolph nose.

"Here you go, sweetie," she said, handing the plate to Biswick. He walked off and I followed him. I felt funny in my stomach like something was up.

I saw Daddy standing all by himself several booths down eating a corn on the cob. Even Daddy had on a light band around his neck and a felt Santa hat. He tilted his head for me to come, but something told me to follow Biswick. I waved at Daddy, trying to smile so he wouldn't worry, and walked on. The image of him jumping off a train as a boy flitted through my mind.

Biswick was seated on a bench watching the dancers out in the street. Somewhere along the way he had tossed his light-up necklace. The dancers all looked like drunken aliens out there dancing to the twist, with light-up bands twinkling around every appendage—heads, wrists, and ankles. They looked very happy—obliviously happy, like one big family. Bug was out there with Tootie McKelvey, holding hands and trying to twist all the way down to the ground. I thought Biswick would want to be out there, too. But I could feel his mood deflating by the moment as he watched them all.

"You can't leave right now, Biswick. Stupendous. Veraleen's not feeling well."

"She wants me to be happy," he said. He took one bite out of a pork rib and put it down.

"She wants you here," I said.

The lights were shining from his eyes. I wanted to believe it was a magical night, I did. And I wanted Biswick to be happy.

"We want you here," I said.

"No, you don't. Not all of you." He was talking about Grandma.

"Oh Biswick. She doesn't even want me here and I'm her own granddaughter." I laughed. "Spectacular."

"Why does she hate you?" he asked.

"I'm not perfect," I answered him. "Imperfection. Fabulous malfunction."

"Nobody's perfect," Biswick said. "That's what they say."

I thought about that. "My mother," I said. "That's why I can't go."

"She's all better now."

I didn't respond.

"You don't want me just like everyone else. All I got in this world is Cheeto and Daddy."

"I let you follow me around, Biswick," I said.

"You're not my friend," he gulped. "And you aren't marvelous." His eyes got big, as though he had remembered something horrible. "You wouldn't even give me that dumb ole smiley PEZ dispenser. And you know what else?" he shrilled. "You never found out who that boy was buried in the cemetery!" He threw his rib plate on the ground and stormed off into the crowd of dancers, pushing them apart angrily with his hands. Bug and Tootie were the only ones who noticed him. They paused a moment and then kept on dancing.

How could I give any more to him? I am not a giver. I am not one of them. And neither is Biswick.

I went inside Mama's bookstore. It was bustling with people who didn't like the cold, mainly the grumpy citizens of Jumbo, like Marva Augustine hiding from her kids, and Pinell Pigg who was still wearing his blue top hat. Lorelei was handing out free hot chocolate in the back and Mama was behind the counter. She smiled when she saw me. That wistful, newly sad, after-accident smile that makes me wonder what Mama has suddenly discovered about me that she wishes she could change. "Where's Bug and your daddy?" she asked.

"Bug's dancing and Daddy's eating," I said.

"Can you man the register while I go grab your daddy for a dance?" How could I say no to that? I had never ever seen Daddy as much as point a toe. This would be good. I nodded my head yes. She grabbed her jacket. "Be back in a little bit." Before she went through the door, she asked, "Where's your buddy?"

"He's out there with the dancers," I answered. "Ridiculous." It was partly the truth. That's the last place I had seen him, pushing through the crowd.

I had barely stepped behind the counter when Lorelei cornered me. "Where is he?" she asked, her eyes big and expectant. "Is he coming?" Her hair, newly blond, was piled on her head. Twinkle lights meandered up and around her hairdo. She looked like a walking Christmas tree.

"I don't know." Why does everyone think I'm the social director around here?

"If you see him, try to get him in here, okay?" She looked desperate. I can't ever imagine being so desperate over a goon, especially one who takes naps in the town dump. She slunk back to her hot chocolate. I was already bored. No one was gonna buy a book when there were free beverages.

I spotted Mona Lisa Venezuela sitting on a bench near the cookbooks reading. I walked over to her and tried to think of something to say. I couldn't. It didn't matter, though. She slammed the book shut and walked out the door. I glanced down. She had been reading a book on medical history. I had thumbed through it myself many times before. I went over to the window and peered out. I spotted them right away; they stood out, my parents. They held each other close, slowly twirling around, and even from here I knew why she had stayed. Daddy twirled her around and I saw him murmur "Helene" into her hair.

* * *

Later that night things were winding down like they always do here, people long departed for home to rest their feet, except for Ramona Grace sneaking off with someone to smooch behind the azalea bushes in the courthouse square and Old Man Blevins, who always falls asleep on the bench in front of the bank because his wife forgets about him, and Frida out in the middle of the street sweeping up the discarded cups and streamers. I stood watching her as I waited for Mama to finish locking up the bookstore. Normally I would join in the cleanup because it drives me crazy to see trash anywhere, but for some reason I felt no gumption, no pull to be out there cleaning. I wanted to stare at the wonderland of lights still strung across the empty street. If I squinted my eyes, they all became one, spinning and spinning. Suddenly I felt the urge to dance, too, like a September firefly. I closed my eyes completely and slowly put one foot out.

"What are you doing?"

I let out a sigh and opened my eyes. Gideon. Gideon with his backpack slung across his shoulder. I think it was the second sentence he had ever spoken to me.

I just shrugged and looked up.

He stood by my side and asked, "Why are you staring at the sky?"

I didn't answer. I wanted to ask him about the pennies at school but I couldn't find the words. I was hoping Mama would walk out with her keys now.

"Refracts. I like the way the light bounces. Around and around," I finally answered. "Like the sky is turned upside down."

"Do you believe in the Ghost Lights?"

"No," I said firmly. "Superstitious."

"Why not?"

I was nervous. "I don't particularly care one way or the other." I shrugged.

"I think you do," he answered.

"Why would you say that?"

He motioned with his head up to the sky. "We're the same. We're both watchers."

I ignored his grand pronouncement about us being alike. "Well, then, what do you think they are?" I looked at the sky, waiting for a long scientific answer.

"I think they are curious observers, like us."

He was so close I could smell his cologne, Pride of the Rose from the Rexall Drug. My daddy uses it too. I couldn't help but look over at him. He blinked a couple of times and I wondered if he saw in my eyes what I saw in his: the reflections of the lights staring back at me, clear and shining, just like Biswick said.

I stood there almost mesmerized.

"You know, you have a really interesting face," he said, smiling.

"Oh," I muttered. I waited for my heart to start racing and my palms to sweat but instead I felt like there were sweet butterflies flying around inside me.

"Can I take your picture?" he asked, pulling his camera from his bag. He had an old-fashioned 35 millimeter.

"It's so incredibly beautiful here, Merilee. I won't ever have to leave to become the great photographer I want to be when I grow up." He focused. I started to turn my head away from him.

"Wait," he said quietly. "Stop right there."

The flash exploded and when I could see again, I saw that Gideon had taken a large step back and was holding his camera reverently, the way Biswick holds Cheeto. He smiled at me before walking away down the street, the festival lights rimming his silhouette.

My grandma believes that a photograph can capture the truth, if only for a brief flash of time. "Don't let anyone ever take your picture," she once said to me. Later that night, when I lay in my bed, I thought about Gideon. What would he see when he looked at that photo? Would he see the truth, that I am an ugly, strange girl? What is true? I thought about the landscape surrounding Jumbo, the wide expanse of gentle grasslands that lip into the mountains who guard the secrets. I thought about the tricks of the eye, the dust devils, the Ghost Lights, even my winking dragon mirage. Was anything true around here? Or was it all a curtain, a shadow, a rumor of light.

Chapter
19

There once was a dragon who was sent away from his family because he was too kind. He flew up to the stars of the heavens and has lived there since, guarding mankind's hopes and dreams, his tears raining down now and then.

I thought about this sad celestial dragon as I rode, bundled up against the cold, to Uncle Dal's on a Sunday afternoon after I'd laid around all day reading *Wuthering Heights*. Uncle Dal had been gone for over a month and it was Christmas Eve Eve, a few days after the Lights Festival. We were out of school now, till after New Year's. My baskets were laden with foodstuffs, all made by Grandma and prettily wrapped with Christmas tinsel and ribbons by Mama. Mama had insisted I go and see if he was home. She told me to just leave the food on the steps of his trailer if he wasn't there. "Idiot, taking off with that nasty dog to God knows where," Grandma muttered at me as I left on my bike. "Too cold, Merilee," she yelled off into the darkness after me. "It's too cold!"

I had missed him terribly, I'd come to realize. I lay awake at night wondering where he was—if he'd come back this time. When I rounded the corner and saw a faint light streaming from Obedias's old barn and Uncle Dal's pickup parked nearby, something akin to a half-sob, half-sigh passed through me.

He was back.

I put the kickstand down and started unpacking my basket. Flynn was lying in the grass outside the barn door. He wagged his tail.

"I've been worried about you," I said as I walked in, Flynn following behind. Uncle Dal was standing in front of the statue, a tool in hand. My breath came out mistily. It was indeed cold, even in the barn.

I was surprised to see that twinkle lights had

replaced the cobwebs in the rafters. I got a shivery feeling up and down my back. He didn't ever really acknowledge Christmas.

Uncle Dal looked over at me. He hadn't expected that I would say anything. I usually didn't, when I came to see him. I noticed his hair, always a little shaggy for Jumbo, was now long enough to be pulled back in a short ponytail and he had the beginnings of an unshaved beard.

"Why did you leave?" I asked as I busied myself stacking the presents on the floor, next to the farm table.

He didn't answer me for a while. He stood staring at the statue.

"I don't know, Hug," he finally answered.

"Uncle Dal?" I said. His face so kind in the lantern light. "I'm not really the hugging type," I told him. "I really hate that nickname. It's preposterous. Ridiculous."

He smiled slightly. The first smile I had seen in a long time. "All right, Merilee."

"Where is she?" This time he didn't even look at me.

"Why?" he simply asked.

"Because I want to meet her."

"I have never thought of you wanting to know anyone," he said. He hadn't said it to be mean. It was just plain speaking.

"I would like to know *her*, though. Because of you."

He waited a while before answering.

"You can't, Merilee," he said. "She's in a cemetery up in El Paso."

I let that sink in for a little while. It made sense. It fit. I should have known, like I know everything else. "That's where you have been going, to see her in the cemetery?" It was a dumb question, I realized, after it left my lips.

"Yep," he answered.

"What happened to her?"

"She got sick."

"Why did you have to take a train and jump off of it?" I interrupted him. I didn't want to hear about any more cemeteries.

"I don't have any money, Merilee," he said. "And I'm not about to ask for any. I barely have enough to get around town here and feed Flynn. So sometimes I take the train up to El Paso to see her. It stops in Whiskey and I don't have the money to get back here so sometimes I make my own stop along the way."

I thought about the trains and how much I missed them. And how things had changed since the day I'd seen him jump. I hadn't been out to watch them since that day. I guess I was afraid of seeing him do it again. And I didn't want to know, I didn't want to have to keep a secret about him.

"Will you tell me about her, Uncle Dal, please? Just say it in thirty seconds, that's all. I won't ask you anymore.."

I could tell he was battling with it. Deciding whether he was going to let go of even a tiny bit of her to me. Flynn ambled over and nudged my hand with his cold nose. I started scratching his back. I waited for an answer. Uncle Dal kept staring at his statue, and I kept my eyes on him.

A minute later he said, "She was sweet, had two freckles on her nose, had big feet like you, and liked to sing off-key with the car radio." I looked down at the Perpetual Foot. A sawing feeling was happening in my stomach and I felt dizzy.

"What was the song you whistled to me, when I couldn't stop bawlin'?"

"Boy, you sure are full of questions today, aren't you? You've been saving these up your whole life, haven't you?"

"I want to know what it was that finally calmed me down, that's all," I said. I glanced down at the tools and saw they were in disarray, like they had danced around in the middle of the night and then collapsed. Some of the rasps had white residue. I stood there looking at them puzzled, like I was seeing something that could not be.

"I don't remember," he answered in such a way that I knew, like Biswick, he wasn't lying, he just didn't want to go down that path in his mind. I looked back at him but kept my eyes from the statue. "Do you have any more questions?" he said now with a slight smile, like the old Uncle Dal. Actually, it was a nice smile, with something strong behind it that I couldn't decipher. I slowly followed his gaze to the statue.

Halfway down, magically birthed from the white marble was a hand—delicate, smooth, feminine, and finely carved, the forefinger draped down in a slight point. It was beautiful. Graceful. Ethereal. Ghostlike.

"Uncle Dal?" I asked.

"Pass me one of the rasps, Hug," he said. I fingered the rasp, thinking about how I'd wished for this day. I took an FF breath. I picked it up and gave it to him and then ran my fingers down over the rough marble till I reached the hand. It was as smooth as Veraleen's river stone. I quickly drew my hand away, like I'd touched fire.

Then I sat down on my milking stool stunned. Uncle Dal started working on one of the fingers.

"Uncle Dal?" He looked over at me. I'd forgotten what I was gonna ask, though. I just sat there for a long, long time.

Before I left, I walked over to the wall below the hayloft. I stared at the ladder, a series of old wooden slats leading up to a dark hole. I started to climb.

"Hug?" Uncle Dal asked from below.

My foot slipped and I almost fell halfway up. I stood there holding onto the slat above me, breathing in and out. Finally I continued till I reached the top. My stomach dropped. It was just a bunch of old hay up there. Smelly old hay.

"You okay?" Uncle Dal asked.

"Yeah," I answered. I took several FF breaths and carefully climbed back down.

I left a little while later and rode home under the stars, thinking perhaps there is room in this world for tender miracles, and wondering, if there is a God, how he chooses which ones to send down to us and which ones he keeps with him.

The next morning, before going early to the train tracks, I went to see Veraleen. I was actually a little scared walking up to her front door, afraid of what I might find. I had had a little gnawing feeling in my stomach all morning that something was wrong somewhere, but it was too indistinct for me to decipher.

Veraleen, though, was fine. She opened the door before I had a chance to knock and she waved me inside. She hustled around her tiny little house, just like herself, first fixing me a cup of tea, then insisting I try her three-layer cookies. When she came back with a plateful, I was disappointed to see she held a lit cigarette in one hand. She took me outside to show me Mamacita and the kittens. I sat down on the dirt floor and reached into the dog house to pet them. Veraleen stood in the doorway still smoking.

I coughed especially loud and I looked at her carefully. She caught my look. "I'm doing just fine, Merilee," she said. "Just fine." She inhaled her cigarette and blew it off to the side.

"It must have been that delicious soup your grandma brought over," she continued, winking at me. The penciling was back on her face. She looked like Veraleen again. "But I'll be leavin' soon, sugar. So someone's gonna have to take those cats."

I followed her back inside the adobe and plopped down on her dilapidated sofa with the springs hanging out while she continued scurrying around. My tummy hurt. I glanced over at her tree and saw there was one present under it. It was wrapped in the funny pages, sort of. There was enough tape on it to wrap a mummy, and here and there hot pink hair stuck out. I wondered what gift I'd give her if I had one to give and realized I had never given a gift before.

"Did you and Biswick have fun at the Lights Festival?" she asked. She was wrapping presents— little boxes of Whitman's Samplers from the Rexall. "Shoot, I need more tape." She went into the kitchen and I heard drawers being opened and slammed shut.

I found myself biting my lip as I thought about Gideon. "Huh?" I asked.

"Biswick," she said a little louder.

"Yeah, I guess he had fun. I didn't see him after a while."

She stuck her head back in the room. "Well, who did he go home with, honey?"

"I don't know. He might have gone home on his own," I answered. Suddenly that knowing, sawing feeling started to come back.

"Was his daddy there making a jerk-fool of himself?" she asked. "Drinking his cowboy Kool-

Aid?" Grandma calls beer "cowboy Kool-Aid," too.

"No," I said, picturing his daddy at the dump and wondering if I should tell her about that. "He wasn't there."

Veraleen walked into the room and stopped in front of me. She had one hand on her hip, the cigarette pinched between two fingers in her other hand at her side. She looked down, piercing me with those blue eyes. "What are you not telling me, Merilee? You look like an egg-sucking dawg."

"Nothing," I answered, knowing right away that wasn't going to suffice. "Biswick left. We had a little disagreement."

"A little disagreement, huh?" she asked.

"Yeah," I answered, trying to remember all that was said. I knew more than anything that he would not want me to tell Veraleen about his mama and what she had done to him. "He was just antsy, that's all. He wanted to go away to the mountains and find the Conquistador tree," I said. "Preposterous."

"There ain't no Conquistador tree," Veraleen said, shaking her head.

"Yeah." I was glad that she agreed. "That's what I told him. It was a stupid idea. We are staying right here where we belong."

"A boy has got to have his dreams and you are squashing them just the way everybody else squashed them," she said as she pulled up a chair.

I was totally confused. "I was just telling him like it is," I said.

"No, you are putting up walls around him so he can't leave. Just like you."

I just stared at her.

"You know." She snuffed out her cigarette in an ashtray.

There was a long, angry quiet while I tried to shut out all she was saying to me in her face, her eyes, her whole being.

"I have to go home now," I said, trying to get up.

"Oh no you don't," she said. "You are going to listen to me, as painful as it is. It's gonna do you some good. Take a breath and bite your tongue, girl."

Ha. I've been doing that all my life.

A shiver went down my back. "It's been my

experience when someone says something like that, it's gonna be something good to write in my journal but that's about it," I told her. "Just something to put in a journal."

"Well, here's something for your journal, Miss Merilee. First, it's better to be wise than smart, and second, you should focus on what is, not what isn't." She ceremoniously walked to the front door.

"And what does that mean?" I said, standing up. "Stupid. Stupendous." I had to take three FF breaths in a row.

"You've set up a nice little existence for yourself here, Merilee. A safe place that you will never have to venture out of your whole life. Believe me, I know. And you're always looking for an excuse to stay in your little make-believe world. Poor Merilee Monroe. Has the biggest bucketload of woes around so of course she can't love anyone. Well, let me tell you—I'm here to tell you the Lord Almighty up above wants you to grow up and love and be loved."

"Ha! Spectacular! You told me," I said between big FF breaths. "You told me kissing don't last."

"You know I'm not talking about kissing. There's all kinds of love, Merilee. The love of family is the most important. And you are never gonna find that faraway magic you've been hankering for if you don't even see the love that surrounds you here." She opened the door for me to leave.

"I don't know why you think you can get on a high horse above me," I said, stomping toward the door. "When you have some sort of secret yourself!" I was about to make my grand exit when a small shadow appeared in the doorway.

We heard a sniffle. Biswick, bedraggled and puffy faced, stood in the doorway. "I've been looking for him all night. I've been everywhere," he sobbed. "My daddy hasn't come home!"

Chapter
20

When I was a little girl I lost my favorite ring, a gum-ball machine cheapo that had a plastic dragon on it. Daddy spent twelve quarters getting it for me at the Piggly Wiggly. I was washing my hands and it slid off into the stream of water and was sucked down the pipe. I had perhaps a millisecond where I could have grabbed it and saved it, but I was paralyzed, watching it all unfold before me and knowing the outcome. After Biswick appeared at Veraleen's door that day, it all unfolded the same way, just like spiraling sink water sucking down something irreplaceable. More than anything in the whole wide world, I wished I could go back to that day at the dump.

Now all I could see was Jack O'Connor lying there on the mattress so tranquil-like, and I could suddenly hear the alarm bells in my mind loud and clear.

"When is the last time you seen him, Biswick baby?" Veraleen asked Biswick.

Biswick choked back a sob and wiped his eyes. "I don't know," he said. "I don't know."

"What do you mean you don't know? Did you see him at bedtime or this morning?"

"I don't ever see him in the morning. He always sleeps."

Veraleen and I exchanged glances.

"Where is he, Veraleen? Where is he? I want my Daddy Jack to come home!" he wailed.

My stomach was now down in my toes and seeping out like blood from a fatal cut. And a roaring hiss, like a mad snake, started rising in my ears. "I think I know where he is," I whispered low for Veraleen only as I grabbed the back of a chair. FF, FF, FF. *Oh God.*

She turned, her dark blue sapphire eyes boring into mine, asking *Where? Where is he? Tell me now.*

I bit my lower lip and swallowed hard. If we went to the dump looking for him, Biswick would see it all. Perhaps he was just sleeping. But I knew better. I reached over, cupped my hand, and whispered in Veraleen's ear, "I think we need the sheriff."

"Ain't no way I'm gonna call that sheriff," Veraleen said as we all jumped in her car. We roared down the road, swerving on two wheels around corners on our way to the dump. I sank lower and lower in the front seat, hoping that if I sunk low enough I would disappear, never to be seen again. Biswick was crying in the backseat.

"I don't want Biswick to see anything," I pleaded, my voice low.

"He ain't gonna see nothing. Don't worry. I just need to check first. That's all. We can't take no chances."

A few minutes later, Veraleen pulled the car to a stop. We were way back on the road, even before all the trash started signaling that the dump was near. She got out, leaned in the window, and said firmly, "You two stay here." Then she marched off.

"Where's she going?" Biswick piped up from the backseat. "I thought we were going to look for my daddy."

"Christmas shopping, Bis," I told him gently. "Just like you." I closed my eyes. I could feel my heart pounding in my chest so hard I thought it would pound out and thump its way down the road after Veraleen. Please. Please. Please let him be all right. Horrendous. Horrendous.

"It's Christmas Eve," Biswick said wistfully. "He always disappears on Christmas Eve. He did it last year, too, and the year before. He'll be back. He will. And he always brings me a bag of Hershey Kisses. That's my Christmas present."

A few minutes later, I heard footsteps. I opened my eyes and saw Veraleen, her eyes all scared and jiggling, a broad fake smile plastered across her crackled face, her gold sheath sparkling. She got into the car, started it up, and said, "Everything's just fine. Just fine. I think we should go home, and get out of this cold." She was breathing so hard as she backed the car up that her breath filled the front seat like a mist. "God rest his soul," she mumbled so low that only I picked it up.

"Aren't we gonna look for my daddy?"

"We're gonna call the reverend," Veraleen answered. "He knows where your daddy is now."

Mama and Daddy and Bug were downstairs in the living room decorating the Christmas tree when I walked in a few minutes later. It was something our family did together on Christmas Eve day. We always get a real tree from down in front of the Piggly Wiggly. Bug and I go with Daddy to pick it out, and when we get home Mama and Daddy always argue over whether it is straight or not in its stand. I had missed the whole ritual. My eyes focused on the Christmas tree where my white angel, given to me by my Grandma Ruth, glittered.

The room was quiet and an eternity passed before someone spoke. It was Bug who looked up and said, "You've missed all the fun . . ." but she stopped in mid-sentence when Veraleen and Biswick appeared at the door.

Veraleen carried Biswick. He was slumped on

her shoulder like a helpless little baby. I glanced out the window and I thought about the poet frozen in the town dump. The silence in the room made me think of one of Veraleen's under-the-breath mutterings. *As quiet as a snowflake on a feather*.

Veraleen motioned with her head that she was taking Biswick up the stairs. I was left to face Mama and Daddy and Bug.

Mama broke the silence. "What's the matter, Merilee?"

"It's Biswick's daddy. Dead. At the dump."

"Gad night a living," Grandma spoke up. I hadn't even seen her, parked on a chair in the corner knitting those blasted snowball caps. "It's going to snow."

Mama told Daddy to go call the sheriff.

Grandma was right. We got snow that night. And some thief stole the baby Jesus out of the life-size Nativity scene in front of Mama's Mexican church. Sheriff Bupp found a single set of footprints in the freshly fallen snow leading up to and back from the manger scene where Mary and Joseph looked down admiringly on the empty straw cradle.

A white Christmas. A perfect Christmas. We woke up to find that one of Mama's dogs, we're not sure which one, had peed on every single Christmas present under the tree. And another ate all the chocolates out of the stockings. We knew Stinky did that because he was under Mama's bed farting.

Veraleen told me later that the poet had died just as I had last seen him, lying there peacefully with a smile on his face. Veraleen said it was just his time for going. Everyone has a time, according to Veraleen and Grandma. What does that mean? That it is all preplanned when we exit? The question in my mind, the one that will always circle around and around like a hungry hawk, was: How long had he been there? Was he just sleeping when I had seen him? Should I have told someone? They could have come and taken him off to jail again. If only I had just done something.

"Ain't no one's fault," Veraleen said to me later that night, Christmas night, a night when most people are enjoying the remnants of a wonderful day. We were all in the kitchen drinking hot chocolate and sitting around the table, waiting for Sheriff Bupp. We knew officially now that the poet was dead. The sheriff had called Daddy late last night with the news, and he had said that he wouldn't have much more to tell us until Dr. Coyote Wilson examined the body. Bug and Biswick were asleep upstairs. Grandma had gone to bed, too, saying that man was a fool idiot and there was no sense worrying about him now. When she left, going through the kitchen door, I had watched her with wonder. She never ever went to bed early, especially when there was a storm brewing and a funeral looming. She always put her two cents in and stirred the pot.

Earlier in the day, when it was time to open our pitiful peed-on presents, Grandma had appeared in her funeral dress and feathered funeral hat, and Daddy had to gently tell her that the poet's funeral wasn't today. And she had actually cried. I'd never seen Grandma cry. No one, not even Bug, felt like opening any presents after that.

"Ain't no one's fault," Veraleen repeated. People repeat things during bad times, I have discovered. It seems to make them feel better to say something over and over. It's as though it becomes truer in the repeating. "He did it to himself." I kept listening for the arrival of Sheriff Bupp and taking deep FF breaths.

"I just didn't know he was that bad off," Mama said as she sipped from her mug. "How could we have known? What has that sweet boy been going through?" I thought about the Porter house and those little marks on Biswick's arm and my heart sank even lower. I heard a car rumble up the gravel drive and the room started to tilt.

"Did you know, Merilee?" Daddy asked. He wasn't accusing. He was just asking.

"Sort of," I managed to mumble. I thought I could even hear footsteps crunching in the snow. "I don't feel well," I said, and I ran from the room as someone tapped on the back door. I went upstairs and gently shut the bedroom door, leaving it open just a crack so I could listen. Biswick was asleep in one of my twin beds, oblivious to all the goings-on in the house. The dogs were sleeping at his feet.

Veraleen protected me. She told everyone that she had seen Mr. O'Connor go off in the direction of the dump before and that she had a feeling he would be there. Sheriff Bupp said that he knew how bad the poet was, that he had found him drunk as a waltzing pissant at the old Dixie Dog Drive In more than once and had decided to let him sleep it off. I could picture everyone downstairs with their heads hung low. They were whispering softly but still their words floated up to me and stung my ears.

"Dr. Coyote Wilson says he's been dead for at least two days, maybe more," I heard Sheriff Bupp say. "Doesn't know yet if it was exposure, or alcohol poisoning, or both. Does anyone know where that boy's mama is?" There was silence. I knew everyone was shaking their heads no. "We can't have no retard boy with no kin flitting about the town. One of his relatives is gonna have to come fetch him or I'm going to call the county authorities to come put him away."

Oh God. Biswick. Where was his mother? I didn't know. And I wondered if Biswick even knew. But I knew more than anyone else about him. And I had a hunch that Biswick's mama was in the same place his father was now. That they were together. And Biswick was here. For us to take care of, no matter what Sheriff Bupp said.

I opened the door and slowly walked downstairs. I went to the Christmas tree and found Sheriff Bupp's present among ours. It wasn't wrapped. It had an old floppy, reused bow stuck on top of it. It looked real good, although it still smelled a little like pee. It was shiny and new. Uncle Dal had helped Biswick with it.

I carried it into the kitchen. Everyone looked at me as if they'd seen a ghost. I handed the present to Sheriff Bupp.

"It's from Biswick," I said, and left the room. I stopped just outside the doorway to listen.

"Well I'll be . . . I had one just like it when I was a boy," Sheriff Bupp said. His voice was filled with wonder. "I got it for Christmas . . . my last Christmas." I peeked and saw he had the toy clutched to his chest, and I saw the boy that had been, before Johnny Bupp got shot by a Nazi and his mama keeled over. "I wanted to be a fireman and save people. To help them." It was quiet a few moments. "Well, I'll be," he repeated, wiping at his face.

Later that night, after Sheriff Bupp left, I was coaxed back into the kitchen for hot tea.

"Where's Biswick's mother, do you know, Merilee?" my mother asked.

I nodded my head no. It wasn't a lie. I really didn't know. I felt sleepy. I kept yawning over and over.

"Has he ever mentioned her at all?" Daddy asked me.

Suddenly I felt angry; they were trying to pawn him off on someone, trying to pass him off. If anyone should have him, it was Veraleen. She sure was awfully quiet. I looked at her across the table. All she had uttered over and over the last hour was "Ain't no one's fault." Why wasn't she grabbing him and taking him home under her own roof? She'd been hugging him and clutching him to her breast like she didn't want to ever let him go for weeks. And yet she said nothing. I looked good and hard at her. And I knew. Her secret was big and it had nothing to do with the fact that she was gonna run off, or that she had lost her job at the hospital, or that she almost had hurt a baby. It was something entirely different. Something deep that even Veraleen couldn't face down.

"Merilee?" Daddy asked. "Are you all right, Hug?"

"No!" I burst out. I wasn't all right. Biswick's daddy was dead.

"Ain't nobody's fault," Veraleen repeated. "The sheriff said he's been gone, been dead, for days." She was still staring at the table but I knew she was talking to me. "Days."

"We've got to find out who his family is," Mama said.

"There's no one," I said, not completely knowing if that was true or not. I didn't want there to be anyone. I wanted us to have him. "No one."

"That's right, baby," Veraleen said. Her eyes met mine and I saw they were full of guilt. Why? Why did she feel guilty?

"Why don't you take him, Veraleen?" I asked. I couldn't believe it. Did I actually say the words aloud? Even Mama and Daddy looked surprised.

Veraleen wouldn't look me in the eyes anymore.

"This is way too early to be discussing what's to become of Biswick," Mama interjected. "I'm sure someone has records of the family. It can all be settled later. For the time being, and however long need be, he will stay with us."

Daddy got up and went to the phone. Mama asked him what he was doing. "Making the funeral arrangements." Mama looked at him in surprise. We all did. I went upstairs and crawled into bed. I tried to draw mental images of my dragons but they were just a mishmash of horns and scales, and I finally fell asleep into an oblivion.

I was up eating cereal early the next morning when the doorbell rang. I opened the front door but saw no one around. There was a Christmas present wrapped in old-fashioned paper on the welcome mat. I leaned down. It read: *Merilee*. I tore off the wrapping paper right then and there.

It was the photo. The one he had taken of me the night of the Jumbo Lights Festival. I held it up and could not believe what I saw staring back at me. The muted lights of that night twinkled all around my face lighting me up with a fiery glow. And I actually looked almost beautiful. Almost. Can you believe it? And for once in my life I didn't have those vacant, lifeless eyes of someone about to kick the bucket. I put the photo under my pajama top and ran up the stairs. I stuck it in my underwear drawer and sat down on my bed. I stared at the drawer for a long time. Then I walked over, took the photo out, and gingerly put it under my pillow.

Chapter
21

Like I said, Grandma loves funerals. But when we were all dressed and ready to go in the Red Rocket, she came out wearing one of those only-wear-at-home housedresses and talking about it being too cold for a funeral. Mama had to help her back to her house and get her dressed in something proper. The whole way to the cemetery Grandma kept muttering, "The snow's too cold, Harley. They can't bury him in that snow. Too cold. Too cold." I wished more than anything that Daddy had just left her at home and I think everyone else did, too.

When snow falls on a graveyard, it adds a cheerful dusting, like powdered sugar over a haunted house. It would seem beautiful, if you didn't know what was underneath. The air smelled lightly perfumed, like clean white sheets hanging on a clothesline. Somewhere in the distance I heard a freight train whistle. Grandma came around when we walked up to the band of mourners standing around the casket like a flock of crows. And she seemed almost happy when the Reverend Ham started into his sermon, shouting "Amen" every time he paused to take a breath.

Lorelei, her hair tucked up under a black Jackie O pillbox hat, sobbed into a handkerchief. She clutched the poet's book to her chest—clung to it, sinfully. Dr. Coyote patted her on the back. Sheriff Bupp stood next to them, his hat held reverently in front of his stomach.

Wadine Pigg looked like Marie Antoinette with her snow-covered beehive. She held her eyes closed when we sang "Be Not Afraid." I thought of something Veraleen had said yesterday: "It was all plain as a pig on a sofa."

I felt something move behind us and turned to watch a white rabbit run across the snow. I

followed his path till he ran past a pair of legs. Uncle
Dal. He was standing outside the rickety gates,
his long hair hung loose and covered with snow.
(Grandma Birdy would have had a hissy fit with a
tail if she'd turned around right then and saw him.)

Biswick cowered by my side, seeking warmth.
But I was jumpy and twitched when he got too
close. So after a while, he leaned over the other
way toward Veraleen, who gladly put her arm
around him. I knew that he kept one hand in his
pants pocket wrapped around Cheeto.

About halfway through the prayers, Daddy
wrapped his arm around me, which I knew wasn't
easy for him to do. I think he'd always felt helpless
after he tried to show me the lights all those years
ago. But he needn't have worried about it. I know
he's helped me in other ways—those soft, silent,
raindrop ways.

On the other side of Daddy was Mama, who
kept silent and still, her eyes unmoving on her
opened Bible. She was humming inside, a low,
plaintive wail, like the Songbird of Sadness. I
could feel it. Like she felt me. Connected. "It's

God's will," she'd said yesterday to me in the kitchen. "Still," she'd sighed, "it's the saddest thing I've ever seen." The cold gave Mama headaches now. I closed my eyes and for a brief moment I felt like I'd just drank a whole grape-cherry slushie from the Sonic over in Whiskey and my brain had freezed up. Then it quickly went away.

I looked at Biswick. It was his idea to have his father buried in the old cemetery. No one protested. No one wanted to deny Biswick anything right now. I glanced over at the row of headstones peeking up from the snow and thought about the day Jack O'Connor had been lying there not ten feet away. And now he was about to be buried in the same place.

Not far over was the tombstone of the nameless boy. I knew the name now. His name was George Charles Williams. I'd found out. I wondered if anyone had ever called him Georgie or Charlie or if he'd ever been hugged. If he had a father, a mother, an annoying sister that talked his ear off. If he'd ever seen the lights. And if he believed in anything beyond this earth.

I looked around for Gideon but couldn't find him.

"Amen!" the reverend almost shouted. We all said our amens but Grandma kept muttering hers over and over after everyone else had finished. It began to snow even harder and I stuck my tongue out to catch a snowflake. Several people popped open umbrellas, and the noise seemed to startle Grandma. "Harley. A bad storm's a-coming. A storm's a-coming." Daddy quietly took her arm and escorted her toward the row of cars, Mama following just behind them, her hand gently laid on Grandma's back. I looked for Uncle Dal but he was gone.

Biswick pulled a piece of paper from inside his coat and handed it to me. He wanted me to read it, I guessed. I glanced at it. It was the same paper I'd seen that day rolled up in the typewriter. *June.* It was deathly silent, except for the crunching, receding footfalls of Grandma and Daddy and Mama. They pounded in my ears. I put the paper back in Biswick's hand but he let it go. It fell to the ground like a snowflake.

Biswick stepped back to Veraleen and we followed Daddy and Grandma to the cars.

June.

Back at the house people started to arrive, shaking snow off their coats, casserole dishes in hand, and they kept arriving all afternoon. The kitchen table was laden with cheddar corn casserole, crunchy sweet potato casserole, macaroni and cheese bake, creamed chicken tacos casserole, Texas turkey tortilla casserole, and my all-time favorite, Wadine's pork-rind surprise casserole. And there were the standard "gatherin'" desserts: sheet cakes, upside-down pineapple cake, blackberry cobbler, and a whole table of gloppy, Jell-O-y desserts full of things like pineapple chunks, canned cherries, and nuts.

Wadine and Pinell walked into the living room, full plates in their hands, and snuck glances at Biswick who sat on the couch, melting into it like a banana slug. He hadn't uttered a word all day. I sat with him watching him carefully. Mama was sitting with us, too, staring at our woe-be-gone Christmas tree that nobody had the heart to take down.

"A Christmas tree's aura changes after Christmas Day," she said to no one in particular. "It's still beautiful, just dimmed," she murmured. She was right. Christmas trees were kinda sad after it was all over, no matter if it was the day of a funeral or not.

Dr. Coyote came over and knelt down to tell Biswick everything was going to be all right, but he didn't respond. When he walked away, Mama going with him, Biswick asked me, "What's an aura? Is it a color?"

"Some people say it's like a glow around the edges of things," I said. I saw in my mind the image of Gideon, rimmed with light, walking away from me the dark night of the Lights Festival.

"Like a ghost?" he asked.

"Maybe," I said, staring at the tree again, at my angel ornament. "You don't believe in ghosts, do you?" I asked. But he wasn't thinking what I thought he was thinking.

"I saw Daddy last night," he blinked. "All aura-like."

"What?" I asked just as Lorelei came by to give him a squeeze. She didn't look so hot. Her hair was parted down the middle like curtains, and it hung limp and deflated over most of her face.

"We never had a Christmas tree," Biswick said flatly, his eyes welling up. "Never."

Later Maydell Rathburger put a plate of food on Biswick's lap and the plate stayed there a full hour. I had to keep swatting away Mama's dogs. Veraleen came and patted Biswick, her big hands covering his whole head, her eyes full of worry. She wouldn't look my way. I kept taking FF breaths, praying for this all to be over so I could go do my litter patrol.

Grandma Birdy sat quietly with her friend Miss Fleta Bell and they looked like twin birds, shaking their heads and mumbling, "Um . . . Um . . . Um," their mutual summation of the whole thing.

Even Sheriff Bupp came and sat in a corner conspicuously without his wife, eating a big plate of food.

Bug came over and took Biswick's limp hand for a while. She actually remained quiet a full five minutes as she somehow knew that was what he needed. Then she let go and ran off into the kitchen, and I could hear her giggling with Tootie McKelvey.

Daddy retreated upstairs. I wished I could retreat somewhere, too, but I knew I couldn't no matter how hard it was for me to stay. I needed to sit there on the couch with Biswick.

The Dean sisters appeared at the same time, each carrying a homemade pie. Myrtle had on thick Coke bottle glasses, thicker than Gideon's. "I'm so sorry, I'm so sorry," Myrtle kept saying to Mama. I'd heard that since Myrtle couldn't drive anymore, Minnie was doing her grocery shopping and they were talking again after all these years. Mama took the pies and showed them on in, patting Myrtle on the back.

I heard the doorbell ring again, and Beasie, Winkie, and Weenie ran off, finally leaving Biswick and me alone with Mama, who had returned, on the sofa. A moment later a worried-faced Wadine Pigg came in and told Mama something. Mama caught the worried look, too, and she and Wadine rushed from the room. I followed and peeked around the doorway of the living room.

Mama was talking to someone at the front door. I craned my neck and saw that it was two sour pinched-faced ladies dressed in tweed standing there looking very official. They had clipboards. I strained to hear what they were saying. Something about "concerns" and "procedures." Then Mama got real mad and said, "Not today of all days!" and her voice carried through the house. Then she slammed the door on them. Sheriff Bupp, who had walked into the hallway when the doorbell rang, nodded to my mother and went outside to talk to the ladies.

Biswick had taken Cheeto out of his pocket and put it on his pants leg next to his dinner plate. He started rubbing Cheeto like a touchstone, and I noticed for the first time that day there was a calmness across his face.

I sat back down on the couch. I wasn't going to leave him again.

That's when it happened. Suddenly Beasie and

Winkie ran into the room, making a beeline for Biswick's untouched plate of good-smelling food. I stood up just in time to catch them by their collars and haul them to the back of the house. I pushed them into the laundry room and shut the door. As I was making my way back to Biswick through the crowd of people, Weenie came dashing from under Grandma's chair.

A look of horror crossed Biswick's face as Weenie grabbed Cheeto off his lap. Biswick jumped up, screaming. His plate of food crashed to the floor. Weenie chomped down on Cheeto like the great white shark from *Jaws*. It all happened so fast. Veraleen picked up Biswick, who was now screaming, and carried him upstairs. Grandma. She was grinning.

Later that night, when Biswick and I lay awake in our beds, he lamented the loss of Cheeto. "It was so mean," he kept saying. I tried to tell him that Weenie couldn't help herself. She'd always loved cheese and I think she just thought it was an enormous chunk of cheddar. Biswick quieted down at last and I thought he had gone to sleep.

But then this is what he said: "He wasn't my real daddy, but I loved him just the same. You want to hear something funny? He didn't talk like he was from Ireland when he was around me; only with his 'audience,' he called it. He liked foolin' people. He was from Al'bama and he was a famous child genius, a piano player, who was written up in the newspaper and everything when he was little. He told me. His parents made him go all over the country performing. He hated it. Hated it. He always wanted to be a poet, but they told him poetry wasn't ever gonna do him any good. He left home when he was seventeen and just wandered. After Mommy June died, he said he was gonna follow his dream and go to Harvard and we did."

The moon sifted through the snow and found my window to shine in. I waited many minutes before I asked. "If he wasn't your real daddy, who was he to you, Biswick?"

"He was kinda my step-daddy I guess," he said. "He found Mommy June in the Chit Chat Lounge in Oklahoma. She already had me in her tummy but Daddy Jack says she didn't tell him. She took him back to her reservation and they stayed up all night gambling and she was drinking away. And they did that for a long time until they got asked to leave. After I was born looking like an alien, Daddy says he felt bad for letting Mommy June drink so much even after he started to see her stomach get big. So he stuck around. He didn't drink anymore. It was only after Mommy June left." He stopped talking and I knew he was replaying scenes in his mind. I didn't want him to be in any more pain. I didn't ask any further.

He started up again. "I don't remember her very much. Not what she looked like or sounded like. I just remember how she smelled, she was always rubbing on her Bonne Bell cherry Chap Stick, over and over, like her lips would fall off if she didn't. And I remember her hands. They were little, like mine. And she liked to hold my hand whenever we walked together."

"So your mama loved you," I said.

"Her name was Mommy June. She wouldn't let me call her *Mama*. She said she was too young to be a mama," Biswick answered. And then, "She left me."

"Where, Biswick? Where did she go?"

"She died," he answered. "She was crossing the street and got squashed by an eighteen-wheeler."

"She didn't leave you, Biswick," I said.

"She left me," he said. "She left me at the apartment."

Later that night I heard the door open and knew it was Bug, probably up to no good. She crept over to my bed and I waited still and quiet with my eyes shut. I was ready. This time I was going to bop her in the face when she reached down to whisper "Velveeta" in my ear. The word never came. Instead I only felt the gentle massaging strokes of a brush and I remained in my pretend sleep as she fanned my hair in a wide arc above my head. The aroma of Love's Baby Soft lingered in the air.

Chapter
22

"**They** were pink," Biswick said, looking up from the leftover blackberry cobbler he was eating. "Her toes." It was just before dawn and we had gotten up early and come down to the kitchen.

I waited and listened as a variety of pink things passed through my mind.

"They were perfectly painted. She spent a lot of time working on her toes. Bubblegum colored, like Bubblicious. One time I had a fungus-amongus on one of my toes and she told me if I spent enough time on my toes like she did I wouldn't have that problem. Maybe it was those bright pink toes that shocked the driver and that's why she got run over."

"Do you have any grandparents back where you were?"

"I don't think so."

"Do you remember anything about being Indian?" I asked him. "What tribe?"

"No," he answered. "I have dreams where I know I'm an Indian and when I wake up most of it's gone and I feel kinda lost."

"Do you feel lost with us, Biswick?"

"No, I feel at home. That's why I don't want to go to the reservation. I don't want to see my granddaddy."

I let these words sink in a little. "Biswick, I thought you told me there was no one, no one left for you."

"Hey, look!" he said, pushing his spoon around what was left of his cobbler. "I made a smiley face."

"Yeah," I answered. FF breath. "Biswick, why didn't you tell me about your grandfather?"

"I'm not even sure he is really alive. He's old, ancient. Mommy June said he spent some time in jail. That's what she said. She called him the old geezer, OG for short. I have dreams about him.

He's always dead in my dreams. I think he's dead. Maybe."

I didn't know what I was going to do with that information. If he had a relative on a reservation, they probably had a claim to him. But they didn't deserve him. He was ours.

"Did you know Indians believe in spirits?" he asked.

"Yes," I said.

"What do you think the Jumbo Ghost Lights look like? Do they look little or like big fireworks?"

"I don't know," I answered.

"Why did Weenie have to eat Cheeto? It was so mean. I could have been in the *Genius World Book of Records*. It was so mean. I don't have anything now." He scooted away from the table and went back upstairs to bed.

I finished my cobbler and went back to bed, too.

There is a time between the setting sun and dusk, called the gloaming, an ethereal time of beautiful light that heralds the coming night. There is also a dividing time between the night and the new morning, a wafer-thin time–in-between time that I heard something scratch at my window. I rose from my bed, glancing over at Biswick, who was still asleep.

I walked to the window. It was an elf owl. I had never actually seen one, but I'd read they sometimes winter around here, up in the mountains. I watched it as it paced back and forth, leaving minuscule footprints in the snow on my windowsill. Pacing, pacing, restless, restless. In an instant it was gone, and I watched it fly into the half darkness toward the Chitalpi Mountains.

I got back in and for a long time pondered all that Biswick had told me. Finally I knew I wouldn't be able to fall back to sleep so I got dressed. I went over to the side of Biswick's bed. I watched his even, steady breathing for a moment and thought how fragile and tiny he looked. Then I went downstairs. Daddy was at the table eating cereal and reading the paper.

"What are you doing up so early, Hug?" he asked over his newspaper. "Is everything all right with Biswick?" He motioned for me to sit down.

"I guess," I said, plopping down in the chair next to him. "Daddy?"

He put the newspaper down. I had never called him Daddy.

"Yes?"

"What are we going to do about Biswick? I'm worried."

"I see," he said, taking a deep breath. "We need to find out if he has any relatives first and if not, maybe Ms. Holliday could raise him."

"That's what I think he wants, but I don't think she's gonna take him." Something gnawed in my stomach, thinking about Veraleen.

"We'll do everything we can for Biswick," Daddy said.

"We will?" I asked, looking into his deep sea-green eyes. Mama was right. He did have ocean eyes.

"Of course," he answered.

I got up from the table and started for the door. But I stopped and asked, "Daddy, can I come and see your tomato plant?"

"Okay," he said with a half smile, like he wasn't sure who I was.

* * *

Mama believes that the animals around here are mighty powerful. God put them here, like Shakespeare put imagery in his plays, as gate-keepers to a larger truth. I thought about my elusive White Feather, my winking dragon, the almost-extinct horn toads, the pacing elf owl, and the roadrunners and rabbits that dart about through the sage and brush seeming to say, "Follow me, follow me, and I'll show you. . . ." But most of all, as I sat on Dr. Coyote Wilson's patient table with the crinkly white paper a few days later, I was thinking about the coyotes that howled outside his bedroom when he was a baby.

"Why did I cry so much?" It was the first time I'd ever gone to Dr. Coyote all by myself.

"Is that why you are here, Merilee?" he asked.

"Yeah."

He looked at me carefully and put down my file. "You were just a baby. A special baby."

"I'm a big problem," I said. "And I'm cursed, too."

"No, you don't have a problem, Merilee. You are

going to be somebody. What is it you want to be?"

I looked down. I thought about all my stories, wrapped around and around in my head. And all the things in my journal. My beginnings. "I don't know. Maybe a writer," I said, expecting him to burst out laughing.

Instead he smiled. "You can be whatever you want, Merilee." A long, quiet moment passed. "I was hoping you would become a doctor, like me. You have the aptitude for it."

"I don't think I would have any sort of bedside manner," I answered.

He smiled. "Most doctors don't, anyway." And then, "Is there something else?"

"Biswick," I said. "His mama drank too much when she was pregnant with him. Is that why he is like he is?"

"Yes, probably it is," he said. "It's called Fetal Alcohol Syndrome. His facial features seem to fit with the syndrome. Where is his mama, do you know?"

"She's dead somewhere." I chewed on my lip for a moment.

"Anything else, Merilee?" he asked.

"Did those coyotes really come and sing outside your window when you were a baby?"

"Yup," he answered, reaching out to help me down from the table. "That's what my mama always said. They were mangy son of a guns with sharp teeth. But she wasn't afraid for me. There were three of them, which means good luck."

"What were they singing about?" I asked as I left the room, but Dr. Wilson had already started reading the file for his next patient.

Later that morning I went to Veraleen's house. I checked on Mamacita and the kittens in the lean-to, all the while feeling that gnawing in my stomach. A few minutes later, I knocked on her door and waited. I knocked again. There was no answer. I pushed the door open. I walked ever so slowly as though I was wading through a big wall of jelly. My heart thundered in my chest.

Veraleen was sitting in a chair facing the back window all serenelike. Her smile was like that smile on Jack O'Connor's face the last time I saw him at the dump. That peaceful dump smile. She was dressed in her old jeans with a huge fancy turquoise belt buckle I'd never seen her wear. She even had boots on. Her hair was down from its ponytail, and sprigs of greenery were tucked in all catawampus.

I followed her gaze to her garden.

The snow had melted away, leaving just a white halo around the edges of the plot. And there in the middle were little blooms, green blooms.

"Are you going somewhere, Veraleen?" I asked, without taking my eyes off her garden.

"Ain't it glorious, Merilee? Ain't it something? I told you miracles happen."

Do they, Veraleen? Do they?

"Look for yourself, honey. There's one right before your eyes."

"Where are you going, Veraleen?" My eyes flitted around for a suitcase. And I saw one, sitting on the other side of her chair.

"It's time I go home, Merilee. I've been waiting all morning, watching my blooms pop up. Waiting, just waiting."

"Waiting for what?" I asked. I didn't want to know. I had to ask for Biswick.

"For the courage, to face them all. I'm waiting for God to give me the courage."

"You aren't going nowhere, Veraleen," I told her. I walked over and pulled a chair up next to her.

"Biswick," she said, the word barely audible, crusty sounding. "You take care of Biswick. He needs you, honey."

"Biswick is yours, Veraleen! He's yours to take care of! Just marvelous! Just marvelous!"

She glanced over at me. "I don't deserve him, Merilee."

"What do you mean?"

She half laughed and it scared me. "I was a no-good mother. I don't deserve him."

"Veraleen," I pleaded. "Please."

"I'm going home. To see what's left there for me. Just waiting for the courage. I've been waiting twenty years."

"You need to stay here and take care of Biswick."

"I need to go home and apologize to people I love dearly, Merilee," she said to me, her eyes tearing up. "My own son. And my husband."

"You're not going to Africa? Or Australia?" I asked her, following her gaze out to the garden again.

"No," she laughed to herself. "I got a big ole heart, Merilee. It loves big and it hates big. That was just a little fib I told you, honey."

"What about Biswick?"

"I gotta go fix things before I can take him on. Things aren't right with me now. Maybe someday."

I started to cry, but muffled it as best I could. "Oh, horrendous," I hiccupped.

"Honey, I didn't want to make you cry. Don't cry, Merilee."

I wiped at my face. "I'm not crying. You do it, Veraleen. You stay here and take care of Biswick. That's just shadows you're trying to chase back at home. Biswick is real. He's here and he needs you. God is on vacation this week so he's not gonna give you any courage." I swiped at the tears that continued to fall.

She stood up to leave and reached for her suitcase.

I brushed at my cheek: "Promise me you'll be back for him," I said. She just smiled. She took one of the little sprigs from her hair, held it up to her nose, and handed it to me. It smelled of lemons.

Chapter
23

"Everyone's got a secret in the cellar," I remember Grandma proclaiming the day they brought Gideon home to his mama and grandma. I didn't know quite what she meant then, since we don't have any cellars in Jumbo.

I thought about that later that same night as I rode to Gideon's house—what kinds of secrets were behind his front door. I'd spent the afternoon curled up with a blanket reading *The Count of Monte Cristo* in my closet where Bug couldn't bother me. I'd snuck out after dinner, my almost-beautiful photo tucked under my shirt. I already missed Veraleen.

I parked my bike and walked up the front

porch. I saw a quick movement in the blinds on both sides of the door. And I saw poor Jim the cat, with a bonnet on his head, peek out in desperation before two old hands pulled him away. The door opened a crack. I could see one eye with blue eye shadow caked in the wrinkles, and at the bottom a black, old-fashioned lace-up shoe. The eye blinked once. I could smell Johnson's Baby Powder.

I was surprised. No one but Gideon ever answered their door. Finally I spoke. "Is he here? Gideon?"

"He went downtown," came a tremoring voice.

"Elsa?" someone called wearily from the back of the house. Then the door shut.

I turned around and walked down the porch stairs. All the stores were closed at this time of night. I got on my bike and rode off wondering where he could be.

I rode up and down the sidewalk on Main Street twice before I found him. Actually, he found me. I was riding past Putt's Chicken Hutt when I heard him call my name. I peered around.

"Merilee!" he called again. "I'm up here."

I looked up just as the chicken's eye lit up and glowed. Blinking, it illuminated a figure sitting on its back. It was Gideon, holding something in his lap. He motioned for me to go around. I rode my bike 'round back and saw a ladder leaning against the building. I carefully climbed up.

"Finally," he said with a lopsided wolfy grin when I reached him, "you've come for me."

"It's not what you think," I told him flatly. "I'm not here to proclaim my undying love." I sat down next to him on the chicken's back just as its beak opened and closed three times. I almost fell off, but Gideon grabbed me. There was barely enough room for both of us. I inched over till I was up against the chicken's upturned tail.

"Yes, you are." He laughed. He knew I wasn't. "Then why are you here?"

"What are you doing here?" I asked.

"Taking pictures," he sighed.

"That's nice," I answered. The chicken's eyes came on again, casting a weird light on the street below. I could see Mama's bookstore from up here.

It was dark again and both of us turned our gaze up to the sky. The stars domed above us like a glittering umbrella.

He sighed really loud this time. "Grandma mentioned she might be ready to go back to her church," he said, fingering the camera in his lap. "No more night forays." Maybe Grandma Birdy actually did see Gideon's grandma that time out by the trash cans. Elsa. Her name was Elsa. I hadn't known that till tonight.

"That's nice" is all I could say. The chicken's beak opened and closed three times again, scaring us a little. We laughed.

"Have you ever seen the lights, like on your own, away from the viewing area?" I asked.

"Yes."

"Well?"

"It's indescribable. It's magical, Merilee. Just magical."

Suddenly a shooting star arced across the sky. "Does it look like that?"

I looked over at him. He was watching me and the happy butterflies returned to my stomach.

I reached up and felt the photo under my shirt. That was magic.

"What did you do to the pennies?" I asked. Scooter hadn't shown up for school the next day and Romey and Cairo wore gloves for a week. None of them ever complained 'cause they knew they'd have to 'fess up about what they'd done to me.

Gideon got a sheepish look on his face. "Grandma found an old bottle of my daddy's Purifying Tonic and rubbed it all over her hands. She says it used to cure the flakes but something must have formed in that bottle after all these years. It was the only good thing my daddy's ever done for me. Veraleen, by the way, gave me some salve for Grandma and it cleared right up."

"You didn't have to do that," I told him. "But thank you." I don't think I've ever, ever said "Thank you" to anyone.

Gideon smiled.

I climbed down the ladder and rode my bike around front, just below him. I blew him a kiss. The chicken's eyes opened and glowed and I saw Gideon touch his cheek.

Chapter
24

I'd been thinking a lot lately about Grandma Ruth. What would have been if she'd lived. If she was with us now instead of Grandma Birdy. Mama doesn't talk about her life before us very much. I wish she did. She did say once that Grandma Ruth believed lying don't do anyone any good, but a little fibble-fable every now and then does everyone some good.

I wonder if she'd approve of the fibble-fables I'd been telling to Biswick a couple of days now about Veraleen being gone. Actually fibbing to everyone. I told them she had some business to take care of in Whiskey and she'd be back real soon. I just didn't want Biswick to know yet. I didn't think he could take it right now.

Although he seemed to have a good appetite. I was sitting in Mama's booth at the Jumbo Chilimpiad drawing dragons in my journal. I watched him run from booth to booth sampling the chili. Almost everyone was there—the Rotary Club, the FFA Booster Club, and the Ladies Guild of the Holy Hands Baptist Church.

"Biswick!" I called after him. "You're gonna get sick!" He pretended he didn't hear me and kept on running.

For some reason Mama had gotten a wild hair and decided to enter the bookstore in the contest. Mama was even wearing an apron with "Hole in the Wall" written on the front. She said she was turning over a new leaf and that she was going to learn how to cook. "Oh, leave him be," she said, looking at me over her cat-eyed glasses while shaking some sugar in her big black Crock-Pot. "It keeps his mind off things."

Grandma Birdy said Mama was sure to win with Grandma's recipe, Hot Breath Mountain Chili. The secret ingredient was a bottle of Thousand Island dressing. I know everyone else's secret ingredients, too, because last year I handed out Tootsie Pops at every booth and it didn't take long before tongues were flapping.

Grandma had planned on coming to help but this morning the sky had darkened and angry storm clouds had marched across the horizon. Grandma said she was gonna wait at home for the bad news. So far the storm held off, but the Chilimpiad contestants had to be squeezed inside the Jumbo school gym 'cause of the ice-cold breeze outside.

Bobo Romaine, Cairo's daddy, was across from us, intently stirring his pot, his eyes shifting around. He was determined to win without cheating. His Three-Alarm Armadillo Belly Chili is the real thing (this time) he says. I don't want to guess where he got the armadillo. I see lots of them flattened like flounders on the old highway. Next door his wife, Mama Peaches, had her own chili pot. Their son Rio, home from the Big House in Huntsville, was helping her set out bowls of her famous peach cobbler. She was hoping to win over the judges. She'd need to, because she puts cream corn and peas in her chili, a definite chili no-no.

Lorelei, her hair looking like a last year's bird nest, appeared with a bag from the Piggly Wiggly. "Here you go," she said handing it to Mama. Mama had forgotten salt.

Mama pulled it out, yanked on the spout, and started pouring in. "Lorelei, why don't you go on over to the Cut 'N' Curl—my treat." Mama kept pouring and pouring as she squinted her eyes at Lorelei's hairdo. I glanced down at Grandma's recipe. It said a pinch of salt, not the whole tub.

"All the shops are closed now," Lorelei said as she sat down in one of our folding chairs. "Another heavy snowstorm is predicted. Actually, a few flakes have already started falling." Two snowstorms in one year. People would be talking about this for generations.

Biswick came running back. "I just had some pineapple chili at Myrtle and Minnie's booth!" He stuck out his tongue to show us a brown chunk of something. I had to turn my head. Already the odors of thirty kinds of chili mixed together and wafting around the gym was about to make me toss my cookies. And Mama's pot was starting to take on an aroma never before smelled by mankind. "I heard someone's got Rattler Snake Chili!" Biswick said as he ran off again.

"Where's Bug?" Mama asked as she liberally poured garlic powder into her pot. Mama was wearing her hair down now, no more girlie ponytails since the accident. I could even smell her Herbal Essence shampoo.

"I saw her outside playing with Mary Alice Augustine. She said they were going home to try to make a snowman."

Just then Ramona Grace Callahan and Scooter Stunkel strutted by wearing banners which read "Miss Chilipepper" and "Mr. Hot Sauce." I hadn't seen the Three Tormenters yet. But Yello was down at his daddy's booth helping him make his Bubba Brown's Black Magic Chili. Secret ingredient: imported chickpeas.

"I'm gonna go try Frida's chili," Lorelei said. She got up and left.

"Traitor," Mama giggled under her breath. "Merilee, honey. Will you dice some onions for me?"

I didn't feel much like getting out of my folding chair but she gave me a "please" look so I got up. I begrudgingly shut my journal. I went to her side and started chopping.

They were playing fifties music over the loud-speaker and Mama started humming along to "Rock Around the Clock" and tapping her foot (not easy to do in clogs). She kept sneaking looks at me. Suddenly she proclaimed, "You look like your Grandma Ruth. I never noticed it until today."

"I do?" I asked. "Stupendous."

"Yes, you have her strong profile. She was very lovely in a different kind of way. They called it 'handsome' back then."

Handsome. Great. I reached up and touched my nose, my big, fat 747 landing nose. But then I thought of Gideon's photo, my almost-beautiful photo, and I felt a little better.

"She would have been proud of you, Merilee." A burning sensation started to creep up my chest as she spoke. "You probably don't have any mem-ories of her, but you would have loved her."

Yes, that's true. I would have loved her. Tears

welled up in my eyes. It was the onion. That's what it was. The onion. I kept chopping.

"Ah, Merilee," Mama said, reaching over and wiping my cheek. "I haven't seen you cry since you were a baby," she sighed. "I know I haven't been the best mother. Believe me, I've been thinking about that a lot since the accident." She put her spoon down. "When you were a baby I couldn't touch you. You scrunched up in agony if anyone tried. Uncle Dal was the only one you let near. And then Veraleen and Biswick." The image of Veraleen backing out of her driveway flitted across my mind again. "Are you okay?" she asked. "You're cloudy today. What's going on?"

I pulled away and kept on chopping. "Why *her*? Why Grandma Ruth?" I whispered. "She would have loved me. Stupendous."

Mama threw some chili peppers in the pot and wiped her hands on some paper towels. "You were about three when she died. She only saw you once. She was going to come see you again but she died. And that was it. She wasn't perfect, Merilee. None of us are. If she had lived, she might not have been the grandma that you've held onto in your mind." She started pouring a bottle of liquid smoke into the pot and I noticed that pink scar on her forehead, although fainter, was still there.

"Mama, I'm never gonna leave you," I whispered as I reached up and briefly touched my forehead.

"Oh yes, you are," she said vehemently, turning her whole body toward me, the empty Liquid Smoke bottle held in midair. "You're going to college. You're going to see the world. But you'll come back, though, someday, Merilee," she said. "There's something special about this place. Magical." She started stirring her chili again. "You've been living in the Shadowlands here."

"Shadowlands. C. S. Lewis. You used to read him to me when I was little. Do you remember?"

"Of course." She shook her head in amazement. "I just don't understand how you remember. You were two, maybe three at the most."

"We live in the Shadowlands. The sun is always shining somewhere else . . . around a bend in the road . . . over the brow of a hill."

We locked eyes just as Dr. Coyote walked up. He asked Mama how she was feeling. "All better," she told him. He asked to sample her chili. She smiled and gave him one of the little tasting cups with the tiny spoons. He tasted it and made a face like a baby eating a lemon. Then he tried to cover it up with a great big cover-up smile. He walked off, a little too quickly. Mama looked confused. "Maybe I put in too many chili peppers." She stuck the spoon back in and tried to fish some out.

There was an announcement over the loud-speaker that the judges, all members of the Kiwanis club over in Whiskey ('cause we know each other too well here), would be coming through in ten minutes. There was a special category this year—most innovative. Maybe Mama'd win that one.

I saw Biswick dart over to the Dearloves' booth. I cringed. Their secret ingredients are deer meat sausage, habañero peppers, and frozen prickly pears. Since no one else was sampling their chili, the Dearloves happily handed him a large bowl. Biswick dug in with gusto.

"Mama?"

"Do you think I should put more sugar in?" Mama asked.

"Mama," I began again. "Veraleen went home yesterday."

She put the carton of sugar down and looked at me. She knew "home" didn't mean back to Whiskey.

I looked over at Biswick. He was holding his tummy. Mama followed my gaze.

"Don't worry about him," she said. "We'll take care of him. Don't worry, Merilee," she repeated. "You've always held the world in your hand and I so wish you wouldn't."

Biswick slowly walked back to our booth. His face was white as a ghost.

"Biswick," Mama said. "You okay?"

He slid down in one of the chairs. "No," he said. "I think the pineapple made me sick."

"I don't think it was the pineapple, honey." Mama smiled.

"Maybe it was the snake," I said.

"I gotta go to the bathroom fast!" he said, jumping up and down. Mama and I both desperately reached for the paper towels in case he was going to vomit.

"I gotta go home!" was all he said as Mama and I stood there stupefied while he ran toward the door clutching his stomach.

Mama put a lid over her pot and waved for me to go after him.

I started to leave but turned back. "Mama?" Mama smiled in that knowing way that means we understand each other. She motioned for me to go on.

I didn't see Biswick. I rode as fast as I could, in and out of the streetlights' shadows in the gently falling snow, wondering if he had made it home in time.

Chapter
25

Grandma Birdy, wearing one of her rainbow snowball caps, sat in her garden chair, her ankles and feet buried in the snow. Her tree looked like a white umbrella above her. I parked my bike and walked over to her. She was looking off in the distance, her eyes gone. She held something close to her breast. I peered closer and saw it was the Jesus baby, from Mama's church.

"Grandma?" She didn't respond. "Grandma? Go inside. It's too cold." I glanced back at our house hoping Biswick had made it in time. Grandma didn't respond and I wondered where Weenie was, her faithful sidekick. Could he be buried in the snow at her feet? She didn't seem like she would notice if he were.

"Too cold," Grandma finally said. I saw a slight movement behind her. It was Weenie watching out her window, his little snout pressed up against the glass.

"Grandma?"

"Huh?"

"Why are you holding the baby Jesus? We need to put him back in the manger."

"He could have died. Everyone knows you never leave a baby out in the cold. So I took him." She looked as though she was seeing right through me. I believed that she had indeed gone around the bend, like Daddy had said, and I was scared. "My baby sister. Born Christmas Day and died that night. My mother, you see, wasn't quite right in the head. Never was. And that night when we was all asleep she took the baby and walked in the snow down the mountain. And when she came home the next day, her toes blue and almost frozen off, she had the baby Jesus in her arms instead."

"Oh God," I murmured. I felt sick. "Horren . . ."

"She'd left the baby girl in the straw manger in

front of the church. She'd tried it once before, with me, leaving me in a basket in front of the church, but Daddy'd found me and brought me home. God only saves you once, not twice."

"Grandma, it's me, Merilee." I didn't want to hear anymore.

"Who?" she hissed, narrowing her eyes at me.

"Oh you." She frowned, a frown I've seen many a time. "It's not Merilee. That was a funny I pulled. Your name is Ruth. I fixed that. I did. No way I was gonna let a grandbaby of mine be named after that New York woman."

I stood perfectly still.

"Your mama didn't know. She was out of it. I'd been waiting and waiting so many years, you see, for a girl to come along. All I had was boys and I couldn't rightly name them Merilee, could I? That was *her* name—my baby sister, and I wanted you to have it. So I told that candy striper while your mama was passed out that your name was Merilee."

I walked over to her and gently pulled her up. I couldn't believe how fragile she felt. How tiny. I tried to pry the baby Jesus out of her arms but she held onto it as though the world was coming to an end. "Come on, Grandma. I'm taking you inside." I put my arms on her shoulders and guided her toward her little house. She looked at her tree. "They took Mama away forever and my daddy, right before he left for good, buried the baby underneath an oak tree out back. I made Avery plant this tree so I could pretend she was right there underneath the roots."

Weenie met us at the door. He wagged his tail and licked at her ankles. I brought Grandma over to her bed and helped her lay down. She handed me the baby Jesus and, not quite knowing what to do, I cradled him to my chest. Weenie jumped on the bed and curled up at Grandma's feet.

She patted my arm and said, "They came from the mountains, my family. Far, far away from here. Backwoods mountains of West Virginia. The cousins all married each other, way back when. That's what started it. It goes away for a little while, and you just hope it ain't coming back." She laughed. "And when I finally started having babies after all those barren years, I worried they'd not be right in the head. Thank God they're not crazy, my boys. I sang to my babies, I did. A song from the old mountains." She hummed a song for a few moments. There was something so achingly familiar about it, and I felt as though I was falling off my tightrope.

She sighed and frowned at me again. "Why couldn't you have been born right? Thank the Lord above my little Bug was a sweet little normal baby." She took off her snowball hat and motioned for me to lean down. She pulled it down over my head.

"I'm fine now, Merilee," she said wearily. "Now scat and get out of here. And don't you be telling any tales about me."

Weenie barked as I left with the baby Jesus in my arms.

I was running upstairs a few moments later. The bathroom door was standing open and the dogs were in the hallway sound asleep. I threw open the bedroom door and stood there. There was no sign of Biswick. Just Bug dressed in her snow clothes.

She was sitting on my bed holding Mamacita too tight and kissing her all over. "What is that?" she asked, her eyes all big. I still had the baby Jesus in my arms.

"Where's Biswick? Have you seen him?" I asked as I put the baby gently down on Biswick's bed.

"He just came from Veraleen's house. He didn't look too good. Said something about a tree and how everyone has left."

"Marvelous." I grabbed an extra coat and turned to go, not before noticing that there was an empty space in my PEZ collection. Mr. Smiley was missing. Downstairs I grabbed a water bottle and my litter stick and ran for my bicycle, almost tripping over my big feet a couple of times. Please don't let him get the wrong idea about Veraleen being gone. Please don't let him head off for the mountains in search of the Conquistador tree. In my heart I knew where he had gone.

I rode my three-wheeler as fast as I had ever ridden through the backstreets of Jumbo. I looked up at the sky and saw the storm was still holding its breath, waiting to pounce.

Oh Biswick, I said over and over to myself as I furiously pedaled. I should have taken him to Cathedral Mountain before. I could have shown him that there was no Conquistador tree, and he would have gotten it out of his mind. I should have said something about his daddy in the dump. I should have told him the truth about Veraleen. I should have taken him home myself.

When I finally reached the base of the mountains about thirty minutes later, the dirt pathway became uneven and my bicycle could go no more. I put my journal in a side pocket of the extra jacket and put it on over the one I was wearing.

Looming above me were the Chitalpi Mountains. My whole life they had guarded me. And now, somewhere, they held Biswick in their arms.

There. A trail. The old Goat Herder's trail. Barely decipherable was an iron pike, marking the point. That's where he'd started. I knew it. I started walking, guided by something deep down inside. It told me where to go, where to look for him. I could feel the way through my entire body. With each step I took, though, more and more snow fell, pelting me and sticking to me. Eventually I found his footprints on the trail, small, like a fawn, barely making an impression. I followed them, thinking about his daddy, what he'd said about Biswick never growing up—never making a mark in this world.

I reached a small flat clearing and paused a moment to call out for him. There was no reply, only my FF breaths, long and worried. The whole wide world had failed him. I trudged on, feeling the biting cold now as I hiked higher and higher. I continued to call out Biswick's name. He was up here somewhere, I knew it. I wondered if he could hear me and was not responding on purpose.

Darkness was slowly descending. I started to feel lost. I couldn't see anything. There was snow everywhere. I thought of something Grandma Birdy used to say: "You ain't ever amounting to anything, so why even try." Well, Grandma, I'm trying anyway.

"Biswick!" I called again. Snow was now covering the tumbled boulders on the slope in front of me.

Then I saw him. Ten yards away. At the top of the rise. He was well dressed for the snow, with a hooded coat and gloves. He was watching something intently.

"Biswick?" I yelled out. "I've been very worried about you!"

"Aaaah. That's silly," he said, still not taking his eyes away from whatever it was he was looking at.

I trudged closer to him in the snow. "What is it?"

"Shhhh." He motioned for me to come closer. As I stepped next to him, he pointed down a ravine. There was a scrawny cedar bush at the base of a bunch of rocks.

"That's it, isn't it, Merilee? My Conquistador tree," said Biswick. "And my treasure. I'm rich now." He didn't even convince himself.

I waited a moment before I said, "There's nothing there, Biswick. Nothing at all."

He frowned.

"I'm sorry, Biswick. I'm sorry."

We stood side by side for a few minutes.

"Where did you get that ugly hat?" he asked.

I reached up and felt the top of my head. I had forgotten. Grandma's snowball cap.

It was getting darker and darker and the wind had picked up, sending the chilling snowflakes whirling about us. I looked around for the way back down, but everything seemed the same. Our footprints had disappeared. My heart began to beat out of my chest.

"Biswick," I said as I pulled at his jacket. "We've got to find shelter." I had to tug at him several times, almost pulling his coat off. We locked eyes. "Come on," I said. He nodded.

We started to walk along the edge of the ravine. "Look," Biswick said. "Over there." A dark hole appeared in the snow just ahead of us. A small outcropping of rocks curled around an opening, like the aperture of an old camera. We got down on all fours and scrambled inside. It was dark, very dark.

We sat down against the rock wall and hugged our knees.

Outside the wind had started to howl eerily. I wondered if we would make it through the night.

What luck. Fabulous. Marvelous. Spectacular.

We watched the small hole of pale light grow smaller and darker before our eyes. Biswick had a little smile across his face.

"What?" I said.

"The elephant is the only animal with four knees. Do you think if he falls down he skins all four knees and has to have four Band-Aids on all four knees?" His teeth were chattering.

"You're not scared, are you?" I asked him.

"No, just cold. That's all."

"Me, too," I said. "Did you know Veraleen's garden bloomed?"

He buried his head into his knees. "Her suitcase and car were gone," he said quietly.

"She didn't leave you, Biswick," I told him. "She's coming back. I promise."

"Nobody comes back."

"Well, she is," I said. "She promised." *Be backs don't come back.*

"They were going to take me away, Merilee. I don't want to go away."

"You're not going away, Biswick."

He lifted his head. "I stole Mr. Smiley, Merilee Marvelous."

"That's all right," I said. "It's yours now. I should have given it to you before when you asked me for it."

He pulled it out of his jacket and held it in front of him. "Wow, nobody ever gave me anything like this."

"Did your mama ever give you anything?" I asked him. I thought about Grandma, and how she had never ever given me anything my whole life, except the hat I was now wearing. *And my name.*

"She gave me a pack of gum one time. It was lime green Bubblicious," he said, his teeth chattering.

"My favorite bubblegum is Bazooka," I said.

"You can't blow bubbles with Bazooka." He shivered.

"I can. I once blew a triple bubble with Bazooka," I said.

"I once blew a four-one with Double Bubble," he said, shivering even more.

The wind was howling, trying to paw its way into our little cave. I could barely see Biswick now.

I was trying to move my fingers around in my pockets when I remembered the journal. I pulled it out and held it in front of me. The silver clasp glittered.

"What's really in there, Merilee?" Biswick asked.

"Just beginnings," I answered. I shoved the journal back in my pocket and knew as I did so if we ever made it out of here alive, I was ready now for more than beginnings. "I'm gonna be a writer someday," I announced.

"When you grow up?" he asked.

"Maybe before," I told him. "You're gonna grow up, too, Biswick."

"We're not gonna make it, are we?"

"Don't be scared, Biswick," I told him. "I'm here with you."

"No, Merilee," he said. "I'm here with you."

"Yeah," I said.

"Do you think Eskimos pick their noses?"

"I think everyone picks their noses, Biswick," I answered between shivers. "It's one of those universal things."

"Wouldn't it be frozen boogers?" he asked.

"I think they're pretty warm in their igloos. It's only cold outside."

"So they only pick their noses when they're in their igloos?"

"Let's talk about something else," I said.

"What does *unibertal* mean?" he asked.

I had to think a few moments before answering. "It's the whole wide world. Universal."

He nodded. "Oh." Then, "Do ants poop?"

"Do you stay up all night thinking about stuff like this?"

"Yeah sometimes. What do you think about, Merilee?"

"My dragons."

"The whole wide world?"

"Yeah."

"Merilee?"

"Yeah?"

"Do you think it's true that somewhere in the whole wide world someone has gum on their shoe?"

"Yeah. That's true. I would say we have gum on our shoes right now."

"It's universal," he said.

"Yeah."

"Merilee?"

"Yeah?"

"I love you."

Tears stung like icicles in my eyes. "Oh Biswick." I knew I felt something for him. Something true and strong. If that's what love meant.

"We're going to die, Merilee. And it's all my fault," he said.

"It's not your fault, Biswick," I told him firmly. *Ain't nobody's fault*, Veraleen had said.

"We're not going to die," I whispered. I thought perhaps I should put my arm around him. It's what a normal person would do. All I could manage was to touch his shoulder with the tippy tips of my fingers. For once I welcomed the fiery jolt that bolted up my arm.

"What's that thingy they put in front of your grave?" he asked. My arm jerked back.

"A gravestone," I answered, taking a deep FF breath. I knew he was thinking about the nameless boy in the graveyard. "I found out. It was George Charles Williams. And I'm gonna ask Uncle Dal to make a new headstone for him."

He didn't say anything for a moment. "I like that name." And then, "What would you put on your gravestone?" I remembered how I had always thought my gravestone would say something about me crying all the time.

"I think mine would say, 'Merilee Marvelous Monroe. Lost Soul. Loved Dragons.'"

"Mine would say, 'Biswick O'Connor, Finder of Giant Cheeto.'"

"Did you have a last name before, I mean an Indian name?"

"You're gonna laugh," he said.

"No, I won't," I told him.

He sighed heavily. "Bigtoe."

"Bigtoe?" I asked.

"Mommy June said my real daddy had one big giant big toe and he had to have a hole cut out of his shoe so it could stick out. That's why they called him Bigtoe. She said she couldn't remember if he had a first name."

I wondered about his Mommy June. If she told him a big pack of whopping lies or if some of it was true. If there really was a man walking around with his toe sticking out of his shoe.

"Do ants poop?" he asked again.

"I guess all animals poop, Biswick. It's universal."

"Oh."

"I'm getting too tired to talk, Biswick. Why don't we whistle back and forth? There's a tribe in the Canary Islands that only communicates with whistling." I made that up.

"Like Uncle Dal?" he asked.

"Yeah, like Uncle Dal," I answered. So we tried to whistle for a while, our shrill attempts blending with the outside howling into nothingness. I started to feel very sleepy. I had to dig deep inside to keep my eyes open. I tried to take my FF breaths but it only made me more drowsy.

I remember in my mind drawing a bloodred dragon that took on a ferocious life of its own, and when it came down for me, picking me up in its monstrous wings, I surrendered into the darkness.

* * *

There was a light. I was awake and there was a faint light. I blinked a few times and adjusted my eyes. It was the Mr. Smiley, still in Biswick's hands, but now all lit up and glowing yellow. Biswick was still fast asleep, his head resting on his knees.

I nudged him and his head flew up. "Oh!" he uttered as he saw what he held in his hand.

"What is it, Merilee?"

"I don't know."

I looked around and saw a glow radiating little fingers of light into our cave. We both stared, mesmerized.

"Merilee?" he whispered.

"Yeah," I answered.

"I can't feel my toes."

"Neither can I," I told him. It was so cold now I felt numb to it and I knew that wasn't good. I had a decision to make. If we stayed here, I didn't think we would make it through the night. If we left, I didn't think we would make it, either. We were in a bind, and there was nothing I could do.

The fingers of light seemed to flicker as though answering me. "Come and we'll show you the way," the light sang to me. "Come. Come."

"Biswick, are you ready to go home?" He didn't answer, but simply nodded his head. We crawled out of the cave and stood up in the snow holding on to each other.

We saw three lights hovering about ten feet away from us. They were the size of basketballs. They spun on an invisible axis and radiated fiery orange light into the darkness. Biswick grabbed my hand. "Merilee?" he stammered.

"Shhhh." I held my finger to my lips.

The balls of light started to move in a mesmerizing dance. Luminous, beautiful, graceful, streaks of light radiating warmth and power. They came toward us and circled around. One slowed down in front of me and I looked in.

There was something there. I blinked. I thought I saw a fiery-veined eye of crystal blue, its black pupil narrow-slatted, reptilian. The eye blinked back at me. *Is that you?* I closed my eyes and when I opened them, I saw that the eye in the ball of light was my own, magnified as though through my binoculars. Biswick's ice-cold hand warmed mine and I saw that he had his own special light hovering in front of his face. My light left me, as did Biswick's, and the three lights joined each other again.

They moved slowly down the mountain, and we followed, protected and warmed. It was difficult, but the lights shone us a trail.

I heard a whistle. A very familiar whistle. I whistled in return. Suddenly I saw three great long arcing beams of light.

"Merilee?" a voice called from the darkness.

"Here!" I screamed back. Biswick clung to me. The beams came closer. It was Sheriff Bupp, with Daddy and Uncle Dal not far behind, all waving around big flashlights.

I ran into Daddy's arms and Biswick ran to Uncle Dal. I hugged Daddy as hard as I could and he hugged me back even harder.

"I knew there was a hug in you somewhere, Merilee," he whispered into my ear.

They carried Biswick and me down the

mountain, and Uncle Dal sang an old song into the night, a song deeply buried within me. It was the song he had whistled to me so long ago, the mountain song Grandma had sung to her babies.

Good-byes

Mama explains it to me this way: people come into our lives, however briefly, for a reason. Like birds, some roost here permanently, and others are just migrating, making a pit stop, before they fly on. What I want to know is why Grandma Birdy, who had to be moved into the Happy Hearts Nursing Home over on Oak Avenue, has to be one of the stubborn roosting ones.

It's been a couple of months since we came down from the mountains. I know this to be true now. My dragons saved me. And who knows, maybe God sent them. Veraleen says we saw what we wanted to see up there in the mountains, that the Jumbo Ghost Lights are like mirrors that illuminate our souls. Biswick says he saw Superman and Santa Claus and a cheeseburger in the lights. Daddy says it was the flashlights we saw. Mama says it was all a miracle. And Grandma says it's all a bunch of hooey horseradish.

Veraleen came back to town to get Biswick. And now they are leaving today. Veraleen decided it would be best to go see for herself the reservation Biswick is from. Maybe he does have a Mommy June waiting for him or an old geezer grandpa. Or a daddy with a big toe. Who knows. I couldn't handle saying the final good-bye so I'm out here by the trains picking up my litter. My VOE still soothes my soul. It always will.

I had a feeling, though, that Veraleen would find me today. I felt the rumble of her old GTO before it turned and came down the road. She brought it to a quick stop and the dust flew up and around like a cloud of pixie magic.

"Come here, Merilee baby, Biswick wants to say good-bye." Her voice boomed out of the car just like she's got a built-in megaphone. She had on a dusty cowboy hat.

I walked over to the passenger side with my head down, leaning on my litter stick like an old lady. I slowly looked up. Biswick. Sweet Biswick had tears streaming down his face.

"You weren't gonna say good-bye?" he asked.

"We said good-bye already," I said. "I told you I don't do *final* good-byes."

Veraleen snorted from her side of the car. "Nothin' is final, Merilee. We'll all see each other again. Now say good-bye, baby," she said to Biswick.

He hiccupped. "Good-bye, Merilee Marvelous." He smiled and put his hand out of the car like he was going to give me a high-five. I reached over and we briefly pressed our hands together in the shape of a steeple. Veraleen gunned the gas and they took off down the road.

I lifted my binoculars and watched the car, like a glimmering gold coin, disappear off into the distance. I raised my binoculars higher and caught the flight of a hawk—*White Feather*—as it soared toward the Chitalpi Mountains calling and calling.

Good-bye.

Acknowledgments

I began this book for my daughter Caitlin, for her unique view of the world. In bringing the story to life, I was also inspired by her cousins Matt and Sean.

To my daughter Lauren, who used to chatter a lot when she was little, and to Cameron, for his profound sense of wonder about the world around him.

My sister Karen, the very first reader, was invaluable with her insight and remarks through many, many drafts, e-mails, and phone calls. As was my sister-in-law, Lynn. Brad Kuhn and Andrea White, my writer friends, were helpful with their enthusiasm, comments, and support. Dianna

Hutts Aston, in her own way, guided *The Very Ordered Existence* to where it needed to be. And thanks to my sister Bonnie, who has the ubiquitous Carlisle storytelling gene.

I'd like to thank Rosemary Stimola, my agent, for seeing great potential in an early draft and believing the book would go far.

Thanks to the Greenwillowites, who feel like family, and to everyone else at HarperCollins Children's who loved the book. Most importantly, thanks to my editor, Virginia Duncan, genius extraordinaire. The story would not be the same without her.

Thanks to Dan, my husband, for his boundless love.

And lastly, thank you to my parents, Acree and Corinne Carlisle, who fostered in me an early love of books and the power of imagination.